THE SOCIETIES BOOK 2

ALLIANCE

SYDNEY REAMES

E-book ISBN-13: 978-1-961057-08-1
Paperback ISBN-13: 978-1-961057-09-8
Cover Design By: Deranged Doctor Design

CHAPTER 1

Everyone I knew, and everyone he knew, was in jeopardy. And Fell had kissed me.

A falling stalactite shattered next to us, small pieces of dust and debris stinging my arms. My eyes flared open in time to see the near-blinding light of our markings before they faded away.

My thoughts reeled not only from the kiss, but everything else that had transpired. Mere months ago I'd been back on Earth pretending Verkent, the alien conspiracy group I'd grown up in, didn't exist. Then the seven planetary Societies that made up a unified group called the Coalition had shown up, making a surprising declaration: these "aliens" and the citizens of Earth were actually the same species. Depending on whom you asked, we

Earthers had either been abandoned or had cut ourselves off generations before. But on Earth, only Verkent kept alive the secret of our shared history.

Fell grabbed my hand and we raced after the others. I heard, echoing behind us, the splash of stalactites dropping into the Rift's Lake of the Dead. The forest walker led us through a tunnel near the lake, and we emerged into the gorgeous forest of the planet I'd grown to love in the short two months I'd lived there. The Rift was the most secretive of the seven Societies that every teenaged Societal (called a Blank), could choose from when deciding where to spend their adult life. When someone I still hadn't identified had altered my decision—my Choice—against my will and sent me here, I'd believed I was moving to a cave. What a shock to discover the real beauty this Society had to offer.

Straw-blond hair whipped around my face as I ran. I kept my legs pumping, determined to keep up as we moved over the soft moss on the forest floor. It wasn't easy, since Fell was the best forest walker in the Rift, capable of moving through the trees quickly and silently.

He had said we needed to find Ama, the older woman who served as the sole Reader for the Riftians. Members of every Society rapidly evolved, or Assimilated, traits unique to their planet. The Riftians got enhanced speed, sight, balance ... and glowing tattoos that appeared on our skin, which held hidden meanings. Ama's job was to interpret those markings—a service I sorely needed. When Fell touched my skin in the cavern, the glowing marks on both of us had grown and spread, in such a way that proved we were Connected. As Ama's pupil, the only one she'd ever agreed to tutor, I had a decent idea of the significance of this. Still, I wasn't about to jump to conclusions until we had spoken to her.

Fell led us to a tree with blackened bark and russet leaves. It reminded me of fall. I'd never seen his home before. We were miles into the forest, far removed from the groves where most Riftians dwelled. The forest walker turned to look down at me, his eyes the bluish-purple of a sky on the verge of night.

"We'll grab my weapons and then meet the others. Is there anything you need from your own home?"

"No. I grabbed everything earlier, when I took Hale." I'd armed my best friend and then sent him on with the others. "Wait. Weapons? What about forest walking?"

"It is my greatest skill. I teach it because I'm the best forest walker the Riftians have. But it's not a weapon. Well, at least not in the same way."

I suspected that Fell would come off as prideful to anyone who didn't know him. But as I'd grown close to him I realized he was, more than anything, objective and thoughtful. He stated facts as they were or as he saw them, without conceit. He was right; of course he would have trained with an actual weapon. It was a requirement for all Riftians. I held my own, a double-headed ax, near my side. Strapped to my legs were a pair of holsters for daggers that were a gift from another weapons trainer, Vanya.

I watched as Fell secured a holster that held two blades, very similar to mine, across his back. It was made of ocala, a specialized material from our planet that was near-indestructible but very rare. Each new Riftian was presented with pieces chosen for them constructed of this precious resource. Many people received just one item. I had been an exception; I'd been given an entire bodysuit, boots, cloak, and bracers. As Fell swapped his typical steely cloak out for a black one darker than the depths of the lake, draped over an ocala tunic he always wore, I realized he'd been given several things as well.

"Ama favored you from the beginning," I observed.

He raised an eyebrow and swept a strand of sleek black hair away from his glowing blue-purple eyes.

"As she did with you. Then again, I didn't get pants or boots, so perhaps you are the true favorite." He smirked as he fastened everything into place.

Smiles were an attractive look Fell wore far too rarely. My new marks brightened in response. Shades of pink, green, and purple danced on the wall of Fell's home. When I'd received the first of my multihued opal markings, I'd worried what they might reveal about me. But they'd become a part of me, and now I could hardly imagine what I'd looked like without them. The light glinted off a weapon in Fell's hand as he pulled it from the holster to examine it.

"And the daggers?" I asked, gesturing toward his blades.

"Vanya had to learn somewhere."

The Riftian he spoke of was a dual master. She was an archer, but also possessed twin daggers of her own. She'd been training me to use my pair alongside my ax. After I saved her younger sister, she had not only given me the daggers I carried but offered to teach me. I wanted to know what Vanya had done that had convinced Fell to instruct her, but right now I had a different, more pressing question.

"You said we're going to the Mists. What will we find there?"

"Ama, for one, and the way back to the Hub for another. It's a rather roundabout way back, but it's certainly better than nothing. Earthers aren't the only ones who have been following the Spear's actions for a while. The resistance have created our own unauthorized Doorways that lead from each of the Societies to a neutral location, so we could meet unseen," he explained, gathering the last of his supplies.

That gave us a serious advantage. I had no idea what the process was for creating a new Doorway, or means of travel between the Societies, but I was willing to bet it was difficult.

"Neutral location?"

Fell nodded.

"As you know, the Societies haven't been able to settle any new planets since Earth was cut off all those years ago. That doesn't mean they didn't have some in mind. There's another place, the Tundra, they call it, where we were able to set up Doorways from each of the other worlds. It was a sort of fail-safe for us. We all agreed to send our resistance members there if the need arose. Which I'd say it has." He walked around the perimeter of the small dwelling, seeming to take one final inventory. He was taller than me, muscular but lean, and silent when he moved.

He was sharing everything without question. We'd been allies before, but sometimes he'd been difficult to read. I decided to reciprocate.

"There's something I need to tell you as well, about the holofilm I brought with me from Earth."

When I'd first arrived at the Hub I'd packed along a holofilm left to me by my father. I found a way to play it, with devastating results. Fell and the rest of the resistance knew it contained the truth of how the Earth came to be cut off. The original Spear, and their leader, had brutally massacred many of Earth's settlers before destroying their Doorway and stranding them on the planet. Much like what the current Spear had tried to do to all of us. In the film, I'd seen many members, including the Spear's leader, get trapped alongside the settlers. Their leader and that of Earth were identical twins—who also just happened to be exact matches for my father and uncle, the leader of Verkent. I'd kept that particular detail to myself, but decided it was only right to tell Fell now.

I relayed the information to him and waited for his judgment.

"You should know it doesn't matter to me," he replied. "Your ancestors' choices have nothing to do with who you are. I see you the same way regardless. My feelings for you aren't going to change."

That last comment *really* drew my attention. While I'd had my suspicions about our Connection, that was his first mention of actual *emotion.* Putting aside my more selfless motivations, I allowed myself to ask him what I truly wanted to know.

"And what are your feelings?" I squeaked out.

The glow in his eyes was intense as he held a hand out, pulled me up from my chair and wrapped an arm around my waist, hauling me up against him. I looked up at him, prepared for another kiss.

Then the door of Fell's home flew open, and he swept me behind him, unsheathing both daggers in one coordinated motion. Silas and Hok spilled into the room, the latter holding his palms up in surrender.

"Right. Should've knocked first. We just wanted to see if you're ready. And if maybe you'd be able to tell us where we're all going?" The hulking Riftian, another dual master, was wielding both a staff and one of his pair of sickle swords.

Fell grabbed his pack and followed them outside but kept my hand firmly in his. Waiting for us in front of his house stood Vanya and Hale, alongside a crowd of Riftians, former Earthers, and non-Assimilators. We'd invited them all to the Rift for the viewing of the Coalition meeting. I had hoped this would protect them from the Spear, but as it turned out, we'd just ended up stranded on the planet together.

Everyone had been equipped with some form of weaponry. Hale handed me back the second dagger that Vanya had given me and I placed it in its holster. My best friend held his own of a similar size, and a row of several smaller knives strapped to his legs. If he appeared overly prepared, he wasn't the only one. Dex and Hok were armed to the teeth. They'd even managed to adhere barbs of some sort onto Dex's still-growing horns. The muscular Verkenter had Assimilated to the Clan. Between the horns and the weapons he held, he looked ready for battle. It would have been comical if the situation hadn't been so dire.

Standing a few steps apart from the rest of the group was Vanya. The crowd held all manner of Societals wielding any number of sharp and fearsome objects, yet she looked the most menacing, with just her daggers and bow. Ever since we met, she had reminded me a bit of a valkyrie. She stood still. Even her hair didn't blow in the breeze, as though it, too, refused to be swayed. Her only visible movement was her leafy green marks, which crackled and sparked like lightning. The matching green from her eyes shone so brightly I couldn't make out the pupils beneath.

I suspected that, inside, she was in turmoil, picturing her sister in danger at the Hub. Ariadna had been so excited for the visit. I wanted to believe the Spear wouldn't hurt kids. Then again, they'd already proved more violent than anyone had predicted. And since Ariadna had Assimilated, they would count her as an adult.

Fell filled the others in on our destination, which he suggested was a full day's walk away. "If we're willing to skimp on sleep tonight," he added.

When Fell mentioned the Mists, the change in Vanya was instant and radical. Her marks died down to near-nothing, and her face pulled into a grimace. After a few moments the light came back as she shook her head. She rolled her neck and shoulders, then strode past the rest of us. She was several steps away as she flung words over her shoulder.

"If that's what we must do, then we'd better get going."

The rest of us trailed after her into the woods.

The beginning of the walk passed in relative silence, broken by occasional whispered conversations. Silas and Vanya spoke to each other, her voice tight and tensed. But maybe I was reading into things. Dex and Hok kept up a discussion with Hale for at least an hour. I caught him looking toward us several times, his face alternating between confusion and a glare whenever I glanced back. I kept pace with Fell at the front of the group. Many of the former

Earthers wandered at the edges, periodically pausing to comment on the surroundings. The deeper we got into the forest, the more frequently I saw flashes of wings or tails off to our sides as creatures leapt out of our way. I'd had my own negative interaction with the wildlife, and yet a part of me was sad as they fled from us.

As time passed, sunlight faded from the trees, replaced by a blanket of shadow. I longed to see the blues and purples that mirrored Fell's eyes reflected in the night, but that was reserved for the Twilight Grove's sky. The rest of the Riftian forests featured trees so large their canopy blocked out the sky.

Our trip to the Mists was the farthest I'd been from my own home since my arrival in the Rift. I wished it could have been for a more lighthearted purpose. I was drained, and even after all my forest walking lessons with Fell I struggled to lift my feet up enough as we walked. I cringed next to him as my missteps increased, the crunch of leaves underfoot far too obvious. I let him lead without interruption, not wanting to break his concentration, and was relieved when he signaled for the group to stop.

As everyone came to a halt, Hok stepped to the center and started directing the camp setup as Vanya ensured our food was divided out fairly.

"All right, everyone, camp here for the night. We've brought enough tents for all of us, as long as people are willing to share. I'd say two to three people per sleeping space should do it," Hok announced. He had the top portion of his sleek, black hair pulled back from his face. His marks shone silver against the dim forest light.

As he spoke, the Riftians who had been hauling larger packs started piling them at the weapons instructor's feet. A line fell into place in front of him as groups separated themselves and started to erect the tents.

"So, you and the Riftian then, huh?" My arms flashed opal light as I turned to find Hale behind me. We'd been best friends since I could remember, but things had begun to change after we'd Assimilated to different planets. I suspected he still had some doubts about my new home.

I *wanted* to talk to Fell and figure out precisely what there was between us. But I *owed* it to Hale to have the conversation with him first. He'd been there for me my entire life.

"Yeah. I guess so. At least, I hope so. It's ... complicated. Assimilation thing and all. Does it bother you?" I chewed my lower lip as I waited for his response. Hale and I had never been anything romantic to each other, but I knew better than to think that meant there wouldn't be any impact. I wasn't going to be dishonest with myself and pretend his own flirtatious banter with Nix hadn't bothered me. It had. I'd met the spunky and petite Crew member when I visited Hale and he introduced me to her. It hadn't mattered then that I had no interest in Hale; I was still jealous. He and I had already become so distant, literally, because of the Choosing. It was just another layer of separation.

Hale ran a hand through his hair, front to back and then reversed. The result was a disheveled, ashy brown mess. Even in the dim light of the woods I saw his form flicker. All Crew members did it. *Shadowing,* they called it. A protection against their Society's harsh sunlight. Hale gestured toward the forest walker.

"I don't trust him. I don't particularly like him, either, but I know that's not completely fair. It's not like I know him well enough to say for certain. It just feels like, like he's taking you away from me. And I know things aren't that way between us. Still, just looking at him grabbing at you makes me mad. It's like he's trying to pull you away from me." Hale had always been direct, but his time in the Crew had sharpened that trait even further. I took his hands in mine, needing him to not just hear me, but understand.

"He's not a replacement. You're my closest friend, Hale. It's not like that's a consolation prize in place of a ... significant other." I still wasn't sure how to refer to Fell. "It's just different. I know things are changing. I don't want to lose you. Can you at least be civil to him?"

He managed a smile.

"You won't lose me. And I'll try, but I can't promise I'll ever like him any more than I do now. He's just so *Riftian*." Hale grinned, and it took some of the sting out of his comments. His face fell back into a frown as a hand clasped my shoulder.

"I'll see you later, Kena." Hale turned back toward the others.

"I think we should talk." Fell's deep voice shook, and I felt it reverberating through me, like ripples across a pond. No small amount of guilt crept over me. I'd been drained by my conversation with Hale, and yet I was eager for a chance to speak to Fell.

"Where did you go?" I asked.

"Checking around the perimeter of the group. There's no saying whether the Spear has members on each planet. I didn't see anyone else but us, though."

I waited for more, and when nothing came I edged closer to the pile of tents.

"I was going to see if Vanya might want to bunk with me tonight," I said, reaching toward one of the remaining pieces of canvas.

His head whipped back around to me. He frowned.

"Stay with me."

"Stay. What?" I blinked up at him, at a loss for a response.

"In my tent. Will you spend the night with me instead?" I wasn't sure whether there was a secondary meaning to the request, but I didn't get the chance to answer.

"She can sleep with me if we need to double up." I could have smacked Hale for his poor choice of words as he strode back over, blankets in hand. Fell's eyes flared as my best friend glared at him.

"Oh, shove off! You know I didn't mean anything by *sleep*, you over-possessive, Lake of Death– guarding crypt keeper," Hale snapped.

If that was his idea of civility than his definition was quite different than mine. I glared at my best friend. He'd picked a terrible time to start the big brother act, although technically Hale was a year younger—a fact I'd often held over his head when we were children.

"Hale, I need to ask him some questions, anyway. We'll share." He left, but he shot a frown over his shoulder at my glowing, black-haired companion.

I helped Fell get the tent set up. A rather simple endeavor, since it was little more than canvas, or something similar, pitched over our heads with flap doors and bedrolls. I stared as he threw blankets down for us. Under normal circumstances I would have crawled under them and fallen asleep immediately. I couldn't remember a time I'd felt so tired.

But, exhaustion or not, I had zero intention of resting until Fell and I had addressed things. I stood, or crouched as the tent allowed, facing him. Neither of us moved to lie down.

"*I* know that both our incomplete marks, now that they're finished, say *soul*. You're the one who used the word *Connected*. What exactly does it mean?" I started.

The glow in Fell's eyes intensified as blues and purples danced on the canvas walls like the Northern Lights. He reached for my hand and pulled us down together. We sat facing each other, close enough that I could see the rise and fall of his chest as he spoke.

"A fair question. And one I can't fully answer without help from Ama."

I huffed.

"Everything here is unnecessarily cryptic." I groused.

Fell dipped his chin towards me.

"What I *can* tell you is that Connected is something that is exceedingly rare. To my knowledge, none of the other Societies have an equivalent. It's only in a mere handful of instances that marks have appeared simultaneously between two individuals."

"And *that* is the part I need explained. Are we business partners? Romantically linked? Is this something the marks control, is it voluntary?" I pressed.

"You always have a choice. That is something inherent to nearly every aspect of Societal life. Just as individual markings reveal pieces of our souls, this type binds those souls together. The few Connected pairs in our history have been great explorers when we first settled the planet, and later joint rulers, and delegates. They were bonded for life. It is considered a great gift. Linked, yes, romantically, but in all other ways as well. You should know that their presence just confirms what my feelings were before. Forgive my openness, but you deserve to understand the true intensity of their meaning. There is nothing you could ask of me that I would not do for you. There is nothing I would not protect you from, all the way to laying down my life. Wherever you are, I will go. Whatever your goals, I will help you accomplish them. There is no one else for me but you."

I didn't move or speak as he finished, and the intensity of this declaration struck me hard. That level of commitment is the type of thing that only happened in stories. Then again, the Societies and their traits had been bedtime stories for me, growing up, and they had turned out to be real. I wrestled with the concept. I'd been drawn to Fell from the first moment he appeared in the training arena. Well before the marks had appeared, I'd felt an overwhelming need to be around him, but also a calming presence when he was near.

"Will you accept? What we are to each other?" he asked as he leaned closer, his hands tightening around my own.

We'd skipped an awful lot of steps. In a day I'd gone from confusion over whether he felt anything for me to hearing him declare he was willing to die to save me. But one key piece had been missing. Love. He hadn't mentioned it, and I couldn't have said it honestly. I cared about Fell, I was intrigued by him, I wanted to stay with him. But I didn't love him. Not that Earther relationships started with love all the time. We'd just done things a bit backwards. It was something I wanted. But I realized that, given the backdrop to this new relationship and whatever horror awaited us at the Hub, it wasn't going to be settled immediately.

I dipped my chin into the slightest nod.

"Yes. I accept."

For the second time that day, his lips pressed against mine.

CHAPTER 2

Before the golden light of day had managed to break through the trees overhead, we were awake and packing. We hadn't stopped for even a full night. I was still worn out from the day before but managed to keep any complaints to myself as I helped clear bedrolls away.

As we continued on through the morning, the light around us stayed grey, the air lacking its usual pleasant warmth. I wasn't the only one who noticed.

"Is it just me or is it getting colder?" Dex shivered, shaking his horned head.

"It's not just you; the air is much cooler in the Mists. We're drawing close." Fell's breath created a cloudy haze in front of his face as he spoke.

"Does the Rift have winter?" I asked.

"What do you mean?" Vanya had been sullen all morning, but at least that piqued her interest. Silas explained the concepts of fall, winter, spring, and summer as we trekked on.

"That's an Earther thing," Hok responded as Silas finished his descriptions. The hulking weapons trainer's arms had silver markings running their length. He gripped his fighting staff like a walking stick as we moved.

"Thank goodness for that. I don't think Dagan are meant for these temperatures." Thea shivered, or at least that's what I assumed it was. The Earther teen's oily skin coating undulated, but it looked more solid than before. Marx, a resident of Twilight Grove and friend of Fell's, pulled his cloak off, revealing markings that matched his emerald eyes. The Riftian wrapped the warm clothing around her. She sighed, and her neon camouflage brightened up a bit. Unlike our markings, which were symbolic, Dagan carried various hues of neon across their skin that served to deter predators on their deep, watery planet.

"We're here." Vanya's words were clipped. She tossed her hair behind her shoulder—at least, what she had of it. The archer kept one side of her head shaved, the other a mix of long, loose strands intermixed with braids. Our group pulled to a stop behind her. We stood facing a row of sycamores. They were imposing, but no more unique than any other cluster of trees in the forest.

"How do you kn—" Dex jumped back as if a snake had bitten him. A tendril of fog had crept out from the trees before us and wrapped itself around his leg.

Several people scrambled backwards. Su Jin shrieked as Thea clung to her. Another former Earther, Su Jin had Assimilated to

Canopy. She had stripes decorating her skin and short but pointed canines. With a sigh, Vanya strode up to the sea of fog billowing out among the roots. She stepped through the tree line, her form enshrouded by the cloud of grey. She disappeared into the fog.

"Well, come on, then." Silas squared his shoulders and went in after her without hesitation.

As we walked, the fog thickened until I saw nothing but the deep, shadowy grey, even with Riftian eyesight. I reached out and locked onto the first arm available.

"Can you see anything?" Hale's voice rang out as he squeezed my arm in return.

I started to shake my head but realized the effort was pointless. "Nothing."

"This way!" Vanya's voice sounded from our left. As I moved toward her, the grey became even thicker. It was what I imagined it would be like to walk through a cloud just prior to a thunderstorm.

I swung my free arm out, searching.

"Fell?"

"Right here." His voice came from only inches away, and I felt his comforting presence as he stepped up behind me and put a hand on my shoulder.

"This place is making me nervous. Remind me again why Ama chose to come?" I asked him.

"Because this is where you go when you want to see the Whispers."

Before I could question him further, we took another step and the fog released us. We stood in a clearing. While soft wisps of grey glided over the ground around us, the thicker, smoke-like wall remained behind. We were quite literally encircled by it, like standing in the eye of a tornado.

"What in the world?" Hale gaped at the grey cyclone that swirled at the tree line in a slow-moving vortex.

"Disconcerting, isn't it?" Hok asked, his silvery marks shining against the flatter grey of the fog.

"Very," Dex responded, as he swiped some away from his horns.

"The Whispers are responsible for those ceremonies in which we send the deceased into the lake, where they disappear into the cave and whatever is beyond," Fell informed the group.

"Likely a stinking cave of dead people, that's what," Hale whispered out of the side of his mouth. I scowled. Fell stepped toward my friend.

"The Whispers possess a certain gift for—"

Vanya scoffed, taking over the explanation from Fell as she and Silas joined our group.

"The Whispers are not *gifted*. More like cursed. They all share the same involuntary Assimilated trait of foresight," she informed everyone.

"Like Ama?" I asked.

"Ama interprets marks that actually exist. Visions come to the Whispers sporadically. They don't have any control over what they see. According to our history, they were once very renowned, but they fell out of favor years ago. I'm not even sure the other Societals remember they exist. The rest of us hardly ever see them, and they reside here unless they're needed for a ceremony at the lake. The onslaught of visions tends to wear on them," Vanya explained.

"The Reader was headed here to gather any information she could regarding the Spear's current activity. Unsurprisingly, she's much more successful at interpreting the Whispers' visions than most Riftians," Fell added as his eyes scanned the clearing.

The Whispers in question roamed about the grove, and all possessed markings like any other Riftian, with one notable exception. Theirs were all the color of smoke, and what looked like steam wafted upwards from their skin. Their eyes reminded me of the swirling mists inside a fortune teller's orb. Simple huts dotted the circle. Ama strode out of one, her sunset orange marks vibrant. The Whisper with her came toward us—*drifted* really was the best word for it. Their cloaks were over-long and trailed on the ground. Without seeing their feet, it was possible they might actually be floating.

The Whisper moving to us had deep brown skin around her marks, long silver hair, and beneath the swirling mists of her eyes I could just make out a shade of summer-sky blue. The grey smoke that wafted off her marks put me on edge, but she was still beautiful. She came to a stop at an uncomfortably close distance, as though she didn't read proximity very well. She reached a hand out to Vanya and caressed her cheek.

"Hello, Mom," Vanya greeted the Whisper as she dragged her boot through the dirt. She looked positively miserable.

"All right, everyone, let's get our supplies unloaded." Silas started to delegate tasks to the others, and drew them away from the weapons instructor.

"Yes, let's prepare some food." Hok moved after him. Between the two of them, they cleared off any curious Societals from around Vanya and her mother.

I grabbed the Reader's hand, tugging her away from the group.

"Ama, the Spear—"

"I know, child, I came here and the Whispers had it figured out, for all the good that did us. I was able to sort out from their visions that the Spear intended to sabotage the Coalition meeting and destroy the Doorways. We were simply too slow. We'll get you all sent off quickly to rectify our mistakes. But first, we must speak." She walked to the edge of the clearing.

Fell followed us. "Ama, don't you need us both? We had questions about our ne—"

"Fell, my brilliant boy, you are one of my favorites, but honestly, you cannot be serious!" She placed her hands on her hips, intimidating in spite of her short stature.

He blinked at her. She put a hand to her temple and sighed.

"You two. Honestly. My own fault, really. I mean, you mentor them both, teach one to interpret marks, push them together, and yet they stubbornly ignore all the signs and—"

"Um, Ama. If you could just explain about Connection," I started.

She waved me off.

"The potential end of the worlds and here you two are caught on semantics. It's enough to drive a poor old woman mad. We've no time for this. You." She pointed, grabbed Fell and dragged him toward me. "And you." She placed my hand in his. "Are meant to be together."

Neither of us responded.

"You're soulmates! You cannot possibly have read that mark any other way! Congratulations and all that, by the way. Now, if we could get on to the more important task at hand. Fell, go help the others."

I let myself be pulled along behind the older woman and stared back at Fell as he watched us leave, with wide eyes. The severity of her statement echoed in me. She wasn't wrong; it had been obvious. Hearing her confirm it so brazenly, though ...

Ama marched out of the Mists and didn't stop until we cleared the fog.

"Now then, all Riftians have at least a modest amount of projection," she began.

"What was that, back there?" I demanded, planting a foot so firmly I might as well have stomped it at her.

"It was me clarifying what you two should have realized on your own, and getting on to more important things."

"You don't think that was a bit of a momentous proclamation to just drop on us?"

She sighed.

"A big deal for *you*, dear, but we are talking about *all* the Societies. I need you to focus. Lives are at stake. *Everyone's* lives are at stake here." I squirmed under her gaze. She was right, and I had to place everyone else before myself, regardless of what she'd revealed. It wasn't as if we hadn't danced around the same term ourselves. I nodded to Ama to go on and remained silent.

"Good. So, Riftian projection. Typically, our subconscious projects onto others we come into contact with how we want to be seen. It can't control or override someone's real opinion, but it can sway them. It's why the other Societals don't push us too much about the fact that we won't even show them our planet. That's something none of the other groups would be able to get away with. It's not so much a method of directing thoughts toward something, but rather directing them away. Away from poor opinions, away from curiosity. At least that's true for most Riftians, who don't even utilize the skill consciously. Do you see what I'm saying?" She leaned in.

"That we don't just Assimilate physically like the other Societies. We can do things that are more inexplicable. More ... magical?" I searched my mind for a more accurate term, but it was all I could come up with.

She waved the term off, as if it were of little importance.

"However you'd like to word it. My own abilities have branched out even further. I've been working to consciously control the skill for years. I can push thoughts onto others, and pull them as well. I can even pluck knowledge directly from someone on occasion. It's mentally exhausting, and physically taxing, so I don't do it often. I honed it by coming to the Mists. Over generations, the Whispers helped me advance it even further. Whisper foresight is the next closest thing to what I can do. There is no one else with this ability, or at least not until now," she finished, grasping both my hands in her own.

"*Generations.* Ama, you said once that you remembered 'everyone' when you heard the song of memory at your home. You didn't just mean the Riftians, did you?"

I'd had a nagging suspicion about Ama for a while that had grown the longer I'd known her.

A soft smile lit her face, but it didn't quite reach her glowing sunset eyes.

"Smart girl. No, I didn't. I remember *all* of them. All the Societals I've come across. Before the Societies were formed, I remember Lone, and all the inhabitants I knew there as well."

I gaped, struggling to respond to this admission. The Ancestors abandoned Lone an innumerable number of generations ago. The Societies were formed out of necessity after they had irreparably damaged their first planet.

"But that would make you ...?" It was one thing to suspect it. Another to have it confirmed.

"Very, very old. I'm not immortal-my aching joints and the plethora of wrinkles I've gained these past few generations has convinced me of that- but just about. The Whispers come the closest to my own lifespan by far, but even they have never made it past seven hundred or so years."

I blanched at this unbelievable number as she continued. If she had really been around before the Ancestors had sabotaged their original planet and been forced to form the Societies, she had seen all of it firsthand.

"Truthfully, when it comes to my own years, I stopped counting quite a while ago," she continued. "It didn't seem as important to keep track when I clearly wasn't continuing to age in the normal way. I do remember that I was a young teen, younger than the Blanks of today, when we first populated the original Societies. I'd lived through the great war on Lone with my parents. They both fought and then served as what we would now call delegates from the original Rift. We created the Choosing quickly, but before the Hub was completed to the extent it is now, children remained with their parents until that age. It took a few generations before we started housing them elsewhere. After growing up in the forests, which became just another secret as time went on, I had no desire to give them up."

I pictured Ama aging even slower than the trees that surrounded her. It was near unfathomable. I thought of everything she had gained. Near-immortality, her ability to influence the other Riftians, the readings she had perfected, over who knew how many centuries. But what had she lost? How many family members, how many friends, how many lovers had Ama had to witness grow old and wither away while she remained, unchanging?

"How can you stand to grow close to anyone after all these years?" It sounded horrible as it passed my lips, but I couldn't take it back.

"This is one of several reasons I like you, Kena. Your perception. You get right to the heart of the more important things. I don't mind admitting it's been very difficult. At first, before I realized what was going on, I had typical relationships. After a lifetime in the Rift, when the last person from what I call my original years had passed away, I was adrift. I spent a good while refusing to let myself get emotionally attached to anyone else. But it was a misery. I couldn't maintain it. Finally I began offering my services to the other Riftians as a Reader. With nothing better to do than observe others, I'd cataloged their markings in my years of near-silence and isolation." She walked a circle around me, lifting my arms and my hair, examining my new marks as she spoke.

"Through persistence and skill, I picked up more and more of what meanings they contained. Once I started, I couldn't help but grow close to some of those I read for. I maintained friendships and relationships, but I used projection to make the others disregard details about me. That way, I was the only one getting hurt by the passage of time. If you ask anyone, they'll remember I read their markings when they first Assimilated, but no one questions how long I've been around, or how I could have read their parents' and grandparents' marks as well. It's quite brilliant, if I can brag about myself for a moment."

It was impressive. Everything she'd managed.

"But you've never taken on a Reader apprentice?"

"Not until you. I had no need of one, and having someone that close could have complicated things. I didn't want anyone prying into my life's work. Then you showed up, and finally, after generations, I sensed someone like me had arrived. That, and the Whispers advised me to take you on, given our many similarities."

I stared at her, and my marks flared to a near-blinding level. Even Ama had to squint against the brightness. As always, she read their meaning well enough.

"No, I don't think you'll be immortal. I meant someone possessing a heightened Assimilated sense of intuition and influence. It's much rarer than you might think. You'll recall that I said I have advanced and perfected the art of projection. It allows me to gently guide and coax people into things."

"Is that what you did with Fell and me?" I demanded.

"Not using any special abilities, Assimilated or otherwise. All I did was boss him into your proximity. You did the rest. No, what I have to discuss concerns you and you alone. It has to do with your fury."

I blinked.

"My ... fury?"

"You've had difficulty controlling how your marks flare or dampen with strong emotion. That's one of the most simple things to master for the majority of Riftians. I think it's because of the intensity of your emotions. They linger in you, just below the surface. Closer than you'd like to admit. You've seen sparks of anger escape before. When you stood up to the Clan member for your friend. When you were willing to argue with Magistrate Warrick to contact Earth and help the others. And why do you think that, in addition to being a Reader, you have such a talent for weapons training?"

The memory came to mind of Sybil in the cave, being taunted by a large Clan Societal, Warrick's face when I'd demanded to call home, and something farther back, from my father. He'd referred to himself as a tornado growing up; all active rage and destruction on the outside, and calm in the center. He liked to say I was the opposite: calm and composed, or at least friendly on the surface, but a storm roiling within. Lifetimes and planets apart, and Ama and my father had reached the same conclusion.

"So, what does that mean for me, exactly?"

"As much as I would love to shield you and the other Societals from it, we are likely headed into a serious battle. I've seen firsthand the ugliness that comes from people turning on each other. Now we have descendants of those same individuals divided among seven planets. Oh, we may put on an act of cooperation and getting along, but there are tensions that run deeply. I worry that in preserving our ways of life and our balance on each planet, we've pulled too far apart from each other. Kept too many secrets, for those who purport to be united. You'll need every advantage you can get."

I tried to follow her train of thought, but I struggled. I wasn't ashamed of my protectiveness of others, but I didn't like it when I snapped into a fit of temper. I liked to plan, and to control. And rage was chaotic.

"And that has to do with me, how?"

"I suspect if you make it up to the Hub, you're going to encounter ugliness. Violence, greed, a lack of regard for others. I'd wager you'll run into plenty of injustices that could spark your rage. I'm asking you to be aware of it. To channel it. Not all anger is a bad thing. If you can focus it and unleash it only on deserving targets, it could help you win this war. But if you aim it at the wrong people, or lose yourself to it, you could cause destruction. I think if you wanted, you could take what I've done and push the skill even further. Influence the others. Use your projection to turn the Spear members' thoughts away from their onslaught, or toward a better solution. Maybe read the others, what their goals are. We certainly haven't been able to figure out all the details any other way, even with the Whispers."

The statement was ominous. While I certainly had hoped to help in some small way, and make sure my family and friends were okay, I'd never imagined myself as having anything more than a very small part to play in the outcome of the Societal planets. After all, who was I to have such importance? Then again, I'd seen on the holofilm that I was likely descended either from the original head of Earth, or the first leader of the Spear. That had been generations beyond generations ago, though, unless …

"Ama, you said you were basically immortal. Is there anyone else who might have this trait? Anyone else like you in that regard?" I pressed.

"Oh darling, *no one* is like me." Her glowing eyes sparkled as she gave herself the compliment, and I breathed a sigh of relief. "While anything is possible, I can assure you I've heard nothing of the sort, nor do I have any reason to believe my prolonged life has ever been duplicated."

I swallowed my trepidation and asked what had been on my mind since my conversation with Fell regarding the holofilm.

"And if it had been done? Do you think you'd be able to tell?" I took a few deep breaths, staring resolutely at the ground as I awaited her answer. I didn't really want to know, but I needed to.

"Well, I can't rule anything out," she replied slowly, and I felt my hands start to shake as I clasped them tighter at her response. "But in this case, I don't think so. Your father and uncle don't have any Assimilated features, Kena. And I do remember both those brothers, as well as my interpretations for them. They were covered in marks. Gold and bronze, as I recall."

I took a few more deep breaths, nodding. Her answer almost chased the anxiety from my mind. Almost, but not quite.

"And what do you want me to do with these abilities, if I have them, as you suspect?" I asked, instead of pressing about the brothers.

"Ultimately? Use them. Right now? Try to become more aware of them. Feel for your projection instead of just allowing it to be. Draw it from your subconscious into your conscious mind, that's all." She patted my arm and strode back towards the Mists. As if it were that simple.

I followed her to the others.

CHAPTER 3

Mealtime with the Whispers was an odd affair. Despite their habit of near-floating through the Mists, eyes glazed, they were more aware than I had initially thought. Ariadna and Vanya's mom was a bit spacey, but perfectly pleasant. The Whispers were all just slightly 'other.'

I sat with Fell on one side and Hale on the other. They hadn't spoken much to each other, but at least what they had said was civil, even if it was little more than requests to pass certain items down the table. Ama sat next to the forest walker. Hok and Vanya brought her up to speed on any details she'd missed and then shared information about the Spear and the resistance with everyone gathered. When their conversation was finished, the Reader stood.

"As soon as we're all wrapped up here, I'll lead you all to the Doorway. The resistance built their own unauthorized ones from each Society to an unsettled planet, and from there to the Hub. While for us it was a simple way to meet and operate without drawing attention, it will now assist us in getting to the others. We'll be traveling to the Tundra, a vast, snowy planet. There, we will hopefully meet resistance members from the other Societies who can aid us in taking back the Hub and rescuing everyone else." She swept her arms out, an orange glow falling over the table.

"But rescuing from what, exactly? What is the Spear's goal here; what do they want?" Thea asked from the end of the table. When I'd first learned about the group, it had seemed wise to keep that knowledge to only a small group of people. Perhaps I'd been wrong. It had left the other Earthers totally blindsided.

"Control, first off. Autonomy, for another. They want to return to a way of life before the Societies, and the Coalition. They think it's too restrictive," Hok volunteered.

"And how does Earth play into that? Why wait until we're here?" Su Jin piped up from her seat near Thea. The Earther had been quieter when we'd first arrived, but defying her assigned planet and choosing the Canopy suited her.

Vanya sighed.

"That we don't know. At the Coalition meeting before this one, four years ago, there were two fairly large arguments. One was how the non-Assimilators were being dealt with."

I noticed how she avoided saying *killed*.

"And the other was Earth. The Hub researchers had located your planet by that point. No small feat, given that any maps of your location amongst the stars were lost when the settlers were cut off. But no one could agree on how or whether to approach you."

Ama took over the conversation.

"Our resistance knew at that point of the Spear's existence, but we had just begun gathering any real information on them. We couldn't be sure, and still aren't, who exactly is a member. A lot of the delegates pressed for Earth's return, and ultimately won. We suspected the Spear, simply because we in the resistance had agreed to leave the planet alone. Still, we couldn't be certain. At that time, though, they'd stuck to political intrigue. We failed to foresee this level of violence or preparation."

The resistance hadn't wanted Earth to come? I tried not to let it bother me. After all, they'd had no way of knowing what the consequences of our participation would be. Not involving the Earthers would have been the safest for everyone.

"Regardless, our focus should be on the mission at hand. We go through the Doorway to the Tundra. Hopefully the other Societies' resistance members are waiting for us. Then, all of us go to the Hub. Once we're there, the first objective is to get everyone to safety. Our delegates, and any others who attended the meeting. There are also the Blanks housed at the Hub to consider. Our second objective is to overpower the Spear and take the station and our planets back." Silas stood and spoke as someone with leadership experience, which he likely had, given his clandestine military service back on Earth.

No one spoke in opposition to this plan, and shortly after his speech we cleared the table and gathered our supplies. Whether everyone trusted the Riftians leading us, or were just too exhausted or confused to argue, no one opted to stay behind as Ama led everyone into the fog. A short way from the clearing we came upon an encased tunnel. It was how the Societies housed all Doorways. Next to it was a small hut, and when Ama opened the door to it we found an abundance of coats, furred leggings, and the like inside. Vanya and Hok divided out the clothing by size and availability. Then Fell spun the spoked wheel that opened the tunnel door. I stood by him as the others began moving through.

"Are you ready for this?" he asked me.

I knew he meant the Hub as a whole, but it felt personal. Pim, a Verkenter who was the closest thing I had to a grandparent, was trapped there. Bayard, a delegate from the Rift I respected, was there as well. And of course Ariadna; I cared for Vanya's sister a great deal. Juliard was another individual I would have to contend with. I didn't want my uncle in harm's way, but my relationship with him was complicated—made worse by a gnawing suspicion that he had hidden something from me. I just hoped it wasn't involvement with the Spear.

As we stepped out of the Doorway on Tundra, I felt a chill so extreme that even the protective, translucent casing on the tunnel didn't keep it all out.

"Hospitable, isn't it?" Hale asked as he gestured to the white and grey waves of sleet that buffeted the barrier.

"Welcoming or not, we're going out into it, so we'd all better be ready," Silas warned. He rubbed the top of his left leg, shaking it in the cold. Since getting an upgraded prosthetic on Rift, he'd had far fewer issues with the partially amputated appendage.

We stepped outside into the howling winds. I clutched my arms around myself, fighting an urge to run back into the tunnel. As I glanced around at the shivering and hunched forms, it seemed most of the others were just as miserable. To make matters worse, we'd been warned that the Doorway to the Hub was miles away. Some of the outlets from the other Societies were even further, and we'd agreed that, despite the urgency, we needed to give the others at least the rest of the day to arrive. We wanted to face the Spear with as many resistance members as possible.

"Remind me again *why* anyone thought it was good idea to build this Doorway so far off from the one to the Hub?" Cassius grumbled as he spun around, trying to adjust furred coverings over his angelic, gold-flecked wings.

I stepped up to help him fix it. He was another member of the group who had every reason to be agitated. His twin, Cassia, had decided to stay back on Canopy during the meeting. We were operating based on a guess that the Spear had destroyed every Society's Doorway to the Hub, as they had done with the Rift's. That, and the assumption that each planet would be able to gather their resistance members and get them to the Tundra. There were lots of steps in the plan where things could easily go wrong.

As we trudged through a veritable blizzard, the wind reached a fever pitch. I was nearly thrown into the snow at one point. Fell caught my arm and pulled me back up. No one spoke for quite a while, or if they did, I didn't hear it over the winds. It was probably a smart decision not to, because the minute I opened my mouth, the chill froze my throat all the way down into my lungs.

"How do we know we're on the right path?" I shut my mouth promptly at the painful onslaught of cold air.

"We're over halfway. I walked this trail several times when we were getting the Doorway set up," Fell confirmed.

I shivered, imagining him making his way through the elements on Tundra alone. Then again, he was doing better with the hike than the rest of us. Where my feet sunk into the snow, his left an indent so slight I couldn't see it without really focusing. The forest walker signaled for us all to stop as we reached a mountainously steep shelf of rock that provided something of a shield against the winds. While still chilled, I was at least able to take in our surroundings with more clarity. Endless snow pretty much summed it up. That, and the occasional outcropping of stony cliffs with large boulders piled at the base. The orange light of the planet's sun shone through but gave precious little heat. It made me homesick for the soft yellow light visible through the Riftian trees.

"We'll rest here. Vanya, Hok, can you get a few tents pitched and bedrolls out? We can each take a couple of hours' rest in shifts. We'll give the others through the night to show up. In the morning, we'll go to the Hub with whoever is present," Fell instructed.

A shadow spread over the group.

"Something's coming!" Dex pointed to the sky. I held up my ax and saw the others draw weapons as well. Vanya had an arrow ready to loose when Cassius grabbed her bow and lowered it.

"Don't! Kites!" he yelled as the newcomers began landing among us. Frost coated their feathers, and several of them shook off their wings, small icicles flying.

Cassius ran forward, clasping forearms with one of them. Each of the Kites' wings and features were unique, and I marveled every time I met one. After all, I'd almost been one of them. Our newest arrival was just as unique. His skin and parts of his hair were a singular shade of a beachy, sandy color. It had that impossibly solid quality to it, not a single freckle or mark, that led me to believe it was actually an Assimilated feature. The rest of his hair matched his wings, which alternated between lightest and deepest blues. Like clear waters in a cove.

"All, this is Shawd, one of my dearest friends at Kite. And a staunch Earther supporter," Cassius explained.

"Pleased to meet you all." Shawd swept into a bow. His wings were stunning. A sandy tan where they exited the back of his shirt at his shoulder blades, and then shimmering shades of deepest to lightest blue as they edged out.

"You made it! Took you long enough!" Smiling, Hok thumped the newcomer across the back.

"We're just lucky we could gather quickly, given our planet's smaller size. That, and wings are a help when your Tundra Doorway is the farthest from the entrance to the Hub." Shawd's tone was accusatory, but he smiled at Hok as he spoke. The larger Riftian just laughed and shook his head, black hair sliding over his shoulders.

"I just hope the others are able to get here," Fell said to me, too quiet for the others to hear. I agreed. There were dozens of new Societals around us. But how many was enough?

The orange sun had set, and a violet moon cast its light from the sky when the next Society arrived. We'd already set up watches, and I was monitoring the perimeter with Vanya, Hale, and Fell as a large group of tattooed Crew made their way into our midst.

I spotted Nix, Hale's possible girlfriend, as she came barreling through the crowd. I thought for a moment she was going to embrace him; then she punched him in the arm instead. Although at first glance she was petite and harmless-looking, she was anything but.

"That's for making me worry! Have you any idea what's been going on? Those anti-Earther ships must have been in on the Spear's plan. They started attacking the rest of us the minute the Coalition meeting was cut off. We took down a few of them, and then managed to get away. Did you have any idea about these extra Doorways? Thank goodness the captains did!" Her words flew out faster and faster as she spoke.

Hale grinned at her as he rubbed the sore spot on his arm, then walked away with her still chattering. I spotted his captain, Karo, whom I'd met when I visited. Next to him stood Everleigh, the captain from our tour before the Choosing. She was a Crew delegate and should have been at the Hub.

"The Crew know that rules are made to be broken," she explained, "and if it weren't for my refusal to attend I'd be stuck up there as well." She removed her coat as she walked into a tent, shaking off the snow that covered it. Her whole right arm had a line of bold black and white tattoos.

The Clan arrived next, the smallest group we'd seen yet. According to the other resistance members, it was a Society where the Spear had a fairly strong hold. I woke Dex for his watch as the newcomers got settled, and he made his way over to his horned and furry-legged companions.

"Derek and Mancio aren't here," he informed me after checking in with his fellow Clan members.

I didn't know what to make of that. The teens had been a pain in my, and everyone's, side. They were rude and intolerable. But they were also Earthers, and at least one of them hadn't Assimilated. That meant they might have gotten themselves in trouble.

"We'll look for them at the Hub, or see if anyone has news," I assured him before I went to rest. Fell was next to me, and I placed my head on his shoulder as I went to sleep. After only a couple days it was a routine that felt natural and right. We weren't allowed a true intimate moment, though, given the limited number of tents we'd set up. There were a dozen others snoring around us.

I woke a couple of hours later, feeling no warmer than when we'd first arrived. I was more than ready to leave the snow planet behind, for several reasons. Cassius found me as I exited the tent.

"Still no Rover or Canopy. What if they've done something to Cassia?" His wings flicked out at the ends as he paced.

"Cassius, your sister is strong. If they couldn't make it to the Doorway, she's probably got everyone organized and hiding on her own planet." Despite all of us being very recent additions to our new homes, I had every confidence Cassia would have involved herself in any resistance going on. Both twins were watchful and intelligent. They had a way of winning people over.

He let out a breath, nodding.

"You're right. And I do have at least one piece of good news. Sybil didn't end up going to the Hub with Pim. I guess she's had enough travel the last couple months. Shawd says she's waiting back on Kite, in case he makes his way back."

That was positive. I was glad the older woman was safe on her home planet. But it drew my attention to the fact Pim wasn't. The man had been like a grandfather to me, growing up in Verkent, and I'd only just begun to rebuild our relationship. I had pulled away from him and so many of the others after my father had passed away and Juliard had all but pushed me from the group. I'd never understood my uncle's motivations, given his tutelage when I was growing up. I worried about them both.

"You need to get moving so you can stay warm." Fell walked up and gestured to Cassius, then pointed to me. "And *you* need a distraction. We should train."

Reluctantly, I followed him past the edge of the group. We stopped near another rock outcropping, which blocked the wind and snow just enough to move without shards of ice hammering against us. Fell had struck on exactly what I needed. With mere hours left before our trip to the Hub, and no truly detailed plan, working with my weapon would help. I thought I'd truly seen the absolute pinnacle of beauty mixed with lethal potential when I watched Bayard's training demonstrations. Fell was something else entirely. As he moved around the sparring circle we'd etched hastily into the icy ground, I found myself mesmerized.

Several individuals joined us to practice. As I stepped back, taking a break while Fell and Cassius sparred, I glanced at the edges of our group. A crowd had formed, watching those of us fighting. I doubted they saw what I did. In the same way musicians express themselves through their instruments, Fell appeared to express everything he was through his movements in the ring.

"Okay, you're back in. I need a break!" Cassius moved to the edge of the circle, a sheen of sweat on his umber skin. I stepped in front of Fell. I'd gone on forest walks with him nearly every day, but I hadn't trained with him. Vanya, Hok, Silas, and the other Blanks, sure. But I hadn't known Fell even owned a weapon until we prepared to go to the Hub.

As we moved around one another in the circle, my awareness of the onlookers dropped away. Fell was by far the superior fighter, but I was proud that I managed to get several jabs in with my ax as well. We didn't say a word, but I could tell by the way he waited after each attack that he was guiding my responses. I got caught up in the exercise, and for the first time since the Doorways had exploded, the clawing sense of urgency diminished.

The longer we sparred, the more hits I landed. I was notably more winded than the forest walker as I gasped for air, but I could hear his inhalations and saw his chest rising as we circled each other. After a span of time I couldn't have named, we wove past one another and brought both our weapons up at once. We came to a stop with his daggers both barely slicing into the handle of my ax as I held the blade inches from his face.

His eyes were blazing with light as I stared up at him, my breathing ragged. I noticed several black strands of hair that had broken free of his normally tamed style. Opal light from my eyes reflected off his skin. He sheathed the daggers as I dropped my ax, his hands moving to my face. His mouth descended on mine, and my fingers tangled into his hair as I pulled him even closer. When we broke free from each other, his heavy breathing matched my own.

Someone cleared their throat loudly behind us.

I cringed, not wanting to look up. Around the edge of the circle, several Societals were politely pretending not to notice anything or continuing to spar. My best friend wasn't one of them.

"Come on! In the middle of the training grounds? We're preparing for the battle of our lives and here you are—" Hale stopped as Nix whispered something into his ear. She shot him a grin, and he cleared his throat before he continued.

"Then again, with all this stress, I'd say we all deserve a break. I'll just ... be in my tent." I rolled my eyes as he left, hand in hand with Nix. The hypocrite. She swayed her hips as they walked away, her short, spiky black hair standing out against the snow.

"Well, the Riftian fighting style is very pretty if nothing else," Captain Everleigh's voice rang out. "Don't worry, you can stay behind us *real* fighters and dance around while we defend you." Around her the Crew members laughed, several Clan joining in.

I seethed and took several steps forward, but Fell caught my arm.

"We'll prove ourselves with our actions." His voice was calm. I was debating whether to ignore him when someone else shouted our names.

"Kena, Fell!" Silas called out as he joined us in the ring. "We have new arrivals."

"From Rover, or Canopy?" Cassius questioned. Silas shook his head.

"From the Hub."

"Spear?" I asked, reaching for my ax.

"No. A couple of undercover resistance members. They've got a bunch of kids from the Hub, and most of the menders. And you'll never believe who led them all out."

We followed Silas over to one of the larger tents. Fell grabbed my hand as we stepped inside. Seated around the space was a group of various Societals. At their center I saw Ariadna, glowing purple, with Vanya hugging her. Next to them was Veronica, a Verkenter who had Assimilated to Dagan, in conversation with Dex. She had a blanket wrapped around her gelatinous form. Beside them was a green-scaled man I recognized as the ruler of the Rovers, laid out on a cot. Standing over him looking like a guard was Sarah.

I blinked. Silas had been right. The privileged, sunburnt, weepy Earther teen was the last person I expected to see at the head of the rescue party. Then again, I had changed; maybe she had, too. Her skin was leathery and reddish brown like a desert lizard, and a black and emerald snake adorned her arm. She reached out to pet his head, and I saw she had talons for nails, blackened at the edges.

At least we'd been able to tell our group about the resistance and the Spear. Everyone at the Hub must have been taken completely by surprise. I walked up to Sarah, the one individual who'd had her eyes locked on me since we entered. I held out a hand to shake, and she took it, grasp firm.

"Welcome. It seems we have some explaining to do."

CHAPTER 4

We had shared our information with everyone, and I had been brought up to speed. I knew Sarah had become a Serpentina, although I didn't fully understand what that meant. I gathered the gist, though: very capable, do not mess with. The title placed her on par with the Rover's ruler in terms of authority. The serpent she carried at her side, a swift viper, carried deadly venom with no known antidote. Sarah supposedly had the same substance underneath her nails.

There had been some grumping from the recent arrivals over the fact that we were turning around and going right back to the Hub.

"But we just got out!" Sarah's friend Saf had opined. She also had a snake, although hers was blue with an orange feathered mane.

Several others had echoed her sentiment. Still, they'd all agreed to go. The small complication was needing to leave some adults behind with all the kids their group had rescued. Several of the menders volunteered to remain on Tundra to help with both the children and the wounded from the Hub. Ariadna had chosen to remain behind as well.

"Are you sure? Sister, I know you don't think of yourself as a warrior. But you can fight! Look at what you accomplished in bringing everyone here!" Vanya encouraged her. She'd been very impressed with Ariadna's ingenuity—using the space behind the Hub walls to smuggle the others to safety.

"Precisely. Th-the kids trust me. I'll stay here. And then if you find any others you can send them to us. We didn't get any families with parents, just lone children," Ariadna reminded her.

Vanya gave an exaggerated sigh, but she smiled.

"I knew you'd say that. Still, at least now I can fight without being distracted by worrying about your safety. I did bring you these. Think of them as a defense mechanism while you guard the kids, huh?"

Ariadna beamed as her sister handed her the flails she'd trained with, spiked maces on their ends. They were an absurdly violent weapon for such a kind-hearted individual, but she knew how to wield them. Her mentor Samell, one of the Riftian arborists, had chosen to remain behind as well.

"We've only got so many first-aid supplies. I'm admittedly less familiar with this planet's limited resources, but I can do my best to help concoct some poultices," he offered as several of the Hub kids climbed over him. Nurturing was in his nature, whether his charges were plants or small Societals.

Fell and I stood off to the side with our newest Kite additions who had arrived from the Hub. I had been thrilled to see my bat-winged friend Ryshal again, and to find out he was a member of the resistance. He introduced me to his partner.

"Acaius, do you remember the Earther I told you about? The one I was so disappointed about when she went to the Rift and not with the Kites? And Kena, this is my husband Acaius." Ryshal gestured between the two of us.

The newcomer was intimidating. Enormous black dragon wings spread out behind him. One was stitched up the center, courtesy of the menders. He leveled a stare at me through vertically slitted violet eyes.

"Charmed, I'm sure." He held out a clawed hand. "Ryshal chatted about you quite a bit after your tour. Seems you made a lasting impression. And who is this attractive gentleman accompanying you? Perhaps the reason you chose to Assimilate to the Rift?" He raised a scaled brow in Fell's direction.

I felt my marks lighting up again. There was no need to be worried about blushing around others; my lack of control over my opal light revealed my thoughts well enough.

After we'd fed our newest arrivals and sorted out lodging arrangements for the wounded, menders, and Blanks, there was no more reason to stall.

Fell sighed as he gave one last glance around the horizon. The group was readied near the Doorway tunnel.

"We'll just have to go without Canopy and Rover. I can only hope they show up and meet us at the Hub. I have a feeling we'll need their numbers."

I shivered as we waited our turn to go through the tunnel. My numb limbs made me question my sanity, but layers would only have hindered my movement once in the Hub. The plan was to breach the station, then make our way to the prison. It had never occurred to me to look for one during the month we'd lived there. Of course the Societies had criminals just like everyone else, and according to

Acaius and Ryshal, that's where the Spear had put the remaining delegates and resistance members, along with any Hub workers who had refused to help them with their takeover of the station.

Vanya and Hok were at the front of the group, Ama directly behind them. I had a sneaking suspicion the older woman was more than capable of protecting herself, but they'd insisted on acting as her personal guards. Hale had joined Nix and several Crew members in the line. He looked at home among their loud and raucous group.

Fell glanced down at me but didn't reach for my hand. He held daggers in each of his.

"Are you ready for this?" he asked instead.

"Yes," I answered, tightening my grip on my ax.

"Kena, I know I don't have much more experience with actual battle than you, but I have trained years longer. This won't be the same as working with Vanya and Hok, or with me. There are real lives at stake, and you need to be willing to land actual killing blows. Can you do it? Either way, I'll watch and protect you as we move through. You don't have to fight if you don't want to."

I reached out with my free hand and wrapped it over his wrist, squeezing lightly.

"I can fight. I *want* to. The Spear are responsible for cutting off my ancestors and stranding them on Earth. They're holding my friends and my family captive. They could have hurt or even killed them by now. They deserve this," I assured him.

"Either way, death stays on your soul. You know from the passing of your father, as I do with my sister. I cannot imagine it's any easier when you're the one to deliver it. But if you're sure ..."

"I am."

One of the downsides of traveling via Doorways was their inability to accommodate more than one individual at a time. We had to be strategic. Especially since Sarah and Ryshal's group had fought their way out. If our enemy had any brains at all, and any inkling of what Ryshal and Acaius had been up to during their time posing as members of the Spear, they'd have increased their guard.

We decided to send in the strongest fighters we had first. Or rather, the Riftians had decided. The others continued to doubt our abilities, although they'd been more than willing to let us risk our own lives at the front of the fray.

Vanya went through first. Hok, Dex, Silas or several others possessed more raw strength, but she had the arrows. The plan was to have her fire rapidly at the guards, hopefully before they closed in on her. She nocked the first arrow and strode through the Doorway silently. Hok ran through next, bellowing like a hardened warrior, with his staff held out. Ama slipped through after them, not even holding a weapon. She was immediately followed by Silas, with his sword drawn. Dex went directly after him, horns covered in spikes and holding a giant mallet. The two were both former special ops of some sort, and I didn't doubt their abilities even if I'd never seen Dex fight.

We were prepared for the Spear to trigger some sort of alarm once Vanya was in. She was good, but not quick enough to down the number of guards Ryshal and Acaius guessed might greet her. The two Kites followed Dex in. Hale's captain, Karo, went next. Everleigh, the Crew's only delegate not imprisoned on the Hub, followed him. Then Fell stepped forward. He paused at the Doorway and turned to me.

"I'll clear the entrance, if anyone has gotten close to it. When you get through—"

"I remember: stick to your side. We'll move as a unit through the fighting," I reassured him.

"Kena, I ..." His voice wavered a bit as he leaned toward the Doorway but still didn't go through. Overcoming my own hesitation, I launched forward, locking my lips with his. Taking time we didn't have, he responded by wrapping an arm around my waist as he pulled me in. I gasped as I broke the contact. Fell stepped away, marks glowing for all to see. I was glad the Riftians had agreed to expose ourselves to the others for who we really were. I'd had enough of cloaks and secrets.

I watched him disappear through the Doorway and reminded myself as I stepped up for my turn that I was capable. Especially with the lives that were on the line. It had only been a few weeks since my last visit, but I felt completely changed. Aside from the increased skill set that had come with training and Assimilation, I had accepted where I belonged. I had accepted myself. I was a Riftian. I was a forest-walking, ax-wielding Reader. These were my people, and I took the attack on the Hub and the Societies personally. It also felt a bit like a chance at redemption. I didn't know whether I was descended from the Earth settlers, or the original Spear leader. I didn't expect I'd ever find out. It was so long ago it shouldn't matter, perhaps, but it did to me. And this time, I would make sure that I was on the right side of the story.

Entering the Hub, for the briefest moment I thought it might actually be simple. Only a few individuals with the white spear symbol emblazoned on their clothing were still standing. Then, another door on the opposite side of the room opened, and more of them piled through it. Some fanned out around the rim of the room, blocking off every exit but the one back to Tundra.

I locked eyes with Fell; he'd waited just at the edge of the Doorway. As he ran toward the Spear members, I followed no more than a step or two behind. He turned as we reached the enemy, so we were standing back to back. As I brought my ax up, I told myself it was just like a training exercise, and that was what kept me going as we moved through the onslaught of Spear members. I quickly got into a rhythm, following the patterns I had performed with Vanya and Hok inside the ring, before a yell broke my concentration.

After years of friendship, I would have recognized the pitch of his voice anywhere. I turned to see Hale, his dagger flying from his grasp. It clattered to the metal floor, far out of his reach. Two Spear advanced on him: one with horns and goat-like legs, the other with leathery green Rover skin. Hale lunged forward, fists out and fighting even without his weapon. He managed to land a punch on the Clan member, but then the Rover jumped out from behind his comrade and sliced Hale across the cheek. My vision blurred, anger spiking through me as I strode toward my friend. I'd abandoned Fell's strategy, but I wasn't going to let my best friend fight alone.

I passed a Dagan with a white spear on her tunic; she merely flinched back, squinting against the glare of my marks, which were growing brighter in my anger. Closing the gap between us, I yelled as I lunged forward and slid under the Rover's arm, placing myself between him and Hale. The lizard-skinned fighter raised his knife and brought it down as I swung upwards with my ax.

I felt my weapon connect with the Rover's stomach. I pulled the ax back as his Clan comrade approached us, slashing out wildly. I jumped out of the way and slipped in sticky, crimson liquid pooled on the floor. To counterbalance myself as much as anything else, I swung the ax back around as he lunged again. His knife glanced off the handle, slicing into my hand. It didn't matter, though. The dagger dropped as the Clan member who'd wielded it fell to his knees. In shock, I kicked him away as he reached for us. Both men lay motionless on the floor.

Hale looked thunderstruck, eyes wide.

"Kena. Wow. I mean, thanks. That was …" He cast a glance at the fallen Spear members. "Something. I know you said you'd trained. I just didn't realize."

I couldn't think how to respond. "You're welcome" didn't seem appropriate, given I'd had to kill someone to save him. Multiple someones. Part of me had been gratified to see them fall.

"You were right. You *can* fight Riftian. In fact, you might even stand a chance against me." Nix winked at me, grinning as she joined us, wiping a blade on her pants as though spilling someone's blood were an everyday thing.

The room had emptied of assailants, at least any still standing. Fell strode up to us and swept a probing gaze across the room.

"We didn't get them all. A lot of them fled. I'd doubt that's a good sign. They've likely gone for reinforcements."

"That would be logical. That, or they're pulling back to gather themselves at a more advantageous location in the Hub. Hopefully not the prison." Silas wiped the blade of his sword on his cloak as he joined us, and I tried to pretend I didn't see the slightly darker crimson staining the red garment. He had been terrified when he'd gotten his first set of markings, which I suspected was because they reminded him of blood. He'd since grown accustomed to them, but seeing the similarity in color now, I understood his initial reaction.

I paced, racking my brain for an idea.

"We check the cameras! It's what Pim or Digit would do. They've got eyes on every inch of the Hub, in the tech room. And I've been there, so I can show you the way. That way, we'll know what we're in for when we get to the prison," I suggested, looking around the group for approval. I longed to see my two tech-minded friends again. I'd only known Digit since we'd been sent to the Hub, but the sassy, Earth-tattooed hacker had been right at home with the Crew. She was also able to master any technological device with astonishing speed.

Cassius was breathing heavily, one wing slightly droopy. Vanya and Hok stood together in front of Ama. The archer had several scrapes on her arms and a blackened eye. Sarah and her snake leaned over Hok, helping to hold him in place. His left shoulder was sitting in an awkward position. He slammed his right fist into it, and the popping noise the blow caused made me feel squeamish.

"There, all better. Ready to go," he said, as if nothing out of the ordinary had happened.

"Lead the way, Kena," Ama instructed.

CHAPTER 5

The soft whir of machinery greeted us as the tech room's door slid open. The Spear workers inside it froze, wasting precious seconds before reacting to our arrival. Hok, Vanya, Captain Karo, and Fell made quick work of the individuals manning the controls.

"Shouldn't there have been more of them?" Hale echoed my own thoughts as several of us piled into the room.

"You're going to want to see this." Silas waved everyone over.

A series of screens displaying various areas of the Hub ran the length of the wall. As I glanced between them I saw Coalition Hall, the cafeteria, an assortment of rooms similar to Nien's classroom, all empty. There was also a horrific wall of cages several stories tall that had to be the prison. It appeared to have only a handful of scattered guards. Then I realized why.

One screen was centered on the arena where the Choosing had taken place. A stage had been erected in the center of the arena floor, with various Societals standing in front of it or seated in the stands. All those in the audience appeared to have white spears drawn or sewn into their clothing somewhere. I couldn't be certain about the number, but it looked like hundreds of them had gathered there. Some had donned masks, but many had their faces and features out on display. I even recognized a few of them.

"Isn't that one of the Rovers we met on our tour?" I pointed out a scaly green individual with a crocodilian tail as I turned to Hale.

"He looks familiar," he responded.

"His name's Stafford. He's one of our Assimilation instructors, and a traitor." Sarah seethed behind us. With the deadly viper and her own venomous nails, she really had become quite intimidating.

"The other instructors are here with us, on the *right* side," she informed us. "Saf and I already took care of our former head delegate."

Their planet's ruler was also out of commission, injured back on Tundra. Sarah was technically their leader here.

"It's another Rover I'm interested in. Where is Magistrate Warrick?" I squinted at the screen, trying to make him out in the crowd. He'd acted strangely from the moment Earthers had first arrived at the Hub a few months prior. He was also my top suspect for who had placed me in the Rift.

Center stage were a few Spear members, alongside a row of kneeling Societals who were clearly beaten and dirty. It was impossible to discern their exact identities, as they'd all had black sacks placed over their heads. I looked for other telling features. At least two had wings, and I could see a set of hooves that peeked out under the robe of one Societal.

Off to the side of the captives stood one individual clad entirely in black, with the exception of a large white spear over his chest. Something glinted beside him, and I zeroed in on a menacing, curved sword in his hands.

"An executioner," I breathed.

"Kena, don't you recognize him?" Hale shook my arm. I looked closer.

"It's Toth." I stared at the Clan Societal who had threatened Sybil and me during our tour. "I mean, I knew he was rotten, but this?"

My confrontation with him had earned me a rose-gold stone from one of the Clan's delegates called a moon quartz. I had it tucked in one of the many pockets built into my ocala bodysuit. I still had no clue what exactly it did, but I knew it was valuable. And not only because it was a gem. The Clan cared about function, not appearance.

The view on screen closed in on the stage and I realized that, unlike the other screens around the room, the feed for the arena must be coming from a live holofilm operator.

"They're airing it." Silas's hushed voice broke my concentration.

"You mean they're filming it?" I questioned.

His lips were set in a thin line, red eyes blazing as he shook his head. He pointed to the corner of the screen, where a green light flashed.

"No. They're airing it. Live. Just like they did with the Coalition meeting. Everyone on the Societal planets can see this."

In the arena, two Spear members hauled the first prisoner to the center of the stage, where they pushed him unceremoniously to his knees, not that he could have stood in the first place, judging by the way they'd had to support him under his arms. Toth stepped behind the prisoner, pulling their blackened hood up and off.

I heard several audible gasps, including my own, as Magistrate Warrick's dirt-covered face filled the screen. He glared past the executioner and towards the holocorder, as if seeking it out. His scaled skin was rough and patchy in areas, and I wondered if that was a Rover's version of bruising. I risked looking away to take in the reactions of the others. Widened eyes lined the room, mainly locked onto the scene that was unfolding in front of us. Silas alone met my gaze. I held the stare between us for a few moments, questioning. I wasn't even certain what I was asking, but somehow he knew. With a frown, he gave a slow shake of his head before turning back to the screen. I felt a pit form in my stomach.

A second Spear member in the arena, masked and garbed in a sweeping red robe trimmed in white fur, took center stage next to Toth. This one was tall, but other than that, the features were impossible to make out. I stared at the mask.

"Hale!" I hissed. He placed a steadying hand on my shoulder.

"I know. I see it, too."

I took the figure to be the leader of the Spear; who else could it have been? The vibrant red wolf mask was eerily similar to the one the original Spear leader had worn generations before, when Earth was cut off. That mask had hidden a face identical to Juliard's and my father's. Which sparked another thought.

"Hale. There aren't any Earthers." I wasn't quiet, and several of the others started mumbling around us. None of the prisoners bore Earth features that I could see, and unless they were hidden by masks, none of the Spear around the arena did either.

The holocorder centered on the magistrate's expression. Warrick, face bruised and cut in places, continued to glare at the camera. He shook his head, then winced, as if even that small act of rebellion had cost him. What had the captives been subjected to that he couldn't even move his neck without pain? The wolf-masked Spear leader inclined his head toward Toth. The executioner pulled his curved sword up. Toth shoved the magistrate's head down, forcing his gaze away from the camera. Then he raised the weapon above his head. I knew what was going to happen, but it was too late to stop it.

The sword swung downwards and sliced cleanly through Warrick's neck.

I heard one strangled *"No!"* behind me as the blade swung down, and turned to see Nix had collapsed against a bewildered Hale.

"We need to get down there!" Captain Karo was the first to truly speak. Unsurprising that it was a Crew captain who'd insisted we abandon our original prison-break plans.

"Absolutely not," Silas countered him. "What is our small group going to do against a force that large? Nothing. We continue with the original objective, and we get as many people from the prison as we ca—"

"Did you see who else they had? Those were our delegates down there that they're slaughtering," Vanya countered her beau.

We hadn't technically seen any such thing, but it was a good guess that's who the other individuals were beneath the black head coverings. Executing each Society's delegates and rulers would certainly be an effective way to demonstrate power.

Silas set his jaw before he responded.

"Be that as it may, the Spear is trying to turn this into a war. We are going to lose people. We need to approach this from a total-loss-of-life standpoint. Not a—"

A voice boomed onscreen. Our new Wolf faced the camera.

"People of the Societies. You were warned that we would be coming. For far too long, the Coalition, and its precious magistrate, have controlled us. And why? It's unnecessary. They preach cooperation and tolerance, yet we all know we are a divided and secretive lot. Think of the might the Societies could wield if the resources and skills of each planet were combined and overseen by a ruling authority that knows what they're doing. Leadership with our best interests at heart. Why wait for settlement of new planets when we have the ability to take more? Why bother with this charade at all when we could use those resources to return home? You have one week to decide. When we arrive on your planets, you are either with us, or against us."

The crowd in the arena cheered, and the holocorder panned around to a sea of waving fists and applause. He'd mentioned settlement. The Societies hadn't been able to Assimilate anywhere new since Earth was cut off. Many blamed the Earthers directly, although in all my time in Verkent I'd never seen any artifacts relating to Assimilation.

"I will lead us back to Lone," the Wolf continued, "a planet that we never should have been forced away from, and which the Spear has worked to return to for generations. Our initial attempt was a failure, ruined by yet another Coalition-backed mistake: the settlers of Earth. Not this time. Behold, the ruler who will guide you into a new era."

The Wolf grabbed his mask and pulled it upwards. I reached out, grasping Hale's hand on one side, and Fell's on the other. I worried for a panicked moment that I would be forced to see my father's face, or Juliard's face, underneath the mask. I was even more shocked when I saw what lay beneath.

"It can't be," Vanya gasped. Kidan, ruler of the Rift, smiled on the screen.

"You Cloaks are responsible for this madness, then!" a Crew member accused from her spot near me, throwing out a nickname that made fun of our planet's modest attire.

"Yeah," a Clan member joined in, "telling us they've got our rulers and delegates trapped in that arena. When *yours* is running the show. You all started this!"

Arguments broke out across the room, and then Karo threw a punch at one of the gathered Riftians. I jumped out of the way of a falling sword as the fighting escalated, although I didn't think it had been aimed at me.

"Stop! This isn't helping anything!" My pleas fell on deaf ears as the yelling and fighting increased. I waded through the crowd of bodies, the tech room being close quarters for so many resistance members, and tried to get over to the Crew captain, thinking that we could get things back under control if Karo calmed his lot down, given they'd started the fight.

I passed Ama on the way, her body glowing brilliantly orange as always. A horned Clan woman began to charge the Reader but veered off before she'd even made contact. Hok fought an enraged Dagan, whose spiny teeth were bared in a growl. He shoved the fish-like Societal away, and they stumbled backwards, their sword aimed straight at the Reader.

I pushed myself in front of her and brought up my ax. The sword slammed into the handle, and I shook beneath the weight.

"Enough!" My yell was accompanied by Fell's and Hale's. They'd both stepped in front of me as I defended Ama. Several individuals did pause, but a good number kept right on brawling. I turned to check on the Reader and saw her giving me a bemused half-smile. Then an alarm started blaring, red warning lights flashing in the tech room.

I looked over and saw Nix, her hand pulling away from a switch on the wall. Her eyes were rimmed red, her face set into a scowl.

"This is the wrong fight to be having. We need to go down there and fight *them*." She gestured to the screen, which was still showing the crowd of gathered Spear members, cheering loudly for Kidan. Hale walked up and wrapped an arm around Nix's shoulder.

On screen, Toth's weapon sang through the air again, signifying that we'd already wasted another life by arguing pointlessly among ourselves. Clouded eyes stared up at the screen as a Dagan's body was pulled off the stage in pieces.

"She was our sea monster instructor," Veronica said, humanizing the delegate onscreen. Veronica's impossibly deep blue eyes were a holdover from Earth, at odds with her oily features and the greyed over eyes all other Dagan had. Her quiet voice faded out.

"She's right. We can figure this out between ourselves later. We're here to rescue the others. Think of those left behind on the planets. They're watching this right now, and so far, all they're seeing in that arena are the violent consequences of not giving in to the Spear. We need to give them some hope," Cassius insisted.

"He's right," Hok added. "We need to get down to the arena."

Several people murmured assent, but one of the Clan shouted out at him, "Who asked you, Riftian!"

"I agree with him." Acaius stepped up in front of Hok and spread his dragon-like wings to their full span. It was quite the feat, and the small room only made them appear larger in comparison. Ryshal joined him, bat wings fanned wide as well, as he reached for his husband's hand.

"If that's the vote, then what are we waiting for? Let's get moving!" Captain Karo lifted a sword in the air and yelled to punctuate his thoughts, and the Crew began running out the door. They were rowdy and unruly, but they respected authority as long as it was their own.

"Are you okay?" I checked with Ama before I headed out myself. She winked.

"Thanks for the help, dear, but don't worry, he wouldn't have hit me."

"You can't possibly know that!"

She knocked on my head with her fist.

"Did you listen to nothing I said in the Rift, dear? *Projection*. How do you think I've been defending myself here without raising a weapon? Everyone after me quickly realizes they'd rather be anywhere else. And how else would I help look after each of you?"

She tottered off, Hok offering her an arm to hold.

CHAPTER 6

Our group convened in the hall just outside the arena where I had waited before the Choosing. Karo, Vanya, Fell, Ryshal, and Acaius had easily taken out the few guards present. Between them they'd also corralled everyone before they ran out onto the arena floor. Or rather, it *appeared* the Riftian and Kites had prevented the Crew from barreling in without a plan. Another echoing thud of a sword hitting the stage sounded through the hall as Silas spoke to the group.

"All right. It's true armies fall when leaders fall. We need to try to either subdue or eliminate Kidan. Anyone going in there needs to be okay with either option. Our other goal will be to get the prisoners out with as little collateral damage to our group as possible.

Decide amongst your Society, quickly, who will do what." He'd taken the change of plan in stride. Once he'd spoken, the groups divided hastily.

"Kena and I will go for the prisoners onstage, if you all can clear a path for us," Fell suggested to the other Riftians.

"Dear boy, of course we can handle that. Right?" Ama raised a brow as she glanced at the remaining Riftians, who all nodded their assent.

The Crew started making their way into the arena. Hok was the first of the Riftians to stalk towards the door. Sarah joined him, striding alongside her friend Saf. The trio broke into a run as they hit the entrance.

As we spilled onto the dirt of the arena floor, made up of soil from each Society, chaos was unleashed. Sarah's snake Charles launched himself before we'd even made it all the way through the entrance. On her other arm was the Rover ruler's personal serpent, who slithered down to the dirt as it headed after a different target. Fell grabbed my hand as we charged straight up the center toward the stage.

As we ran, I glanced around us, and between the Societals fighting one another I spotted the glinting lenses of holocorders. Their lights were on, which meant those back on the planets could see us.

"I will stay by your side the entire time. No one will get close to you." Fell squeezed my hand tight as he made the promise.

In that moment, the potential violence wasn't even my biggest concern. Part of me simply craved vengeance. For the Hub, for what they had done to the delegates. If the original Spear leader had still been around, I'd happily have fought him for his crimes as well. The thing that bothered me most was what had happened to the Earthers. They had to be somewhere. If not the arena, then surely in the prison. The alternatives were that they'd all been killed, or released. Neither was good.

As we reached the stairs to the stage, I saw Vanya put an arrow through a Spear member who had raced after us. His clawed hands dropped. I started to scream a warning as a Dagan snuck up on her, an eerie protrusion on his head, lantern-fish style. Silas cut him down before he was within striking distance.

"Where is Kidan?" I yelled over the din as we rushed up the stairs to the stage and the bound Societals. He wasn't anywhere visible, but the stage was truly theatrical in style. It had a long black curtain set up as a backdrop.

"We'll look for him, Kena!" Ryshal promised as he and Acaius flew past us. I saw Cassius and Shawd on their heels as the four of them wheeled through the air. Fell and I raced over to the prisoners.

The row of formerly impressive rulers and delegates that kneeled before us onstage had their wrists and ankles bound behind them, bags over their heads. Fell wasted no time slicing skillfully through the ropes. I moved behind him in a defensive position, pulling bags off of heads and helping leaders to their feet; those able to stand, anyway.

I staggered as we reached the last of them, the one next in line for execution. His sapphire marks gave him away before I'd even pulled his hood off. Bayard, head delegate for the Rift. I'd been so focused on Warrick that I hadn't even noticed him onscreen. Maybe it was the adrenaline from the moment, or maybe it was just relief that at least one of our leaders had clearly been uncorrupted by the Spear. I choked back a sob as I wrapped my arms around him.

He looked thinner, and he had purple circles under his eyes. His voice was hoarse when he stepped back and spoke.

"Get me a weapon."

I handed him the daggers strapped to my thighs, and he moved offstage into the fray. I had no idea what he was actually a master of. In training he'd used whatever weapons we had out for the day. He did just fine with his borrowed option, though. His movements lacked their usual fluidity, but he was still lethal as he cut through the crowd. Riftian justice indeed. The other leaders who were able to move made their way off the stage and into the battle that unfolded beneath them. Resistance members waited at the bottom of the stairs and led the more injured individuals toward the exits; they handed weapons to the others. Ryshal and Acaius landed next to us.

"No one backstage," Ryshal confirmed before he helped Keldrin off the stage. I'd seen the Kite delegate get stabbed when the Spear had first blown up the Doorways. His left wing was twisted awkwardly behind him, and while he moved on his own he had a pronounced limp. Acaius supported a woman with glistening silver hair, run through with green strands. She had shimmering emerald wings. I guessed she was Nimue, the Kites' queen.

I watched the freed delegates and resistance members funnel down into the fray. Bayard's marks flickered whenever he made impact with his foes, the only sign that doing so was hurting him. I turned to the few remaining delegates as they made their way to the stairs.

"Kena! Fell!" Vanya's voice somehow carried over the crowd. She waved an arm at the opposite end of the stage.

Kidan was long gone, but his executioner wasn't. Toth was making his way to us, flanked by several others. Fell charged at them, daggers swirling as he held off our attackers.

"Go. We'll fend for ourselves if needed." An injured Clan delegate looked up at me, one horn broken off as he glared at the oncoming group. I hesitated only a moment before I ran after Fell.

The forest walker spun around his opponents, daggers dancing as an extension of his arm. He engaged three assailants at once while I took down a Crew member, knocking him off the stage with the butt of my ax. Next, I sliced through a Dagan that had tried to bite into me with needle-like teeth, the bottom jaw unhinging to create a hideous maw.

There were still six Spear onstage, and Fell hadn't slowed at all. I had improved since I first picked up the ax, but I was breathing heavily. Toth's eyes locked onto mine. They widened for a moment before he broke away from the group.

"*You.*" His gaze narrowed into a glare as he pushed past one of his comrades, snorting through bovine nostrils.

I guessed I wasn't the only one who had remembered his threats to Sybil, and my subsequent threats to him, on our Societal tours. At that time I'd hefted a pick-ax and promised retribution if he hurt her. The difference was that, at that time, I wasn't capable of backing up my words. Not that he knew that. I played into what I hoped was an advantage as he got closer. I widened my eyes and skittered back a few steps. I let the ax droop in my hands, and exaggerated my breathing.

"What's the matter, Deserter? Realized you don't belong here?" The word grated at me. I hadn't heard the insult for Earthers in quite a while. I had Assimilated, and I was just as much a Societal as he was. Whether he liked it or not.

"Seems to me there aren't Deserters and Societals now. Just those of us on the right side, and the rest of you trying to wreck everything," I retorted.

I needed to goad him into action. It was my best shot, given how much larger he was. I yelled and lunged at him, clumsily. I made sure to drop one of my legs as though the weight of my ax had thrown me off balance. He swept my weapon aside easily with his own. His sword was much larger, the blade long and wide where it curved.

Toth laughed. He was arrogant enough to toy with me instead of going straight for the kill. I risked a quick glance behind him. Fell was down to two Spear, a Crew and another Riftian, not one I recognized.

"You're weak. We could all see it the moment your kind arrived. Failures, all of you. Couldn't Assimilate on your own planet, and then you came seeking ours. As if we didn't have enough problems to contend with, overthrowing the Coalition. I have no idea why Kidan pushed so hard for including you. And aligning with you for this takeover—it's useless to us. He may think we need the numbers, but we don't need any of you!"

That statement actually had distracted me, and I barely managed to sidestep his next blow. The curved edge of his blade sliced into my ocala bracers and left behind an indention. Thank goodness for the superior Riftian defensive wear. As he brought the weapon down again, I slid to my knees and pushed forward, bringing up an arm so the dull side of his weapon hit the bracer. Then I swept my leg out and knocked his hooved feet from under him.

He rolled and managed to upright himself, while keeping a hold on his weapon. More agile than I'd given him credit for.

"What do you mean, you aligned with us?" I demanded in between blows.

"News to you, is it? Earth's little task force kept you in the dark, did they?" He bared his teeth at me in a grin as he shoved against me. The blow hurt, but his words were worse. His statement only added to the doubt I had in my uncle.

I was finished playing games.

Toth charged me, his sword gripped firmly in both hands. I yelled and spun at the last moment, knocking the weapon away from him and sending him off balance again. That time, though, I struck his shins as I swept around. His sword flew off the stage and into the melee below as he dropped. He huffed and struggled to push himself up.

I held up my ax, but hesitated. Ama's words about rage echoed in the back of my mind.

"*I* am not the weak one here," I said, looking down at him.

He spit at me. I ignored it.

"Stay down. We'll find a spot for you in the prison when we take it over." It was the most generous offer I was able to muster.

Instead, with a grunt, he hoisted himself up and charged, lowering his own horns. I hadn't anticipated it, and I knew as I brought my weapon back up that I wasn't going to be able to prevent him making contact.

I swung anyway but didn't hit anything but air. Fell had come up behind Toth with his daggers. He clipped my assailant at the heels, then brought the blades across Toth's neck before kicking him offstage.

The forest walker offered his hand and pulled me toward the stairs. I looked behind us where Toth had fallen, a confusing mix of emotions fighting for space in my mind. I was grateful to be safe, but a small part of me was disappointed. Not in the outcome, but that I hadn't been the one to do it.

"I know it's difficult, Kena, but you have to be willing to kill. If something had happened to you—"

Fell let the sentence hang as we moved down to the arena floor and joined the others. Spear members just kept pouring from the stands. I circled up alongside Fell, Hale, Nix, Silas, Hok, Dex, and Vanya. We slashed, stabbed, and lunged, but for every Spear that went down, another took their place.

"We're losing!" Hale shouted as his form flickered, shadowing in the lights of the arena.

"A brilliant observation, Shadow. Remind me again how it helps us?" Hok managed a wry smile as he teased my best friend even in the face of death. *Cloaks, shadows, deserters.* The snide nicknames were present in every group.

"Not the way I wanted to go, and not so soon. Still, I'm happy to be among friends if the worst should happen." Silas gave voice to what I'd been thinking as we fought on.

I squeezed Fell's hand as both our marks lit up. We were forced to step back as the Spear continued to close in. I dropped Fell's hand to get a better grasp on my weapon. He lifted his daggers as I heaved my ax overhead, prepared to fall alongside him even as I lamented that we'd failed—without getting the chance to have a relationship. Not truly. I was never going to rescue Pim. I'd never settle things with my uncle.

A series of yells sounded from the entrance to the arena. Several of our attackers glanced away, breaking formation just enough for me to see a crowd making its way into the arena. Cassius was at the front, wings flared wide, with his sister alongside him. When I'd last seen her at the Hub she'd sported a tail, having begun her Assimilation in the Canopy. Now her umber skin had steely grey areas with near-black whirls, like a leopard's. As she shouted, her canines were impossible to miss, even from this distance. Many Societals had sharpened teeth, but hers were near saber-tooth length. Her grey ears matched the markings on her arms, furred on the top of her head. She threw herself on the nearest Spear and put her fangs and claws to use. She held no weapon, but she didn't need one.

More camouflaged, striped, spotted, furred and feathered Canopy people ran into the arena after her; scaly and leathery Rovers with reptilian features were just behind. They all had shields strapped to their arms and held spears or swords as they advanced. I saw Sarah and her friend Saf break through the crowd and join the newcomers. Sarah had her own snake on her arm, but also the one the Rover ruler had originally carried with him. She held it out toward the others, and I saw Saf pointing and speaking. Then the freshly arrived Rovers began chanting.

"Serpentina! Serpentina! Serpentina!" they yelled with each step as they advanced, pounding their leather shields.

The Spear members that had encircled us rallied. They took fighting stances, seemingly prepared to do battle from both sides. We launched back into motion.

As we fought our way out, I saw Veronica and the Dagan had joined Sarah and the Rovers. The two groups could not have looked more mismatched if they'd tried. Gelatinous ink-colored amphibians alongside dry, reptilian beings with claws and in some cases prolonged, gator-like snouts. Even so, they presented a united front as they waded into the fray, side by side. At this new development, several of the Spear members began breaking away from the group in a run as some screamed to the others to hold their ground.

We'd made it to the final layer of enemies that surrounded us when some of the Spear's Dagan fighters joined the attack. Two pulled out a net full of hooks and barbs. They moved to toss it on our group, and we had nowhere to go. I saw it arc through the air, and several of us lifted our weapons. Our only hope was to try to slice through it.

Bayard jumped in front of the net. He caught its barbed edge with the hooked end of a weapon he must have picked up from the arena floor, and twirled it in large circles through the air to bunch it up. The weapon soon became a useless, tangled mess, which Bayard cast aside, moving in front of Nix. She held one arm gingerly, and I saw a sliver of bone poking out from the side of it. One of the Dagan grinned as he advanced on the two; I saw that he was holding something between his needle-like teeth.

Too late, I realized what it was. Darts, with puffs of pink and purple at the edges. We had some in the Riftian weapons shed, but I'd never seen them utilized. The Dagan spit into Bayard's face. Before the darts could embed themselves in his skin, they exploded with small pops of color, like miniature powdered fireworks. Bayard flung his arms out, shoving Nix back. Hale threw himself on top of her.

The powder hit the Riftian delegate, and he screamed as it encased his eyes. He fell to the ground, hands clawing at his face.

Fell and I made it to the Dagan member at the same time. I heaved the ax and brought it across for a sideways blow towards his gut, while Fell brought his daggers down from over the Dagan's shoulders. The gelatinous Spear member fell sideways, clouded eyes devoid of life.

I raced over to Bayard and hauled him up.

"Kena, be careful! We don't know if the powder will transfer!" Fell yelled after me, but I didn't feel a sting. The substance had settled.

We'd taken the arena. There were dead and wounded on both sides, and several bound Spear members were being guarded by some of our resistance fighters.

The first battle against the Spear had been a win for the resistance, but it hadn't felt like one. As I helped Bayard out of the arena, angry red welts covering his face, it just felt like loss.

CHAPTER 7

After a few of our group were sent out to scout, it became clear the Spear had chosen to barricade themselves in various parts of the Hub. I'd lived on the station for a month prior to the Choosing, but hadn't appreciated at the time how truly massive it was. I'd been too concerned with the Societal tours and the threat of death that had hung over our heads should we not Assimilate.

"The Spear has control of the Blank and family housing, the classrooms, and sadly for us, the cafeteria," Ryshal reported, "but we've managed to block them from the storage room with Tundra's Doorway, and from re-entering Coalition Hall. Not sure how long we'd hold it if they really put an effort into getting it back, though. They seem to be biding their time."

"That bothers me. Aren't all of them here? Or should we be expecting more of them from somewhere?" Silas asked.

"They could still have some of their number planted on each Society. Although that's complicated by the fact that they blew the Doorways. Then again, they announced that they wanted to go to each planet at some point. And then apparently back to Lone. Could some of them already be there, waiting?" Dex asked, his furred legs caked in arena dirt while the barbs from one of his horns hung off to the side.

"I'd wager they have both those things set up. They clearly planned better than we had any knowledge of. And that makes me worried that they suspected some of our resistance members were snooping around, because they knew enough to keep those individuals out of it. That, or there's a select few in the Spear's leadership actually privy to this plan," Hok added.

I knew what I had to share, even though I wanted to do almost anything else.

"I think I know something that may help," I said. I told the group what Toth had said, about Earth being involved, and about the numbers.

Silas nodded, a grim expression on his face. His deep red marks had shone so brightly I'd had to squint when I first mentioned the task force.

"It surprises me, but it shouldn't. Verkent has always been curious about the Societals, but the other Earth leaders, it never fully made sense. We knew they'd asked some of those they sent up here to look into Societal tech, weaponry, and the like. It seems they hedged their bets. Rather than trusting the task to a ragtag group of us, it's possible they made a backroom deal: trade their forces for the knowledge? One of the Societals' biggest complaints with us is that we've overrun our own planet. We outnumber them ten to one. Perhaps the Spear is smart enough to use that to their advantage, even if they aren't exactly fond of us."

"So if they gave Earthers the ability to lead up a fighting force en masse in exchange for our technology, and perhaps a share of some of the planets, your task force may have been willing to bargain?" Fell asked, his voice level.

"I know my father would have. In a heartbeat," Sarah confirmed. Her snake hissed as if punctuating the point.

"But they put all your lives in jeopardy! Even if they didn't know about the killing of non-Assimilators, and that's a big if, they had to know you'd be at risk during this fight." Vanya's eyes widened.

"Again, my father would have considered it an excellent trade," Sarah said, with a flat expression. Charles's hooded face flashed from her hair.

Silas paced for a moment.

"Ultimately, our new plan is the same as the old plan, the way I see it. Kidan said into the holocorder that the planets had a week. I say we operate with that as our timeline. If Kena's information is correct, I'm betting that's when they expect their Earther reinforcements to arrive."

Cassius nodded.

"So we break out the prisoners, and make getting everyone to safety our priority. If we can gain control of the Hub and subdue the Spear, we'll be the ones with the leverage." The gold on his wings shimmered as he spoke.

"If not, we'll be facing an enemy with forces that greatly outnumber our own, and all the technology of the Societies behind them to boot," his twin finished, her voice slightly altered as she spoke around her large canines.

We'd set up makeshift first-aid stations in the various delegate offices of Coalition Hall. I went to see Bayard, who as head delegate of the Rift had been placed in his own office. He looked ghastly.

Searing scars covered his closed eyes, their vibrant blue light extinguished.

"I've numbed it for now," a Dagan mender whispered to me as I looked down at the Riftian, "and gave him some medication to make him sleep through the worst of it."

"Will he live?" I asked without glancing back.

"Yes, he will. We were able to combat the toxins in his bloodstream," she assured me.

"And his sight?" I thought I knew the answer, but I felt compelled to ask anyway.

"Hard to say. It's possible it's a permanent loss. Sometimes we tip our weapons on Dagan in puffer toxin. It's highly acidic, but effective against some of our larger predators."

I knew what she meant. Dagan's sea monster and flying dinosaur-like residents were part of why I'd decided against their planet.

There were several reasons I'd fallen in love with the Rift after being sent there. Every individual I'd been instructed by excelled at their respective skills. Vanya and Hok with their fighting style, and Fell with forest walking. Bayard, though. It's not that I'd been particularly close to the delegate, but he'd always treated the Earthers, and everyone, with respect and dignity. And it was while watching him fight Hok during training that I'd first realized the potential in being a Riftian. Before I Assimilated and became more immune to the projection of others, I felt a strong pull to him. Fell was the only person who provoked a stronger response.

I left him to rest and walked by the others. People were scattered, some napping on the floor along the walls or on desks, while others kept watch. The situation was dire, and it wouldn't be possible to stay on the station with our enemies forever, but people had to sleep. As I passed the sea of faces, my thoughts moved again to those who were missing. Not just Juliard, but Pim and Digit. The urgency I felt to go after them nearly overrode my good sense, but it was useless without the rest of the group.

"He was my uncle. I've barely spoken to him since he became magistrate, but I always thought he'd be there if I wanted to mend things." I overheard Nix talking to Hale as I passed. Warrick was related to her? I was intrigued, but I understood complicated familial relationships. I had no intention of prying.

I made my way past the other offices to the one at the end of Coalition Hall: Warrick's. Sarah and several of the Rovers were standing in front of it. As she turned to me, it struck me that her emerald eyes fit her leathery, rusty lizard skin better than they ever had her pale, freckled face. Hok was next to her, pressing on a panel by the door.

"We can't get it open. We were hoping there might be some useful information in there. On the Spear, or the resistance, or anything, really. But it's locked tight. The only good thing is that it might mean the Spear was out of luck as well—unless they're the ones who sealed it." Sarah gestured to the wooden entrance, which featured jeweled inserts from the Clan mines. It mirrored the entrance to Coalition Hall itself. Behind the façade, though, the actual door was made of an impenetrable metal that slid into place.

"Do we have any idea what it would take to open it?" I asked.

She shook her head. Her friend Saf, blue snake on her shoulders, stepped up.

"It's got a palm scanner. But it's not set to Warrick. Whenever anyone else tries, the screen pops up with a message."

"Show us," Fell instructed as he stepped up behind me.

Hok pressed his large palm to the scanner, and a message wrote its way across the screen.

For the one whose choice was taken, but who made the choice anyway.

Fell squeezed my shoulder.

"It could mean you."

In spite of the wording of the message, I was inclined to disagree. The magistrate had not cared much for me. At least, that was the impression he'd given when he spoken to me before the Choosing. Until I witnessed his execution on the stage, he had been my top suspect for leader of the Spear, and for the individual who had sent me to the Rift. Still, it was worth a try.

I stepped up to the pad in the wall and placed my hand against it. I waited for an alarm or an error message. Instead, a soft hiss of air escaped as the door slid open. I stared, wide-eyed, at my hand, not removing it from the pad.

I shook my head and moved into the room. Behind me, some of the others started to follow, but Hok slammed a hand over the entrance, blocking everyone but Fell.

"He left it to her. Let her take a look first."

Several of those gathered began to argue, but then Silas and Dex joined him, forming what would be an intimidating wall for most. The crowd continued to grumble until I heard Sarah's voice.

"She goes alone." It was followed by an intimidating hiss, and everyone went quiet and began to disperse.

The office was neatly organized, every item on the desk spaced evenly. The shelves held books, small statues, and all manner of what could have been Rover items, arranged in an aesthetically pleasing manner. Still, he'd left me a way to enter; surely there was something he wanted me to find.

I made my way around the perimeter first.

"A book, like what Nien gave you, perhaps?" Fell ran his hand over a shelf of them.

Nien had instructed all the Earthers during our preparation for the Choosing. He'd also given me a cryptic book full of markings that resembled Riftian symbols. I had failed to make any sense of it.

"Maybe."

As we made our way around the shelves, I considered Warrick's actions. He hadn't been aggressive, but he had been forward. He'd approached me early on and singled me out among the Earthers as someone with a position of leadership in Verkent. He respected titles and roles. Warrick had known we'd broken into his office and the library, but he hadn't turned us in. Instead he'd kept that information to himself, as far as I knew. At the time he'd claimed it would cast a poor light on him, given his support of Earther participation in the Choosing, if we'd looked like a bunch of petty thieves.

Could it have been something else, though?

He was aware we knew about the Spear, and he knew I was suspicious of him. The thing that had first tipped us off was Silas finding the group's symbol stamped on the underside of a desk drawer, hidden unless you were snooping. Which we had been.

I moved over toward the desk, shoving the late magistrate's chair out of the way. It rolled across the floor, making a soft thump as it hit the wall.

"Silas!" I called toward the door. He made his way over and crouched down next to me in front of the desk.

"Where was the symbol on this desk?" My marks wavered, flashing bright opal light as I asked.

Gently, he nudged me aside. He reached forward and pulled out the second drawer on the right side of the desk, then twisted his head to look up at the base of it. His red markings flashed.

"This is the one." He moved back as I approached.

The symbol looked as if it were burned in. I tried pressing it, like a button, but that was ineffective. It didn't twist, nor could it be pulled up. I was beginning to grow frustrated when Fell came up with a suggestion.

"It's got a circular border, like the medallions. You all would have been provided one when you first started Societal tours. They would each have had seals from the different planets."

He was right. Every Society had a sigil. Before our first tour, we'd each been provided a medallion with one emblazoned on it. I'd ended up with an orange bird from the Kites. But the Spear wasn't a Society; they didn't have an official seal. Unless ...

I sprinted out of the room, past the others. Down a small hallway was a library in Coalition Hall. I ran directly to the very back shelf—a small, dilapidated piece that stood in contrast to the towering metal shelving units around it. Hastily, I pulled open a holocorder case, the one I'd used to view the film I brought along with me from Earth. It had revealed the truth about how our planet had been cut off from the others, and the first appearance of the Spear.

Warrick had been ahead of us at every turn and had thrown that in my face. Whether he had been a friend or a foe, I had no doubt he'd stay consistent. It was the only place that made sense. One last dig at how he'd always been able to predict my moves, and a taunt that no one else would understand.

Sitting in the case, on top of the holocorder, was a medallion. There was a circle around the edge, but unlike the ones for every other Society, it had small, Riftian-style markings. The background was red, and in its center was a white Spear. I grabbed it and sped back to the magistrate's office.

I hoped that when I placed it against the symbol in the desk, it would act as a key. Sure enough, as I pressed it inward, from the side of the desk a door popped open.

"What's in it?" I asked from my side of the desk.

Fell crouched down and pulled out a holofilm, holding it up to the light.

Silas yelled out to the others.

"Someone grab a holocorder!"

CHAPTER 8

I loaded the message from Warrick's desk into the holocorder someone had brought in. It might have been wiser to keep this a private viewing, but I trusted the others. At least Verkent and the Riftians. I didn't know the other leaders well enough to put my faith in them yet, but sharing whatever was on the film seemed a good next step in fortifying relationships.

A soft whir sounded as the projection started. Warrick's face appeared in front of us, hovering in the air. I still hadn't gotten over how clear the holofilm made everything. He might as well have been standing in the room as he began to speak.

"I'm hoping this message isn't necessary, but just in case. I've set the office to answer to you and you alone, Kena. You're likely wondering why. It's not as if I've been overly friendly with you, and there's a good reason for that. If you're viewing this, it means the Spear really has acted in some way. The only positive is you've also hopefully realized that I'm not a part of it, let alone in charge of it. I am guilty, though. I allowed its members to influence me. Not knowingly, of course. I wasn't aware of what the organization was, or its purpose, until I was in too deep. I can't pinpoint who's leading them, but I know several of the other planetside rulers and Hub delegates are involved. I don't have many people left I can trust with certainty, not that it's in the Rover nature to hand out trust to others to start with."

A scoff sounded across the room, and I followed the noise. It had come from the Rover area. Sarah was surrounded by a small cluster of other reptilian Societals that, based on their stance, might well have been guarding her.

"*That,* alongside other prejudices, is part of what's led to my downfall. At least if you've found this tape. I didn't have allies, not real ones. I hope you do. You'll need them. The Spear has managed to come this far because they're able to set aside petty Societal differences and work together across planets. If you hope to beat them, you'll all need to do the same. When you showed up, it was natural that those of us on the Hub would take an interest. In the Earthers, that is, but particularly those of you in Verkent, who had known about our existence prior. You were likely to be the only ones who knew any of our secrets, or held any answers regarding our failed settlements. Some saw your group as a potential ally, others as a dangerous adversary. And I know you've been treated as both or neither. I personally chose to go straight to the source. Your uncle was maddeningly dodgy when I approached him, but I thought perhaps I would be able to gain information from you instead."

That plan had failed utterly. I'd disliked Warrick. Gone behind his back to the very uncle he hadn't been able to win over, even with all my complicated feelings towards him. As if Magistrate Warrick had realized the same thing, he ran a hand through his unruly red hair on the film.

"I admit I didn't go about it the best way. My approach seems to have alienated you further. Know that wasn't my intention. I was pressed for time. I don't know what they have planned, but I suspect the Spear will try to heavily influence this Coalition meeting. Whether from the sidelines, or directly in a way that reveals themselves, it remains to be seen. I *do* know they've influenced the Earthers being here. I was heavily pressured to involve you all, threatened even, by individuals I now know were working for the Spear. That can't be a coincidence. Despite my statement about allies, I would caution you against relying on Earth's task force. I think they've been won over by our enemies. We'll have to see once the meeting begins."

We had seen. He'd underestimated his enemy, and it had cost him his life.

"I've been looking into our past since your arrival; trying to beat the Spear to whatever answers they're looking for. One thing I have realized is, the non-Assimilators aren't the fault of over-population. They're not because of stolen information on Earth or any missing information at all. The two things aren't linked. It's some sort of substance being slipped to Blanks at random that inhibits their ability to Assimilate. The Spear have been using it for years to create fear, and anger against Earth and the system. Quite brilliant, actually, but a tragic loss of life. We could have prevented so many deaths if we'd realized. One of the other Rovers figured it out, and I fear retribution from the Spear if they realize what Sorvay knows."

A gasp sounded from Saf. I connected the name Warrick mentioned with the injured Rover ruler we'd left back on Tundra.

The one who had given Sarah his serpent. At any other time, I'd have seized on the information. The Blanks didn't have to die; it was the whole thing we'd hoped to prevent before the meeting. After what the Spear had already done though, it was a moot point. It was obvious they were content to slaughter us regardless of our status.

"I plan to reveal this information at the Coalition meeting. It's a gamble, and one that may force the Spear's hand. But at least then everyone will know the truth."

Except he'd waited too long. The Spear had disrupted the meeting before he'd ever gotten the chance to tell what he knew.

"One more thing. Tell my niece, Nix, that I'm sorry. Her safety was among the threats I mentioned. She's strong, and vibrant, and I'm quite proud of her. I would have loved to have been closer to her, if I hadn't worried it would put her safety in jeopardy. There is one thing I can do for her now, however. The current ruler of Rover has a snake familiar who is hardly ever seen with him. It's a rarity among our kind, not only to have one, but especially for the snake to be willing to part from us once bonded. My serpent puts even his to shame in that particular aspect. No one at the Hub knows I have her, and I did everything I could to keep it that way. She slips through the walls here, gathering information for me, waiting in the vents to protect me. I'm leaving her in my office for this meeting, in case things go wrong. The Spear are too numerous for one serpent. She's in an aquarium hidden behind the shelf with the globe; spin it so the arrow points to the Canyons from Rover planet, and it'll slide open. She's likely spitting mad at having been confined, but she should be in good health. Even though my niece is Crew, I'm hoping they'll bond."

A small sob sounded across the room, and Nix hiccupped. She held up an arm with a cast around it, and I pretended not to notice the tears that flowed down her face. As the holocorder shut off, Hale made his way over to the globe of the Rover planet that Warrick had mentioned. He spun it so the arrow on its frame pointed to the cavernous canyons that housed some of Rover's more gigantic creatures. When he did, the shelf behind it slid open, and true to Warrick's word, there was an aquarium. A small, slender black snake blinked up at my friend. Nix stepped next to him, flipping open the lid. The snake stared for a moment, then leapt forward. Nix let out a yelp but stayed where she was. The snake wound its way up her arm and peered into her eyes, then rested its head against her shoulder.

"The snake's a nightwinder," Sarah volunteered from across the room. "They burrow into the dunes on Rover, so it makes sense that she was at home concealing herself in the walls here."

"Does she have a name?" I asked.

Hale pulled a small card from the side of the aquarium.

"Kaos," Hale read. Nix reached out and scratched the serpent's chin.

A sharp knock made me jump, and I turned to see Vanya rapping her bow against Warrick's desk. Once she had everyone's attention on her, she used the weapon to point to the snake.

"Very touching, and it gives me an idea." Her mouth curved into a smile, leafy eyes glimmering.

To her credit, it was an excellent plan, inspired by what her sister Ariadna had done, leading the children out of the Hub by smuggling them through the walls, and the capabilities of the snake. Kaos had used the same passages to travel all over, spying for Warrick without anyone being the wiser.

"So that's how we break into the prison, now that they know we're here. They've got to be expecting an attempt, and most likely an attack on the entrance. There's only one way in and out, that they *know* of," she explained, pacing the floor with her bow slung back around her shoulders. Silas watched her every move.

Unsurprisingly, not everyone liked the idea.

"So we sneak in through the walls, then, like cowards," Captain Everleigh complained. The Crew's other delegates hadn't made it; or at least they hadn't been rescued from the stage. A couple had joined the Spear, and the delegate who had toured us around initially, Track, had been found without a head. Captain Everleigh was officially the head delegate.

"No, we approach in the manner that's least likely to get a bunch of us killed off. It's safer for the prisoners as well," Hok argued. The silver-marked Riftian had nearly as much control as Fell over the symbols that adorned his tanned skin, but I saw them growing ever so slightly brighter as he glared at the scarred and tattooed Crew captains.

"The walls could work. It's how we managed to get everyone out before, and how we were able to take down the Spear guarding the kids without being followed," Sarah argued, both snakes on her arms hissing as she finished. In that rescue attempt, she'd also killed her own delegate who had sided with the Spear, not that I blamed her.

"She's right," Veronica joined in from Dagan's group, "but that means we have to consider they *could* be expecting it. After all, we came out of the wall when we charged the Doorway for Tundra." The neon blue camouflage shapes on her arm were a perfect match for her eyes. Both made her stand out against the others on her planet as they murmured their assent. Similar to the Clan, a lot of the other sea dwellers had sided with the Spear, her head delegate and most of the Society's ruling council among them. The few individuals around her were anywhere from teens to twenties in age, as far as I could tell, though Dagan ages were admittedly hard to guess, given they looked a bit like a deep-sea fish mixed with a sludge monster. Not that I'd ever said such a thing to them.

"I can attest to the fact that no one who saw the wall panel open when the kids ran to the Tundra Doorway are alive to tell the story. That being said, I'm going to have to vote with the Shadows on this one. Large wings and cramped walls are a poor combination." Ryshal grimaced in Vanya's direction as he spoke, holding his hands up in a conciliatory gesture.

"We Clan members seem to be a fair bit of the problem here. So we'll go with whatever is voted the best idea," Dex said with a shrug across the room. There were only a few other Clan with him, and none was familiar to me. Their head delegate, who had given me the moon quartz, had been on our side but was dead as well. Nearly everyone working for him and most representatives from their planet had sided with the Spear.

"All in favor of using the walls?" Fell put the question to the group, wasting no more time. A good portion of hands went up in the air. More than half. Tense silence reigned for a few moments.

Captain Everleigh strode into the center of the group, clapping her hands together. Her body language was hard to read, more shadow than solid in the dark light of Warrick's office.

"Right, that's us outvoted, then. No use crying over it; everyone get prepped!" The tattooed Crew, many still cursing and grumbling to themselves, made their way out of the office. They were impulsive, and reckless, and condescending, but I had to hand it to them. They moved on from disagreements with surprising speed.

I walked over to Acaius and Ryshal, putting a hand on the latter's bat wings as the others funneled out of the room.

"I am sorry, I know how uncomfortable it will be for you all to squeeze yourselves through the walls. But I think Vanya's right. It's our best chance at sneaking people out without a bloodbath, like in the arena."

He sighed, and his wings spread out as he raised an arm and ran his hand through his hair.

"I know. It's the answer that makes the most sense. Although, between here and the Tundra, I'm realizing how some of our features we prize so highly on our own planets are a hindrance in others.

That's always been true; it just never mattered like it does now." He grabbed Acaius's hand and the two walked off together.

"I know what he means. My leathery skin keeps me cool on Rover, but it slowed me down on Tundra. Every movement on that icy hellhole was an effort," Sarah commented as she, too, swept past us.

Fell slid in next to me, matching my pace.

"They're right, you know."

"Maybe in some instances, although *your* skills seem to have been nothing but positive this entire time."

"And just what skills might those be?" He grinned, his gaze dropping to my mouth.

I'd meant his ability with the daggers that I hadn't guessed at, or the way he was able to sneak up on our enemies without being heard. As he leaned in, though, those thoughts fled.

CHAPTER 9

We'd obtained a glimpse of the prisons onscreen when we first arrived at the Hub, but we had no way of knowing whose cell we would exit into from within the walls. Not that it mattered. Anyone inside was someone we had to rescue. The last screw came undone and Dex lifted a panel back and out of place. Several groups of resistance members were doing the same thing along the wall. As we moved to enter the prison cell, a few faces looked back at us. One was familiar.

I stared up at my previous Hub tutor in disbelief. Aside from Warrick, Nien had been one of my few real suspects in the mystery of who had sent me to the Rift instead of honoring my actual Choice to join the Kites. With the magistrate gone, he'd moved into the number one spot. His mouth opened wide, small tusks jutting out, as we started to spill into his cell. He wasn't the only one who was surprised. On the Canopy instructor's arm was a single glowing Riftian mark of canary yellow.

"How did y—"

"Down, Kena!" Fell yelled as he swept in front of me and, with his blades, sliced a spear that spiraled through the bars toward us. Its halves fell to the floor as the forest walker launched himself toward the front of the cell. Only seconds into the mission and we'd already been spotted by the guards.

Karo, along with his Crew, made quick work of the lock, and the bars swung open. The others in our group exited and spread out as they moved on to the other cells. I was supposed to do the same but locked eyes with Nien instead.

"How did you get a Riftian mark? And what was in the book you gave me, Nien?" Once I started questioning my former instructor, I was unable to stop. I swept another gaze over the mark, trying to read it. He pulled a grey sleeve down over it before I got the opportunity.

"Kena, this *really* isn't the time for such a discussion," he snorted at me over his tusks, then reached for a shock stick, taken from a fallen guard, that someone had tossed us. I followed him into the fray, where he parried and then lashed out, striking an assailant on the wing.

I hadn't seen Juliard yet, or Pim, or Digit. Warrick was dead, and my tutor, whom I'd alternated between trusting and suspecting, stood there, supposedly on our side. After missing the mark so badly with Warrick, I wanted proof I could trust him.

"I disagree. Now is as good a time as any." I swung my ax indiscriminately at the Spear guards that charged us. "How did this happen?" I gestured to his arm with my weapon as I posed the question again.

We had come out on the second floor. The prison had cells five stories high that formed a rectangular border around the walls. Nien and I continued to fight our way to the stairwell, but he responded when there was a quiet moment.

"I helped the resistance build the illegal Doorways to Tundra. Our first set was from the Rift to the snowy planet. It took a long time. It was pretty hands-on. They had to make an exception for me, to allow me past the cavern and into the forests, at least into the Mists."

"That shouldn't have mattered! Everyone Assimilates once. To only *one* planet. You told us as much. Also, how did you help set up a Doorway? You could barely operate the holocorders in class!"

"I may have downplayed my abilities a bit. I was under suspicion from the Spear. I'd integrated myself with their group to gather information, and it earned me my spot teaching you all. I had no intention of hurting the Earthers, Kena, but I'm not going to apologize for the deception."

His form flicked out of existence for a moment as someone furred and fanged, also from Canopy, charged him. They looked around frantically for the instructor, who reappeared and struck them over the back of the head. I'd almost forgotten some Canopy denizens could camouflage themselves so well they were invisible to others. Nien turned back to me, and it struck me that his sunburst-colored eyes suited his yellow mark. I shook the thought away, glaring at him. His plated brows drew down as he returned the expression.

"Tricking you was necessary. I wanted to get the best opportunity to observe you and figure out whose side you might end up on. If I didn't want anyone to be suspicious, I had to make sure academics and curiosity looked like my only motive." He knocked a charging Dagan across the head and the Dagan fell to the floor, neon purple swirls gleaming against the dulled metal.

With a start, I realized we were out of Societals to fight. We stood there, surrounded by bodies all wearing a white spear. In the distance, Hok, Silas and Dex formed a wall of muscle as they corralled a good dozen Spear toward the cells, to lock them in. Vanya and Fell were activating the doors of those that already held Spear members. We were winning.

I turned the instructor's words over in my mind. I thought of all the hours I'd spent with Silas poring over the book he'd given me, thinking it had meant something. Had it all just been a ploy to win me over?

"I trusted you! I actually liked you! I believed that you wanted to befriend us, but you just wanted to use us like the Spear if it turned out we were convenient." I spat the accusation at him. I needed to leave him and go find my friends. Pim had to be in the prison somewhere, and Digit. Yet, I felt stuck with the instructor. He'd been my last suspect for how I'd ended up in the Rift. I'd felt so guilty at questioning his motives, too. And he wasn't even sorry at having deceived us all.

He stomped a foot as he started to push past me toward the stairwell.

"We didn't *have* any loyalty to Earthers! For all we knew, you were just another potential threat the Spear could weaponize, and we were right! It doesn't matter, though, because I did end up caring about you, all of you. Most of you are valuable additions to the Societies you chose, and I—"

"That's right! *Chose!* I didn't get to choose. All this blasted secrecy going on with you all. I knew something wasn't right. Nien, I actually suspected *you'd* sent me to the Rift. I've been wasting time digging through Ama's tomes, trying to find a way to read the book you gave me. Was that just a distraction, or a way to gain my trust? If you had just told me tha—"

"I did."

I dropped the handle of my ax to the floor and leaned down against it for support.

"*You did what?*"

"I did send you to the Rift. I altered your Choice before Warrick ever got a chance to see it. I knew you'd suspect him. The resistance didn't know whether he was involved with the Spear or not. So, I let you think it was him. If you'd have openly accused him, it might have thrown him off guard enough to give something away. But I'm the one who's responsible."

Nien was on our side, yet he'd forced me into the Rift. It didn't matter that I was happy there. It didn't matter that I had Fell. He hadn't known any of that would happen.

If things hadn't worked out, I could have been trapped there, never able to rejoin my family or friends elsewhere even if I'd wanted to. Nien was the first individual I'd ever seen with traits from two Societies, true. But most Societals were allowed to move planets under certain circumstances. Not so with the Rift; there, it was stay or die. Nien had volunteered me for a lifetime of potential misery and loneliness without my consent, or a death sentence.

I glared at him and willed my marks to life. Dimming them might have been difficult, but increasing their light was as easy as losing my temper. Nien stumbled back a few steps, blinking as the opal light that spilled from my arms temporarily blocked his vision, but *I* finally saw everything for what it was. I didn't raise my weapon as I backed Nien into a wall. Despite all my anger, I had no plans to hurt him. We needed him, especially if what he'd said about the Doorways was true.

"What could you possibly have to gain? I was one person. It didn't matter! But my life mattered to me. What did I ever do to you? Why me?" I demanded as I closed in on him.

"Kena." I heard my name on Fell's lips as he wrapped his glowing arms around me from behind. Just his touch was enough to soothe

the hurt I felt over Nien's betrayal. "It'll be okay. We can explain." Until he said that.

Fell at least had the decency to look guilty, eyes to the floor, as he continued. "That's not what I meant. What I mean to say is—"

I pushed away from him, extricating myself from his arms.

"You *knew*? And you lied to me about it?" I tried to blink away the tears forming in my eyes and failed. Fell reached for me, and I threw my arms out to block him.

"No! Do *not* follow me. I don't want to see either of you."

Color drained from his face. He dropped his arms as I turned to stalk away.

"Boyfriend troubles?" Hale's voice was lighthearted, but his expression told me he was serious. During all the mayhem I hadn't even noticed that he and the Crew he'd rallied had joined us. Nix smirked from behind him, one arm in a sling and the other wielding a curved blade.

Fell followed me, trying to reach out to my hand. Hale blocked his path as the forest walker spoke over him.

"Kena! We have to talk about this. If you'll give me the opportunity—"

"She clearly isn't interested in talking to you right now. One step closer, and I'm happy to add you and Nien to our list of problems that need to be taken care of," Hale offered.

Fell sighed. "You can't be serious! We do not have time—"

"Does this mean I finally get to put those Riftian fighting skills to the test? Delightful!" Nix's smirk grew as she moved next to Hale. I could hear the three of them bickering as I retreated toward the cells. I had more important things to deal with. We weren't in the prison to fight each other. We were supposed to be rescuing people. The delegates, the Hub workers, and any other resistance members or Earthers caught in the crossfire. Verkent was my family, the ones who didn't lie to me. They were the ones I needed to focus on.

"Kena!" I saw a blur before a body slammed into me, enveloping me in a hug. I stepped back to see that it was Digit, the petite, tattooed hacker that had joined our group when we'd first come to the Hub.

She filled me in while she dragged me to a corner cell. The Spear had taken several of the Hub workers, along with herself and Pim, and tried to force them to help set up some things in the tech station.

"They needed you to help program ships to move Earthers up here?" I asked as she finished. She nodded.

"Yes. They needed Earthers to help integrate their tech to ours. But we double-crossed them. The ships started just fine, but we messed up the coordinates. They're waiting on backup that's going to be delayed."

"Just how delayed?"

"We couldn't alter things too far without getting caught, but the path we sent them on should take a few extra days to arrive."

Kidan had said in his message that the Societies had a week. That increased the total window to maybe ten days if we were lucky. And we'd already spent one of them in the arena and sleeping in Coalition Hall. It wasn't much, but it was something. And the delay could cost them.

"I should warn you, we didn't agree to help right away. They ... were angry." Digit chewed on her lip, eyes downturned. "I managed to keep most of their attention on me, but Pim still got some of it. He's refusing to come out of his cell."

I took a closer look at Digit. She already had a gnarly scar on one cheek, but that was courtesy of the Crew. I realized the eye above it was swollen shut. She held out a hand to me, the fingers bruised and bent in odd directions.

"They said if I wasn't going to work for them, I wasn't going to be hacking at all," she admitted, staring down at the damaged fingers.

"How can you stand it! Go to the menders!" I yelled, wanting to help but afraid to touch them in case I made it worse.

She didn't even flinch.

"I plan to, but I needed to make sure someone went for Pim." I hugged her, careful of her hands. All this time, I'd been bickering with Societals and she'd been looking out for the Verkenter. She guided me to the door of the cell before heading toward the others.

As I entered and saw the elderly Verkent member curled in on himself in the corner, the sickened feeling in my gut was replaced by anger that burned deep. I took a breath, soothing the beast and the waves of light rising off my marks like flames, at the thought of sweet old Pim being interrogated. Ama had warned me against rage, but I was determined to make anyone responsible pay, and dearly.

"Pim. It's me, Kena." I kept my voice soft as I approached. He was crouched down into himself, wearing a tattered grey Hub jumpsuit. His wings appeared mercifully unbroken, but there was a space on the left one that was devoid of feathers. I clenched my teeth as I tried to swallow down the fury that threatened to rise again.

He blinked up at me from the corner of the cell.

"Kena?" The confusion in his voice broke me.

I threw my ax down, and it clattered on the floor as I ran to Pim. When I touched one of his smoky-colored wings, he pulled away. I wondered if he'd been hiding in the corner of his cell, scared of the noise and chaos around him after what he'd been through. For a moment I couldn't see straight, but I breathed out, willing myself to be the calm and caring person he needed at that moment.

"You're all right. I'm going to get you out of here. We've taken over the prison. I'm going to get you to a mender." I knew I was only speaking of his well-being physically; we had no way to erase this experience from his mind.

He gave me a blank stare, then shook his head. His eyes went wide and he clutched at me.

"But how did you all make it back here? It's not safe! Kena! They're sending reinforcements from Earth. Kaiser, he backstabbed some of the Earth's task force. He's working with the Spear. And when they get here, they plan to—"

An alarm started blaring, and red lights blinked on the walls.

"We're going to have company!" Hok yelled from outside the cell.

"We need to hurry. Can you walk on your own?" I kept my voice steady and held out my hand. Pim trembled as he took it. He pulled himself up to his full height and gingerly tried putting weight on his left leg before shaking his head.

"Hobble, maybe, but not without help." He winced as he tried one more step forward.

"That's fine, I'll be right here," I reassured him, "I've got you now."

I pulled one of his arms over my shoulder and supported most of his weight as we made our way out of the cell. I glanced around before exiting; his cell was on the ground floor of the prison. So far, it was only resistance members and released prisoners milling about. Several moved toward the prison's entrance, preparing for whatever the Spear sent at us. I led Pim toward the cell where our group had entered, determined to get him through the walls and to a mender as soon as possible. I just had to figure out how to get him up the flight of stairs to the second level.

Hale waved at us as we made our way across the center of the cellblock. Silas spotted us as well. I smiled as they came toward us, relieved to have their help. Silas could probably carry Pim if needed. I was so focused on the two of them that I didn't have time to register where the soft whistling noise came from before a spear flew in front of me and buried itself in Pim's chest. The force of it pulled him from my arms and down to his knees.

"Pim!" I dropped beside him, my hands fluttering over the wound. "Pim, it's going to be all right. We'll get someone to help, we'll—"

He wheezed once, coughing blood before he slumped over. His pale blue eyes slid shut. Hands shaking, I held one over his face, but he wasn't breathing.

I screamed, but the way it echoed off the walls made it sound as if it came from someone else. I could not possibly have made such an animalistic noise. Ama's home had chimes outside that played the melody of different emotions. If suffering had a sound, I imagined the wailing coming from me had to be it. What I saw could not have been real. The prison was secure; the door was guarded. Pim wasn't dead. Not after everything he'd been through. Not when he'd been in my care. We'd been so close. It wasn't right. Silas's arm touching my shoulder brought my screaming to a halt. He and Hale knelt over Pim's body, but my best friend shook his head, confirming what I already knew.

I looked up at where the spear had come from. A heavily tattooed Crew member was smirking from the level above us. He pulled aside the grey jumpsuit all the prisoners had worn, and beneath it was a red tunic with a white spear.

I saw Vanya take aim with her bow.

"No. Stop!" That time I knew the sound was my own voice.

"She's right. We need at least some of them for information," Silas added as she lowered the bow.

My response was for Silas, but I kept my eyes locked on my enemy.

"That's not why."

"Kena, what? We have company!" Silas interrupted his own question as more Spear assailants reached the entrance to the prison. Several resistance members fell at once, and I couldn't understand why.

"Puffer poison!" Dex yelled. I envisioned more Societals with scars like Bayard's, all because of the Spear.

Many of the others turned toward the door. Not me. I watched as the Crew member who had killed Pim stalked the railing. Some of the newly freed prisoners flinched back as he passed, and I guessed there was a good reason for it. A guard, then.

Running a hand through his hair, Captain Karo stepped up next to me.

"He's from our Society. We'll take care of him."

"No, go help the others. He's mine." I yelled the last words up at the Spear member. To my surprise, he responded, leaning over the railing above.

"Realized I'm more useful breathing, then, have you? I hate to disappoint, but if you're hoping some Riftian's questioning is going to get me to reveal anything, you're sorely mistaken. You'd be better off letting the captain there face me. You stand no chance."

Thanks to my forest walker training, which had included scaling trees, I made my way up the metal structure to his level easily enough, ignoring the stairs and dropping on the catwalk directly in front of him. Fell would have been proud.

"I believe you. You're not going to give us anything. The only response I need is for you to answer for your crimes. That man was family to me." I informed my adversary, not taking my eyes off him.

His smirk returned.

"Then you have poor taste. That old codger was past his usefulness to us."

I said nothing, but the marks on my body flared so brightly that his smile faltered, and he flinched momentarily before regaining his composure and putting a sneer on his face.

"How do you propose we handle this, then, Deserter? You have no weapon, and neither do I, now that I've been relieved of my spear."

He was right. My ax was in Pim's cell. I clenched my fists.

"I won't need one. Are you telling me a Crew member thinks himself too weak to take on a Cloak with his bare hands?" My goading worked. He scowled at me and waved me forward.

"Let's settle this, then."

The next moments existed inside a bubble. I tuned out the fighting below as we traded blows back and forth, neither of us gaining ground. We moved past several cells, until we reached one with another fallen guard. Something glinted at her side. My opponent bent and retrieved it. A short sword. His smile returned as he began hacking away in my direction. One of the blows landed just above a bracer, and the blade sliced into my right arm. I cried out and stumbled backward.

I heard Fell yell my name from below, as if, even over the din, he recognized my voice. I saw him start moving toward us. But he had to contend with the crowd that had filled the prison floor. I let the arm hang limp at my side; perhaps the trick I'd pulled on Toth could work twice. My attacker's form flickered. If I had to guess, I'd say he was enjoying himself. He gloated as he closed in on me, punctuating his sentences with heavy steps.

"You Riftians. Even in the Spear, you think you're so superior with your supposed *intelligence*," he spat disdainfully, "as if you're so much better than the rest of us. And an Earther to boot. Once we make use of your planet's superior numbers, we won't need any of you."

"Isn't your leader a Riftian?" I continued to back away as he stalked toward me.

"Kidan's warrior-like attitude fits with us much better. He should have joined the Crew. If anything, he proves what we're trying to do. Stuck on that useless planet because of a choice he made years ago, when what we all really need is to go home."

I tripped over another fallen prisoner behind me and fell backward. Pim's killer stared down at me.

"At least other Societies have some fight in them. If you had half the ferocity of a Crew member you would have let that captain try to gut me. But you're soft. You're not capable of doing what has to be done in order to defeat us. Which is why we'll win.."

He had his sword lifted over his head, ready to bring it down on me when I moved. I wasn't sure if it would work, but it was my only option. I threw out my uninjured arm, and put all the anger and hurt behind my statement. I squeezed my eyes shut, waiting for impact in case I was wrong.

"Stop!"

When I didn't feel the sting of a blade I risked opening my eyes. He had done what I'd told him. I hadn't been certain it would work. After all, Ama had been very clear there were limits to projection. That it wasn't mind control. But the Crew member frozen in front of me was evidence otherwise.

"How? Riftian trash!" He spat at my feet. It appeared my control only went so far.

My marks blazed, and it took all my concentration to keep him still. I fed every bit of anger that pulsed through me into the effort, all the grief. I felt my energy, like a physical thing, draining from my body. How had Ama kept up the effort for any amount of projection close to this? I had limited time.

"When I can move, you will be sorry," he swore.

I glared at him, unable to bring myself to feel pity even as I held him still.

"I don't think I'm the one who's going to have regrets here," I stated.

"You all deserve what's happened to you. All the Earthers, and all those who followed the Coalition blindly. All this for some old man?"

He slashed out at me again, but the sword made no contact. I'd been so shocked that I'd dropped control. The new surge of anger caused by his comment helped me gain it back.

"Drop the sword," I yelled. He did. "Now climb the railing."

I knew I was toeing a line, but I wasn't able to bring myself to care as he did what I asked. He swayed as he stood on the metal rail, looking down at the floor beneath.

"Deserter filth. If you think I'm going to ask for any mercy from you, I won't."

Though it took every ounce of self-control I had, I dropped my arm, and with it my hold over him.

He could have climbed down, but instead he attempted to lunge at me. The movement threw him off balance, and his arms wheeled in the air for a moment before he fell. I made no effort to reach after him, and I wasn't sorry when he hit the floor.

CHAPTER 10

I had no idea how long I'd been standing, staring over the railing after the Crew member, when someone approached me.

"Are you okay?" There was a light touch on my shoulder, and I saw twilight markings in my peripheral vision before I even turned around. Fell placed the handle to my ax in my hand, and I took it without thinking.

Part of me wanted to shrug him off. I was still upset with the forest walker, but I needed him. I owed him a conversation at the very least; to hear his side. On top of all of it, drowning out any other emotion, was grief. I shook my head, unable to put into words all the things I felt. Fell wrapped his arms around me and pulled me toward him, letting me cry.

"I will be here for you in whatever way you need, but we do have to go," he whispered into my hair. "We've got the prison entrance blocked and all the prisoners out, but we can't hold it forever. Hok and Silas suggested moving everyone back to Coalition Hall. If we utilize the library stacks, there should be enough space to fit everyone, and it's a better idea than dividing our limited numbers." He kept his voice soft, as if coaxing a timid animal. Like I'd done for Pim.

"Is anyone else hurt?" I pulled my head out from his shoulder and started to move with him toward the still-open panel in the wall.

"Some. The Spear managed to take out several resistance members and prisoners when they came through the main entrance to the prison. Our losses here weren't as bad as in the arena. We were able to funnel them through the entrance, and keep almost everyone clear of the puffer poison. There are several gashes and bruises. A couple nasty breaks, but most of the injured should recover."

But not Pim, I didn't add out loud. He'd meant more to me than almost anyone else. And I'd failed to save him. Worse, I was responsible, at least in part. I should have gone to him sooner, instead of arguing with Nien. I'd let all the tension and frustration that had built over the recent months out at the worst time. Then, I'd been so eager to get Pim out of his cell and safe that I hadn't checked to see if our path was clear. I was new to fighting, but I should have at least known to do that much. And there was nothing I was able to do to take it back.

"I should have seen him." I stopped and looked at Fell. "I should have *known* there would be Spear hiding out, waiting for us. They're underhanded and cruel. We've seen it over and over. But I didn't stop to look. I just wanted to get him safe. And now—"

I had to take a few deep breaths to prevent breaking down in tears as we neared our exit.

"Fell." I had to tell him before we were around the others. "There's something else. When that Crew member who hurt Pim ... when I fought him, I made him stop."

He laid a hand on my shoulder.

"You did what you had to do. This is a more serious situation than any of us has ever been in. It's natural to feel conflicted, but it was his life or yours."

I shook my head.

"Not that way, and I'm not conflicted. I'm not sorry about it. But I *made* him stop. It was like projection, sort of. Except instead of it happening subconsciously, I was wielding it. I *told* him to stop. And he did. Then I told him to drop his weapon. And he did. Then—"

"You asked him to jump?" Fell's voice gave nothing away. I wasn't sure what he would have said if the answer had been yes. I suspected he would have supported me even in that. The thought was both bolstering and unnerving at once.

"No. I let him go. But I could have. That's what I'm saying."

An echo sounded through the prison.

"Kena, we have a lot to discuss. But they're breaking through."

I followed him through the hole in the cell wall and we sealed the panel behind us.

"So," I started as we made our way back to the others, "you said earlier that 'we' could explain." I knew we had to address what I'd done to the Crew member, but that also meant dealing with Pim, and I'd reached the limit of what I was able to handle in that department.

He sighed as he ran but didn't put me off. This was one of the features I most appreciated about Fell.

"I worded it badly. I'll admit that. I want to be very clear that I had no idea when you arrived that you'd been forced into the Rift. *That* is something I'm happy to hold Nien accountable for, you just say the word. What I referred to was that I knew he was part of the resistance and gathering information for us."

That was much better than I'd feared. I'd let my frustration with Societal secrets override my trust in Fell. *That* was a mistake I could correct.

"I'm sorry. I should have trusted you. What kind of information?" I asked.

"Mainly whether he thought you all were aware of the Spear, or at least the task force who sent you. He was trying to unravel whether you'd be an enemy, an ally, or just a potential hindrance. Then there was the question of whether you all knew how to fix the settlement problem. I know none of you has any idea why we can't settle new planets, but at least now we know non-Assimilators were a Spear-made issue. But I swear to you, Kena, I was never aware of any personal details, and I wouldn't have condoned Nien forcing anyone's choice."

I grabbed his hands, and our marks lit the space along the walls.

"I'm still upset, but not at you. I trust you. I need you to know that."

He nodded, seeming to accept it, as he kept going.

"To be honest, he hadn't fully made up his mind about Earth as a whole by the time the Choosing hit. I'm as confused as anyone why he did to you what he did. From everything we'd heard, he thought you all largely trustworthy, at least those of you actually up at the Hub. We still had questions about the motives of those who sent you, but the people here were all right, with a few minor exceptions."

Derek's face popped into my mind as he said it, and I felt disloyal. The Earther teen and his friend Mancio had been rude and unruly since we'd arrived, but there was no evidence that anyone up in the Societies had been any less shocked than I had with what the Spear had done.

I had a follow-up question prepared when we were both thrown to the floor. The walls shook. I heard the clanging of falling metal and unnerving creaking noises. Fell managed to catch me with one arm while shielding me, pressing me against the wall. As another wave of movement shook us, he cursed.

"They've figured out we're in the walls. We need to get out."

"What?" Despite the callousness with which I'd handled the Crew member, I was far from a hardened warrior. The creaking noises that came from the metal around us reminded me that we were on a station in space. I had no desire to find out what happened if the walls gave way.

"They won't create a hole. That would be catastrophic for everyone here, including them," Fell said, as if he'd read my mind, "but they would damage this inner layer of wall enough to try and cut off our movement throughout the Hub. We'll just have to exit early and hope we're able to make it through whatever numbers they have between us and Coalition Hall."

The metal shook again, and the passage in front of us caved in entirely.

"It doesn't look like we have a lot of time to think about it," I grumbled as we started undoing the screws on the panel nearest where we stood.

I could hear shouts and noises from outside as we worked. With the last screw out, I held my ax in one hand and pulled the panel with the other. Fell stood behind me, daggers at the ready. We stepped into the open hallway. We'd been behind the others but clearly weren't the only ones who hadn't made it back to Coalition Hall before the cave-in. Panels popped open in several spaces as resistance members spilled into the fray.

It felt like we'd been fighting an endless battle since we arrived at the Hub. Which in a sense was true. I longed for an actual solution, not that I planned to find one in the hallway. As I dove into the fight alongside Fell, I spotted the twins off to our left.

Something that looked like a trident caught the edge of one of Cassius's angelic wings, ripping out feathers as it twisted the appendage. He dropped to a knee and the weapon's owner, a Dagan fighter, raced toward him. Cassia went into action, a feral sound escaping her lips as she sprinted at her brother's attacker.

As Fell and I ran to the fallen Kite, the crowd of Spear attackers converged on Cassius. A horned Clan member pinned his injured wing down with a hoof as Cassius thrashed wildly, swiping out at the Spear member with his one available wing.

"Duck!" I yelled, swinging wide as Fell lowered himself, our movements in tandem. He slashed at ankles while I went for chests. Multiple Spear members dropped or pulled back, but it wasn't enough. We weren't going to be able to break through all of them. I could see Cassius over their heads, bellowing in defiance as one of the Spear made it through his one-winged defenses and slashed at the Kite's shin. Cassius wavered but refused to drop.

Cassia turned and growled at the Dagan who had wielded the trident against her brother. She ripped her claws across each new foe with apparent ease. I'd almost reached the twins when I saw that one of the Spear members had managed to get their hands on a bow. I hadn't seen anyone use such a weapon with anywhere near Vanya's skill level, but this individual was so close in range it I assumed it would be inconsequential. The first arrow tore through Cassia's ear, but she yowled and kept fighting. Her attacker, a blue-winged Kite, drew another arrow, this time aimed at her throat. I moved to leap in front of her.

With a bellow, another Kite caught the attacker first. I stopped, even amidst the fighting, in disbelief as Sourface, of all people, dove into the melee from above. The grey, dingy-winged Hub instructor, whose real name was Iduna, had openly despised Earthers since our arrival. Still, she barreled into the Spear members attacking the twins, bearing down as they all fell in a heap. One, at least, was left unconscious as the others tried to scramble out of the way of her slicing wings. Though they'd typically been kept tucked behind her, as she moved I realized they were sharpened at the edges, more weapon than feather.

When all Spear fighters in the immediate vicinity were down, Iduna landed. With her scowl and ramrod straight posture she looked more stern than graceful, as she approached the twins.

"But why? You hate us." Cassius stretched his injured wing and motioned across to the other Earthers in the group as Iduna stepped toward them.

The grey-haired woman swept a stray strand back from her blood-spattered face, somehow managing to look official even with her literally ruffled feathers and crimson-splattered attire.

"Because. Despite any misgivings, and I had many of them ... you *did* Assimilate. That makes you Societals. Furthermore, you're all here defending that system, while these *insurrectionists* attempt to tear it down. We have rules for a reason, you know." She looked down her nose at some of the Spear bodies scattered around us.

It was almost comforting to find out that her disdain for us hadn't been faked.

"So she's on our side now then, huh?" Hale leaned in close as he passed me. I threw my arms around him, thankful to have proof he'd made it through the melee safely.

"She's on the side of the Societies, at least."

"Does this mean we aren't allowed to call her Sourface anymore?" He grinned, winking at me. I even managed a laugh in response.

The reprieve was short-lived. We'd come near enough to the door that the injured resistance members could duck into Coalition Hall, but there were still plenty of Spear to fend off.

"We're wearing them down!" I heard Hok's yell as we continued back toward the doors.

"Are you all right, Kena?" Fell questioned, next to me. I gave a limp nod. For him and the others, I was determined to carry on until we were all safe.

Fell shoved me behind him as several Spear members rounded the corner. There were six of them. Two men from Clan, a woman from Dagan, a woman from the Rovers, a purple-feathered man from the Kites, and one individual who still wore full Spear regalia. This last one had a red cloak and a ridiculous red and white crocodilian mask, complete with a jutted-out nose. The glimmering teeth looked almost real, and the mask had a spear emblazoned down the snout. As I watched this crocodilian-masked Spear slicing through the crowd with a scythe, like some Societal reaper, something struck me as odd. Then I realized they were undercutting their fellow Spear members, not the resistance.

Fell fought off all the enemies to our front, joined by Dex and Silas. The fake Spear member made his way toward me, at last pulling the mask off. I'd been distracted before, but as his face came into view I lost track of the battle completely.

"Juliard," I exhaled in surprise. My uncle stood before me, in the garb of our enemies. The Rover he'd come in with was a talented fighter, or at least quicker than her comrades. She unrolled a leather shield that had been strapped to her back and pulled out a barbed whip.

"Behind me, niece!" Juliard yelled, and moved to shield me. He dropped the crocodile mask on the floor and gripped his scythe with both hands. As I went to duck under his arm, he ran forward. My uncle slid under the Rover's whip, catching it with his scythe and pulling her down. As Fell finished her off, Juliard swung his weapon up and into an attacking Dagan.

Fell and my uncle stared at one another for a moment before moving toward their next targets.

The purple-winged Spear had moved behind Fell. He unfurled his feathers and revealed a weapon hidden within: small darts, no doubt poisoned, each labeled with a little white spear. I reached for my ax as the Kite cast Fell a predatory glance. I was determined to reach the forest walker first. I screamed his name as I sprinted toward him.

The Spear drew his weapon as I raised my own, and his eyes slid to me just before the throw. I realized too late what he planned. The darts sailed from his hands not in Fell's direction, but my own.

Fell screamed as he lunged toward me, but the sound was drowned out by another voice.

"No!"

Blurry figures moved in front of my vision as the darts collided with my bodysuit. I fell backwards and landed with a painful jolt on the ground as the air was knocked out of me. I heaved and tried to suck in breaths that wouldn't come. Beautiful twilight hues flooded my vision, and I knew Fell was standing over me. As small whiffs of air started making their way back into my lungs, I lifted a hand and pulled out the darts. There was no blood. I patted my chest, for a moment thinking the moon quartz I carried in one pocket had been responsible for protecting me. The gem, however, was unscathed. The ocala had done its job. Whatever was in the darts, and I still suspected poison, it wasn't the clouded puffer poision that had hit Bayard in the arena.

I looked up to see Fell breathing deep, eyes wide.

"It's okay. I'm okay," I told him. Or at least tried to. My voice was a hoarse rasp and I winced when I spoke, clutching what I was certain would be very bruised ribs when I got a chance to look. Those darts packed a punch.

Behind Fell, there came a feral yell and a pained shriek. As I looked up, I saw a pile of crooked and ruined purple feathers jutting up from the now-dead Spear member. There was a grunt as one of the wings moved and a figure emerged from underneath. He was facing away from us, but I recognized my uncle.

I tried to yell his name, but it came out as another hoarse attempt. Ignoring the painful protest from my ribs, and the more verbal ones from Fell, I pushed myself up and moved toward Juliard. I stopped clutching my aching side and held out my arm. In that moment it didn't matter what his motives were, or what questions I had. I had to make sure he was all right. I wasn't going to lose anyone else.

"Uncle Juliard!" I tried again, finally close enough for him to hear.

"Kena?" His voice sounded hopeful as he turned to me. When his eyes met mine, I stopped in my tracks.

No. No, no, no.

Bronze light glowed from my uncle's eyes. His red cloak fell as he twisted to look at me, and as he reached an arm out, light spiraled down to his wrists as well. It shouldn't have been possible, and yet the proof stood in front of me. I recognized those marks.

"No." The word I'd been repeating in my head managed to escape my lips as I halted and took a step back. It couldn't be real. Juliard glanced down at his arm and grimaced. When he looked back up at me, his expression hardened.

"Kena. We have a lot to talk about."

Before he could say anything further, I ran.

CHAPTER 11

The path to Coalition Hall had been fully cleared. I sprinted past offices, ignoring the voices yelling after me. Hale, standing with Nix, tried to grab me as I ran past, but I kept moving. Silas, Hok, and Vanya were resting on their weapons, looking like they were about to drop, but I didn't pause. I headed for the library, though I knew running was useless. No amount of distance was going to undo what I had just seen. My ribs and lungs screamed in aching rebellion as I forced my injured body past the holocorder stacks. I didn't stop until I reached the aged bookshelf at the back that held the oldest films. With nowhere left to run, I dropped to the floor. I pulled my knees up against myself and cried, dry-heaving against the stabbing pain in my chest. I knew it was from the impact of the darts, but for just a moment I imagined my heart had actually broken.

There had to be an explanation. Had Juliard somehow managed to Assimilate since getting to the Hub? He couldn't have, though, not without touching the planet's surface, and I hadn't seen him in the Rift. Despite all the secrecy and deceit that had taken place so far, I knew in my bones that if he had been there he would have found a way to get to me. The obvious answer wasn't possible. I refused to accept it, because it couldn't be true. Except ...

"Ama." I made myself finish the thought out loud. "He could be like the Reader."

She'd said she didn't think it was possible, but perhaps even she was wrong sometimes.

I stood up so quickly I felt light-headed. Swaying, I put an arm down against the bookshelf for support. I was in worse physical shape than I'd realized, but it didn't matter. As quickly as I had made the choice to run, I decided to go back. A steely determination settled in my bones, replacing the denial that had sent me fleeing. I wasn't Kena, Juliard's indecisive niece, the one who ran out on her family and friends. I didn't want to be the Kena who had let her emotions distract her in the prison when she should have saved her friend. I was a citizen of the Rift. Capable and strong. Maybe not fearless, but certainly brave enough to face whatever truth Juliard had been hiding. A truth I was going to force him to reveal, one way or another.

I moved back through the stacks, absorbed in my thoughts. My Riftian hearing picked up on near-silent movements, giving me just enough time to sidestep, my arms wheeling as I tried to stay upright. A gentle hand kept me from toppling over. The moment it steadied me, I could tell who it was, and a sense of calm swept through me.

"Fell." I gazed up to where he stood, and his face broke out into an uncertain smile.

Another hand grasped one of my own.

"He said you'd need us." Hale gestured to the forest walker.

From behind them both, my uncle stepped into view. His glow was muted now, but I could still see the bronze marks that ran along the exposed parts of his body.

"Kena, we need to discuss this." His tone brooked no room for argument, but there was no reason for me to counter it. I had every intention of talking things out as well. Still, I felt my temper flaring again and was in no mood to attempt to dampen it.

"You're one of *them!*" I accused, putting as much vitriol as possible into the last word. "You're one of the brothers, aren't you?" My angry tone faded as I put into words the question I feared getting an answer to. I felt my lip trembling.

The answer was clear on his face before he spoke it aloud.

"Yes." His voice was measured and calm. He didn't even try to deny it.

Juliard sighed, exhaling tension and strength as his shoulders slumped.

"It may or may not comfort you to know that you were able to bring forth a secret I've kept hidden for ages. Even after the Societals showed up again, and then the Spear, I managed to suppress my true nature through it all. But when I saw you get hit, when I thought they'd managed to harm you ..." He held up his glowing arms.

"It doesn't comfort me at all, actually." I was trying to sound cold, but my concern for someone else close to me at the mercy of the Spear kept me from achieving that goal. Around Juliard's marks I noted a lot of purple and green bruises.

"It was never my intent to lie to you, Kena. This is simply what we'd been doing for generations. By the time you were born, we weren't Riftians anymore. Not really. We hadn't been for a long time. When your father and I were first stranded on Earth together—"

I held up a hand, cutting him off with the most important question.

"But which brother *are* you?"

He blinked several times, head tilting, but he didn't respond. I was done waiting for answers. Putting more force into my voice than before, I repeated the question.

"*Which. One?*"

"Kena. You know about me, so I suppose you've seen the holofilm of what happened. There's no other way you would have found out. I wish you'd told me your father had left it to you. I could have prepared you." He held his arms up and out, and the light poured from them until the whole room around us was lit with a warm, bronze glow, all the way to the cavernous ceiling.

Bronze

The answer hit me. I knew. I'd just been too shocked when I'd seen his markings to remember. Or maybe I hadn't wanted to. When Earth had been cut off all those years ago, two Riftian brothers had fought each other over it. The Cloak, the leader of the Earth settlers, had glowed bronze while he fought. And the Wolf, the original leader of the Spear, whom I'd despised, had glowed gold.

I saw my uncle reach for me, felt Fell's arms close around me from behind, but whatever they were saying didn't reach me. I stumbled back. The tears poured out, and I didn't even try to stop them. He was right. I *had* known. And that was what was wrong with the entire situation. It wasn't that he was Riftian, it wasn't that he was immortal, and it wasn't even that he had lied.

I managed to respond through the tears, my voice more like a howl than speech.

"You're the wrong one!"

He held his arm out again, even as I batted it away. The bronze light illuminated everything I didn't want to face.

"I know this is a lot to take in. And I know I have some explaining to do regarding my actions. That being said, we are short on time. Let me help the resistance first. Then I can tell you everything. I promise when I've finished to answer any questions you have, truthfully. And if we figure this all out and you don't want to see me again, I'll respect your decision," Juliard finished.

He had offered to give me time, which was being far more reasonable than was typical of him. I, on the other hand, was a wreck, which is why I agreed. I wasn't ready to explore the extent of what the information meant, yet.

"All right."

At my consent, the tension dropped from Juliard's features.

"Thank you. First, we need to get whatever leadership you've got gathered together. I have important information."

It didn't take long. Fell and Hale went after the others, while I did what I could to pull myself together. Once they were all ready, I swiped us into Warrick's office. The room filled to the brim with resistance members as we piled in. Fell, Vanya, Silas, and Dex all stood together. Next to them, Hok chatted with Sarah and her friend Saf. Captains Karo and Everleigh stood next to Hale and Nix.

"Who is who here?" my uncle asked.

The group went around introducing themselves. There were plenty of representatives from the Rift, although as I craned my neck and looked around, I noted Ama was missing. I'd have gone into a panic if I hadn't seen her in one of the offices as I ran to the library earlier. The Crew and Rover contingents were also strongly represented. The Kites' queen, Nimue, was flanked by several from her planet. Ryshal and Acaius were at her side, Cassius and his friend Shawd bordering them. Iduna stood at the edge, her sour features looking out of place. I couldn't look at them all without remembering who was missing. Pim's wings had been simple but beautiful, a fading grey, like smoke rising toward the sky.

Next to the Kites stood the Canopy grouping, with Cassia at its edge. Her furry, right ear was missing a large chunk. Everyone had already sacrificed so much. Nien stood awkwardly to the side, with his tusks and yellow, glowing mark that left him a member of no single Society.

The Clan and Dagan were largely leaderless. Veronica stood next to some of her fellow inky-skinned and neon-marked kinsmen. I squeezed the piece of moon quartz in my chest pocket as I remembered Ugdol, a Clan member who would have sided with us. I wished one of the other leaders of their Society had been at the Hub. Or at least one that hadn't sided with the Spear. I wanted to know how to utilize the gem I'd been given.

When introductions were out of the way, Juliard explained his own identity. Several people shot glances in my direction as he revealed himself not only as an actual Riftian but also the leader of Verkent, a member of Earth's task force, and my uncle. Once the gasps and whispers quieted, he launched into a speech. Even in this crisis, he was in his element.

"I began to suspect several of my other task force members, including that militaristic oaf Kaiser, before we'd even arrived at the Hub for the Coalition meeting," he said. I remembered the Earther, who had expressed an open disdain for Societals before we'd been sent up. It seemed he was willing to set his prejudices aside for the right kind of profit. "The others were taking private calls and meetings on video with some of the delegates. Between that and the information my niece shared regarding the execution of non-Assimilators; I knew we were walking into a serious problem up here. I pride myself in thinking on my feet, so when they attacked I followed the other Earth members who joined the Spear—" He held up his palms as some started to shout him down. "—not to participate in anything violent, of course. But I wanted to save my niece and the other Earthers. I knew my position was precarious, and in order to do that I'd have to convince them I wanted to join."

I glanced around the circle. Juliard listed the large number of individuals from our home planet that weren't to be trusted; Sarah barely blinked when her father's name was spoken. I gathered their relationship was far worse than my uncle's and mine had ever been.

"I wasn't initially successful." Juliard rubbed his jaw, where a deep purple bruise bloomed. "But eventually someone noted my resemblance to the original Spear leader. Their organization may not have film, but they've kept illustrations. I didn't reveal the truth, but I played it up. Stated I was a descendant. Tried to make it seem as though I'd led Verkent this whole time to keep the belief alive, in hopes that the Spear and Societies would return. Eventually I won them over. I'm sure you lot have worked out that one of their goals is a return to Lone. Earth provides them the numbers to subdue the planets, and in return Earth gets the advancements and technology they're after, without having to give in to the leadership of the Societals. The key thing is, they're going to get rid of the Hub to do it. They're waiting for the arrival of a fleet of ships they supplied to Earth, and at that point they're planning to destroy this station and go after each Society systematically, one by one. That way, it's near impossible for the resistance to fight back."

Shouts rang out around the room at his proclamation. Everyone talked over the others for a few minutes before order was restored, primarily by the Riftian contingent.

"They have a point. Why should we trust you?" Hok leveled the question at Juliard.

Fell squeezed my hand as my uncle walked to the center of the room, a move I knew he meant as an attention grab. As if he wasn't at the center of it already.

"Can we all be candid? Let's discuss the Spear just like we would any Society. You all have plenty of stereotypes about one another, some of which are typically accurate. Apply the same logic here. From what you've seen so far, ask yourself what the most likely outcome is." Juliard gesticulated with his hands as he moved, enunciating every thought with a gesture.

"He's right. We know the Spear wants not only Lone, but control over everyone else. Many of our fighters are here, along with their former prisoners. We ruined their live executions in the arena, but I'm willing to bet they'd broadcast destruction of the Hub. Especially if they could show all of us trapped onboard. That alone would be enough to bring the other Societals to heel." Fell's quiet presence, or projection, had everyone focused on him. He didn't stand or pace like my uncle; he just stayed in the same spot, holding my hand, as he delivered his opinion.

Silas appeared thoughtful, one hand on his chin.

"Whether you're right or not,"—I noticed he didn't accuse my uncle of lying so much as being misinformed—"it doesn't hurt us to respond as if they *are* going to destroy the Hub. We're wasting energy here, anyway. We came to rescue who we could, and we have. Objective achieved. We've also got most of the minds behind the Hub's tech. While I hate to abandon it, it's just a location. Either way, we'd do better to get out of here and build up more forces on the planets themselves. Create some unity in person."

Several individuals nodded their assent.

"You don't have long to decide," Juliard insisted.

"We have a little extra time. I messed with the navigation on the Earther ships. Pim and I both did." Digit joined the room, her hand heavily bandaged. A tear slid down her cheek as she spoke of the deceased Verkenter. He'd been so happy to find someone who liked tinkering with computers as much as he did. Next to Digit stood Ama, glowing orange.

People around the room were already discussing the timeline, sharing snippets of half-formed plans in several conversations, when my uncle noticed her.

"Reader?" Juliard's eyes widened. I'd almost never seen him surprised, but this had done it.

"You!" Ama gasped.

CHAPTER 12

"Let's ... reconvene in the library. This is a lot to discuss, and everyone should be informed," Fell suggested as he stepped away from me and started to edge others toward the office door.

"Yes," Silas agreed, seemingly catching on. "Everyone go around the offices. Let the others from your Society know what's going to happen. If we're going to be prepared to handle the Spear, the Earthers, *and* the loss of the Hub, we'll need every last Societal."

The general grumbling that took place whenever any unified action was suggested began, but with the help of Sarah, her snake Charles, Cassius, Cassia, Hok, and Nix all pushing their factions into agreement, the room emptied until only five of us remained. Fell stood on my left and Hale on my right, as my uncle approached Ama.

"The Reader is still alive?" Juliard demanded of me, while gesturing at her.

"Your Uncle Juliard is a Riftian?" Ama's voice was equally demanding as they both stared me down.

"I—"

I had no desire to get in the middle of whatever argument or discussion or debate they were on the verge of; so instead, I drew their attention to something else entirely. "I used my projection to control someone in the Spear."

"What?" they spoke in unison as they moved toward me.

I summarized what happened in the prison, Hale and Fell each squeezing one of my hands while I explained what had provoked my powerful surge of emotion. Juliard actually shed a tear when I mentioned Pim's death. The two had known each other their whole lives. Or at least, all of Pim's life.

"Damned shame. That man was pure compassion. Not a mean bone in his whole body. A Kite, you say? It fits him. And what about the Spear that killed him?"

I relayed what I'd done.

"And then he fell from the railing. But I didn't tell him to jump. I'd released him before that."

Ama's sunset orange marks stayed steady as she leaned over, staring at Juliard instead of me.

"We will settle this later. Agreed?" She offered him a hand.

"Agreed." He accepted it, shaking once. He hadn't even flinched in the face of the Reader.

As soon as she'd gained his consent, she turned her attention back to me.

"And *you*, we need to work on this skill. Train you up. Help you put it to use," she decreed.

I had mentally prepared for some serious scolding after she found out that I had not only failed to temper my anger but used it against someone. I'd thought her whole plan had been to guide the Spear toward a better means of settling the conflict.

Juliard swept an arm out, preventing the Reader from getting any closer to me.

"Are you mad, woman? She can't *use* it. That path only has one possible conclusion, and it's a bloody one. My niece will *not* take a single step further down the same violent road that her father took. I forbid it." Juliard's marks flared bronze as he shouted down the Reader. It was as if, having been let loose after so many years, they were determined to make themselves known.

"Forbid it do you?" Ama scoffed. "And just how do you intend to stop her? As if you've any right. Been up here helping her adjust to Assimilation, have you? I just happened to miss the part where you've been up here looking out for her best interests? No? She's got an ability the rest of us couldn't dream of. She's every right to utilize it."

I was taken aback at both reactions. Ama was pushy, but she'd not steered me wrong in the short time I'd known her. Juliard was the one who had been willing to damage our relationship to maintain control of Verkent. He had saved me on the Hub, but he'd also put me in danger by sending me there in the first place. And he had done all of that without telling me the truth. It was my father's holofilm that had provided that.

The moment I thought of my father, I felt the urge to run back to the library, or the Rift. I needed time to process what I'd learned, but I knew it was a luxury we didn't have. My uncle wasn't the Wolf. He wasn't the one I should be upset with, and yet, I couldn't separate my frustration with my father from my anger at him.

I squeezed the hands of my best friend and the man I was Connected to. Both Hale and Fell returned the gesture. I hadn't saved Pim. I didn't know how to face that, but it was true. Still, there were so many other people who needed me. Beloved Verkenters,

Riftians, and Societals. I had a chance to help them all. To avoid making the same mistake twice. I released my hands and moved forward to stand between the bickering older Riftians.

"I want to work with Ama." I turned to the Reader. "You have taught me how to read markings, and you haven't led me astray. You saw the truth about my being assigned to the Rift, and you didn't hold it against me. You've been honest about what you've seen in me, which is more than I can say for many Societals. If this ability could help us win against the Spear, then I want to try. If it could protect everyone, then any cost is worth it. Teach me to control it."

The Reader beamed, her warm glow encasing me as I turned back to my uncle.

"Juliard. I am my father's daughter, but I am *not* my father. And I'm not you. For the good of everyone here, and for myself, I need to be someone else entirely. And that means accepting and using the skills I've been given." I planted my feet on the floor, hands on my hips, as I stared up at my uncle. Really he was only a few inches taller than I was, though he'd towered over me in the past. Perhaps that had all been my imagination.

He let out a sound from the back of his throat, something between a sigh and a growl.

"Very well, niece, but don't say you weren't warned." He scowled. I ignored it.

I had turned on my heel, content to leave him to argue the rest of his issues out with the Reader, when Juliard reached out and grasped my shoulder.

"And I know who you are and who you're not. You're better than both of us." I didn't know how to respond to that, so I let it hang in the air.

Fell grabbed my hand, and Hale followed as we headed for the library. When we arrived I saw the others had made quick work of modifying the space. The fireside chairs and bookshelves still dominated the front of the room, but that was the only thing that remained the same. The rows and rows of towering metallic shelves that housed the Hub's many holofilms had been pushed and shoved to the perimeter, leaving a large space in the center of the cavernous room.

Several piles of blankets, pillows and the like had been piled haphazardly at the edges of the room. Encircled by all the stuff stood the Societals. We'd left two bickering Riftians behind and traded them for a whole room of arguments.

"I vote we charge in now! They're not expecting us. Also, what are a bunch of Riftians going to teach us about fighting? I don't know about you all, but we Crew members have been steadily training since day one. And it sounds like you've been doing, what exactly? Walking around enjoying the pretty leaves?" Captain Karo had seen everyone fight, and he had to know he was wrong. Still, he was probably as exhausted as anyone.

"At this rate they're going to spend longer arguing over a plan than executing one." Hale leaned in as he spoke.

"It seems likely. But they're wasting time we don't have. I just wish I knew how to get them to stop, not that my word would convince everyone." I sighed. Despite my tough response to my uncle, I still had no idea how to control my newfound ability. Even if I had, bulldozing my enemies was one thing, but projecting my will onto those I had sworn to help? I didn't want to go there.

Nix joined Karo in his attack on the Riftians.

"Yeah, just what would you Cloaks be able to teach us, anyway?" I never knew with her if she baited others because she believed what she said, or if she just enjoyed the conflict. She had several piercings running the length of her ear, and they glinted in the overhead lights of the library.

An arrow flew past her face, leaving the faintest graze on her cheek. Nix grinned as she wiped the single drop of blood that spilled away. Kaos, the snake Warrick had willed her, hissed from the girl's shoulders. Her look was devilishly delighted as she pulled out her short sword and charged at Vanya, who was still holding her bow aloft.

"Well, if you can't settle it with words ..." Hale shrugged.

Vanya blocked the first few blows expertly with her weapon, which happened to be wrapped in ocala. Nix hesitated for a moment, stepping back and looking down at her sword with a frown on her face. No doubt she was used to the weapon being much more effective. Vanya took the opening to sweep Nix's feet out from under her with the bow. She landed on her butt, wincing.

That was enough to set Hale off, in spite of his previous statement. He ran in and placed himself between the two before I could stop him. Karo joined in and engaged Hok, who had stepped up to help his fellow weapons specialist. The ship captain managed to attempt three strikes before Hok snapped him on the wrist. Karo dropped his sword, which Hok flung away with the edge of his staff. As it skittered across the room, Vanya leveled an arrow at Karo's windpipe.

The only other captain present, Everleigh, had been watching the entire event unfold with a calculating gaze. She sighed, eyes rolling like an exasperated parent, before she drew her sword and moved forward.

"Aw, hell." Digit rubbed her unbandaged hand down her face as she watched the others. She might well have been the only Crew member present who wasn't itching for a fight.

If the Crew hadn't been making fun, I would have felt sorry about what happened next. As Everleigh drew nearer, Vanya reached one hand into her holster and, quicker than a viper striking, threw a dagger at Nix. It caught her sleeve, and the force of it threw her back to the ground. Hok had swept Hale's legs out from under him.

Captain Everleigh had just enough time to close the remaining distance before Vanya saw her. The captain tried for a lunge, but Vanya was too quick. She ducked and lashed out with her bow, knocking Karo in the windpipe with that instead of an arrow. He coughed and dropped to his knees. Then she struck upwards and hit Everleigh in the gut. Both captains sputtered and sucked in air for a moment. Then Everleigh spoke, her eyes watering.

"We train with the Cloaks. They can fight."

Vanya offered the captain a hand and she took it, pulling herself up.

Hok spun his staff before planting it by his side again as if it were a harmless walking stick.

The pirates and the Riftians settled into exercises together, but it only took five minutes for yet another argument to break out.

"And why are we listening to you? A bunch of flitty, floaty, feather-brains have no idea what it takes to survive a planet that requires true grit." One of the lizard-skinned Rovers leveled the biting comment at Cassius.

He retorted as Sarah walked toward the feuding duo to smooth things over.

"It's not easy trying to get everyone to set aside their differences and work together. Especially when they've never really acknowledged before just how much bitterness there is between certain groups." Ama's orange glow fell over me. "Come. We have work to do. Bring a few volunteers with you. And not the forest walker; we need someone who will be disinclined to listen to you. I think that will be the best way to truly test the limits of your projection."

I pondered my choices. Hale, Silas, and Fell were my first and most obvious picks. But Ama was right. I needed individuals who weren't going to just agree with me. I needed independent thinkers with strong will.

"Where should we meet you?" I asked the Reader.

She placed a hand on her chin for a moment.

"Your uncle is still stewing in Warrick's office, and I doubt you'd want to try this for the first time in front of everyone. Let's use the Riftian office, if that is agreeable?"

I nodded. Bayard was the only inhabitant that I knew of, and I'd wanted to check in on him anyway. Even without his sight, his input would be invaluable.

Several minutes later, I led Cassia, Nix, Digit, and Vanya into the office. The quartet of women were perfect for our purposes. Digit was tenacious and feisty. Nix was annoying and pushy, which is exactly why she'd be a challenge. Cassia and I had always managed to be on the same page, but she was strong-willed and careful. I imagined she'd be difficult to overpower, even with my newfound ability. And Vanya was an obvious pick. She was one of the quickest and most capable fighters I knew.

The office was dim and quieter than the rest of Coalition Hall. Bayard's desk and chair had been pushed to the side. The delegate leaned up against a wall, the scars over his eyes a searing red where there had once been a calming blue. Unlike many Riftians at the Hub who had chosen to reveal their marks, he still wore long sleeves that kept his covered.

"Will it bother you if we train here?" I asked.

"Not at all. I'm very interested to see,"—he cringed, and I felt myself do the same in response—"to *observe*, your skills. Ama shared that you're working on some perfected form of projection? How intriguing."

I shifted my weight, self-conscious under the potential scrutiny of the best fighter I'd ever witnessed.

Ama instructed the other women to line up across the room from me and to charge at me, one at a time. The idea was to start with them where I'd first begun using my skill: a *stop* command. It took several tries, and Nix actually bowled into me on one attempt before I got it right.

"Just trying to motivate you, Cloak." She grinned as I rubbed a sore shoulder. The following time, when she ran I channeled my annoyance at all her verbal jabs and threw out an arm.

"Stop!" I yelled.

She skidded to a halt so quickly that she fell over. Cassia leaned down to help her up.

The saber-toothed woman went next. As she got close she leapt, tail arcing in the air as she aimed at my throat.

"Sto—" Her features froze, but she still collided with me, unable to change course. After extricating myself from her tail, and from under her fangs, which had mercifully missed me, I pulled her up.

"Impressive," she conceded as she went back to the line. Digit let me stop her several times in a row, expressing thrill at the entire prospect. Then again, she was the only one in the group who had actually found herself in the Spear's clutches, and she still had bruises and mended but scarred fingers to show for it.

Vanya was tougher. Not because I couldn't control her, but because of how quick she was. I had to build up my energy and emotion, then throw out a command before she'd come within striking distance.

"What else do you think you could do, Kena?" she asked after I'd stopped her for the fourth time.

"Make the Spear throw themselves off the station?" Digit smiled, but her voice got tense. I related to the desire for revenge, but that was exactly the type of thing I wanted to avoid—letting the ability overwhelm me.

"She has a point," Ama put in, "not with the station bit, but you're picking this up faster than I could have anticipated. We should have you try another command, or work against a tougher opponent." I felt my eyes go wide as the Reader herself moved to stand in front of me.

Bayard took a few unsteady steps forwards, sweeping his arms in front of him and then grabbing her shoulder once he'd located it.

"Excuse me, Ama, but I would like an opportunity to experience this myself before you move on. If you have no objections?" She started to shake her head, then responded verbally instead.

"No. Of course not, Bayard. By all means." She helped position him in front of me and stepped back. He tilted his head, and as I changed my footing to a more secure stance, he ran. Riftians had increased Assimilated hearing in general, and he certainly took advantage.

I brought an arm up, determined to stop him.

"The Spear members are on the move! We think they're headed to the Tundra Doorway. If they breach that all the wounded and kids are in danger. We need to move *now*!" Acaius leaned into the office doorway, dragon wings folded at his back. Behind him, Cassius, Hok, Dex, and Silas ran toward the entrance to the hall.

I lowered my arm as Bayard walked back toward the wall, arms out as he traced his way back to a chair.

"We can try again soon, once this is fixed?" I asked as I grabbed my ax and prepared to join the others.

"Soon," he agreed, sinking into the chair. I wanted to offer to help. I knew it had to be killing him not to be able to fight, but I had nothing comforting to say.

I left Bayard alone in the dark office and joined the others.

CHAPTER 13

"We're lucky Warrick's office had access to the holocorder feed for the whole station, or we might not have caught them in time." Silas filled us in on the issue as we sprinted down the halls. He wore one of the Hub-issued grey jumpsuits, sliced off at the knees. His ocala prosthetic was on full display.

I supposed I owed my uncle a thanks. Juliard had spotted the Spear on one of the magistrate's screens, a group of them massing together. The big trick was getting to storage room that held the Tundra Doorway first.

"Digit, can we beat them there?" Silas asked the techie. She'd been equipped with a small handheld screen and was typing away furiously with one hand, looking at the Hub's schematics. She nodded.

"Yes. Coalition Hall is a lot closer to the storage room with Tundra's Doorway than where the Spear was holed up in Blank housing. Take a right!" She yelled instructions at the group as we moved.

We came to a fork in the hallway. As we spilled into a larger walkway from a path on the right, I turned to see several Spear members converging from the left.

"Duck!" Vanya yelled as she loosed several arrows at once over our heads. Four of the five found their marks and sent the front row of our pursuers tumbling.

"I love it when you do that." Silas winked at her and blew a kiss as he continued to sprint.

"Did all the Riftians just view this whole experience as a dating service?" Hale huffed, breath coming in short bursts as he ran next to Fell and me.

"Would that be such a bad thing?" Hok countered, and I caught him shooting a side-eyed glance at Sarah as she slashed her blackened nails into a Spear member from Kite, who fell to the floor covered in blackened marks.

Our group made it to the storage room that held Tundra's Doorway with the Spear on our heels. Ryshal and Cassius's friend Shawd were the current guards. They spread their wings to shield everyone. Once we'd all made it inside the room, the Kites slammed the door shut.

"Blockade!" Shawd instructed, blue plumage glinting as the other feathered members of the group began stacking chairs and tables in front of the door.

"It's no good. Several of the Spear died when we did the prison break. Lots of them fell in the arena. Saf and I took out a few ourselves when we rescued the kids, but still they just keep coming."

Sarah glared at the door, her snake Charles flaring his hood as he hissed toward the barricade.

"All people have a breaking point. We'll find theirs," Dex insisted, expression grim as he hauled a heavy shelf across the room.

"They're not *people*. They're Spear members," Nix argued as she helped add a chair to the growing pile. She fumbled it a bit with her cast, and Hale shoved it the rest of the way up.

I frowned but said nothing. I had no right to talk, given my actions in the prison.

Hok walked by carrying a closed storage tub, which he threw onto the mess blocking the door.

"The Serpentina is right. They *will* get in here. What's our plan for when they do? Try and hold them off, and hope the wounded can catch whoever inevitably slips through to Tundra? Retreat to the icy planet and rally defenses?" He tallied off the options, none of them sounding palatable.

Fell reached down and grabbed my hand. He had his other wrapped around a dagger.

"We cannot afford to let a single one get past us. So far, their cruelty has been beyond our predictions. They cannot be allowed near the children or the wounded on Tundra." His eyes, which stayed steadier than any Riftian I'd ever seen, wavered as he spoke of the kids.

His determination sparked my own. We needed something drastic.

"We blow the door." I said it under my breath to myself at first, but I saw him turn his gaze down to me. I let go of his hand and stepped to the center of the group. A loud banging sounded in the hallway as the Spear began their assault on the entrance.

"We destroy the Doorway!" I shouted. A few of the Kites continued their work, but most people around the room stopped and turned. With dozens of eyes on me from a variety of Societals, I struggled to hold my stance, not to look at my toes.

Dex paused in front of me after he dropped another tub onto the pile.

"Listen, I'm all for a dramatic and half-baked idea, but we have no backup. You may have missed all the infighting in the library earlier, but we never exactly decided what to do about the Spear's plan to destroy the Hub. This Doorway is really our best option out of here if worse comes to worst. Are you saying we just retreat now and let them have the station?" The lights in the room glinted off the spiked metal on his horns.

I shook my head.

"No. I'm saying we make a stand. Fell is right. The Spear is formidable, and they've been two steps ahead of us the whole time. If we leave now, who knows how far ahead they'll be by the time they reach the planets? We can't take that chance. So we blow the Doorway, and beat them at their own game. We don't let them near the menders and kids. Earther ships are arriving soon, but given how distrustful the Spear is of them, there's got to be another plan in their back pocket. Digit, aside from the Earther ships, is there any other way they could leave the Hub?"

As quick as I'd asked, she had typed a few things onto her screen and a 3D replica of a small ship hovered over the pad. She pointed to various items on it.

"The Hub is equipped with a whole slew of what we'll go ahead and call lifeboats, or escape pods, whichever you'd prefer. Those would be their best bet to transport their numbers and make sure they could be well clear of any fireworks when they destroy this thing." She clicked another button, and the 3D rendering of the ship sank bank onto her tablet screen.

"Could we use them to get somewhere else? Somewhere other than the Earther ships?" I asked. She started to nod, and smiled.

"I see where you're going with this. Yes. You certainly could. They're preset to autopilot themselves to the nearest Societal planet, which in this case is the Canopy."

"Right. So, that's the plan. We blow this Doorway, which will keep the kids and wounded on Tundra safe. Someone's going to have to go through and warn the others so they don't suspect the worst. Then, if we can't overthrow the Spear before the Earther ships arrive, we make sure we beat them to those escape ships when the time comes. We reconvene on Canopy, and once we're planetside we can use the Tundra Doorways from there to reach out to the others." It wasn't a fully formed plan, but it was a lot better than hoping the Spear forces didn't overwhelm us and take over the snowy planet before we'd even left the Hub. We'd only just sent wounded from the prison through the Doorway; those waiting on Tundra weren't in any position to defend themselves.

"I vote we destroy it," Acaius said. He stepped to my side, wings flapping open as several others shouted him down.

"It's not a vote, you mad, winged reptile! This Cloak is trying to trap us all on this floating death station." One of the Dagan I didn't recognize spoke out. Veronica shushed them, but the arguments began regardless.

"He's right! He's right!" I yelled. No one listened. Ama raised a brow at me as she walked toward me. Several of the other Riftians followed her, forming a semi-circle around us.

"We should listen to the girl," she said, voice quiet but firm. They didn't stop talking instantly like the guard in the prison had, but the chatter slowly died down. Several of the others stared up at us with bewildered expressions as arguments tapered off. Whatever she'd done, and I suspected she'd turned their attention away from their protesting, it presented me with the opening I needed.

"The Dagan is right! We've got to stop this bickering, and this is as good a time as any. It needs to be a unanimous decision. Not because you all agree with my plan, but because you agree with helping one another and defeating the Spear."

"Um, Kena. Very touching and all, but they're breaking through!" Hale yelled from where he was helping the Kites shove against the door.

I sped up my speech.

"Warrick warned that the Spear had set aside Societal differences to align with one another. We need to do the same. These issues are real, but they're also petty when compared to the fate of all Societies hanging in the balance. We all have friends and family at risk in this. Can't we lay down our disputes long enough to help them? We don't have to be the same, but if we can't have an alliance where we can back each other, the Spear *will* win. And the Societies will fall. It's your *choice*," I finished, throwing memories of the Choosing ceremony back at them.

For several moments, the only sounds were the bangs and clangs of the Spear outside the room.

"They've breeched the door!" Acaius yelled as a small gap opened behind the piles of furniture and shelving.

"I'm with you, Kena! Queen of Verkenters, and leader of the alliance!" Sarah shouted from the front. Some of the Rovers looked reluctant, but they followed her chant all the same.

"I don't like you Cloaks. Or the sea monsters. Or the feathers, for that matter," Karo started, "but I like the Spear less. Far less. I'm with you, girl. Queen of the alliance."

The pirates began chanting, their forms flickering and shadowing over their bold black and white tattoos. The few Dagan and Clan that hadn't been former Earthers took up the chant.

Su Jin and Cassia led the Canopy.

"Queen of the alliance! Blow the Doorway!"

I was overcome. I hadn't intended to put myself in charge, just to get them to agree.

Juliard stepped in front of me.

"Seems you've won them over, niece. Very impressive, better than even I could have done. And you didn't even have to force them." I ignored the last bit. He held a giant scythe at his side, as he had in the hall.

"That's your weapon, isn't it? You mastered it before you went to Earth?"

"Yes, but it's not the only weapon I stole away with when I ran out on the Spear." He reached into his pocket and pulled out a small metallic sphere. "It's a bomb, of sorts. Fairly certain this is the kind they plan to rig the Hub with. Toss it in the tunnel with the Doorway and it will shut it down well enough. But we'll all want to clear ourselves out of this room, just in case."

He dropped it into my hand.

Fell picked up on what he said, and the other Riftians moved through the crowd. Digit and Nix began opening a panel in the wall for everyone to make their way out of the room and around the Spear.

I rolled the sphere in my hand and stared at my uncle.

"If this is what they're planning to use on the Hub, how do you know it won't blow a hole in the station? That it will only damage the Doorway?"

He shrugged.

"I don't. I'm basing it off numbers. They've got a whole stockpile for the Hub. One inside a tunnel with the Doorway isn't likely to do as much damage. Then again, it could be the end of us all. Your choice niece." There was a glint in his eyes, and I wasn't certain it was just the bronze.

"Wait! Someone has to go warn those on Tundra!" Vanya shouted.

"I'll do it." The teal-eyed Rover, Saf, spoke up from Sarah's side. "Someone has to check on our planet's ruler anyway. And it would be an honor to guard the wounded Rovers for the Serpentina." The girl's snake, orange feathers flared, wove out from her hair. Without waiting for approval, she ran into the tunnel.

"I'll go with her, for the Canopy wounded." Su Jin volunteered as she stepped into the tunnel.

"And me!" Thea volunteered, form undulating as she moved close.

"You hated the Tundra! It basically solidified you!" I argued.

"I'll watch her," Marx, a maker from the Twilight Grove, stated as he stepped up and wrapped his cloak around her. Fell nodded at his friend before he too disappeared into the tunnel.

"If that's everyone, then?" Cassius waited at the metal door to the tunnel, glistening gold and white wings folded behind him. One was still a bit misshapen at the edge where the trident had scraped away some feathers.

"Niece, throw the sphere!" Juliard instructed.

I tossed it into the tunnel and Cassius slammed the metal door with the spoked wheel shut.

"This way!" Cassia yelled from where she and Vanya held a panel open to the wall of the storage room. We ran toward the open space. We made it inside the wall but hadn't sealed ourselves in place when the floor shook. I watched as the metal tunnel containing the Doorway creaked and collapsed in on itself.

The shaking jostled loose the last of the resistance's barricade. As the Spear broke through, I caught the glinting black light of Kidan's marks before Vanya slid the panel back in place.

CHAPTER 14

We managed to make it back to Coalition Hall without having to engage the Spear, for once.

As our group moved around the delegates' offices I saw Bayard resting against a wall. His head tilted to the side as we got closer.

"Kena, I—" He leaned past me, and I turned to see Juliard stomping up behind us, scythe in one hand. "It can wait," Bayard said instead, going back into his office. I didn't blame him. The actual Riftian ruler had turned out to be a villain. Juliard, former leader of the Earth settlers, had to seem questionable to the delegate, showing up after all this time.

I made my way past every office to Warrick's at the end of the hall. I swiped it open and stepped inside.

"Kena, we'll need to get started on—" Juliard started before he'd even crossed the threshold. It was on the edge of my tongue to tell him, or command him using projection if I had to, that I needed a moment.

Silas did it for me. He laid a hand on Juliard's shoulder.

"It's late. None of us are going to be any good in this fight if we don't get some rest." My uncle looked unconvinced, taking another step toward the office. "And I know we need to sort out the food shortage. You surely had to oversee that for the settlers, so you're most likely to have the expertise," Silas insisted.

"Well, that is true. All right, first thing in the morning then, niece!" Juliard said before marching himself towards the library and our limited food stores.

Silas winked at me as he turned to follow the older Riftian.

I stood in the near-empty room, the silence deafening in the absence of all the others. Fell was several feet away, just standing and looking at me. The glow from his eyes lit the floor, and if I closed mine I could almost pretend I was back in the Twilight Grove, sitting by the fire next to him.

We stayed like that, staring each other down for a few moments, before he moved. Swift and silent as ever, he'd closed the distance between us, one hand reaching into my hair and the other around my waist as he pulled me close.

I let the kiss take me away for a moment. Away from the Hub, and the Societals, and the Spear, until it was just the two of us. When Fell kissed, he did it like everything else in his life, expertly. Of course I'd kissed others back on Earth, but nothing else compared.

As we broke away, Fell breathing heavily, he stared into my eyes. He reached both hands up to cup my face.

"You are beautiful," he murmured. "And I am honored to stand by your side as you lead us."

I felt my lip tremble. I tried to push past the feelings that welled up, but I wasn't able to.

"I'm not a leader!" I yelled, pulling at my hair. The urge to rip it out, or rip myself from the moment, was overwhelming.

I dropped into a crouch, and my head fell into my hands. I spoke toward the ground.

"I'm not a leader," I repeated. "I wanted to be one in Verkent, after my father died. Maybe Juliard was right to block me out back then."

Fell's hand rested against my back.

"You don't mean that."

I took a few shaky breaths.

"No. Well, maybe. If things had been different, if none of this had happened ... then yes, I would have still wanted that position. Now, though? There's so much pressure. From Ama, and the Earthers, my friends, even myself. Just a few months ago, I wasn't even certain you all were up here. I believed it, but no one had proven it. And now, it's like everyone's looking at me for answers, expecting me to save them. What if I can't? I'm just one person. Surely there's someone better qualified?"

He let out a soft laugh behind me, and I was so shocked that I froze. I turned to glare at Fell.

"It's not funny!" I snarked.

He didn't seem put off; in fact, he kept right on with the comforting, repetitive movement of his hand circling my back.

"No, forgive me, it's not humorous. Not the idea of you as a leader. It's just that you're wrong."

"So you think I can do all this, then?" I swept an arm out.

"No," he said. I felt my eyes dampen and blinked to clear the tears away. As I opened my mouth to retort, he actually placed a hand over it.

"Allow me to explain, please." I nodded and he lowered his hand.

"You can't do this, not alone. But you shouldn't think you need to. I personally think you're a great leader, and that it's something you've already been doing. The problem is that you have the definition for that role wrong in your head. A leader doesn't have to be some blustering voice at the head of an army. You don't need to be a delegate, or the magistrate, or anything like that. Your fellow Verkenters, and by extension the Earthers, respected your opinion even after your uncle deposed you. They trusted your intuition, whether or not you'd been around them for years. That's because of your character, and the way you treated them. You've made their protection a priority since the beginning of this process, including when you invited all the non-Assimilators to the Rift. *That* is the quality of a leader. Not having people openly acknowledge that you're in charge, but being able to influence things for the better because others respect the perspective you bring."

I thought for a moment about what he said.

"I've made mistakes, though. I didn't share what I had learned about the Spear sooner. I didn't question my uncle about it, or bring it up to anyone else. I stayed away from Verkent for too long. Perhaps if I'd been with them before, instead of only appearing when it benefitted me, I would have been in a position to be on the task force myself. Then I could have figured some of this out earlier. And," I voiced the worst thing of all, "I failed Pim. I let myself get distracted by all the Societal secrets and intrigue. I was selfish, and I pushed Nien for answers in a moment when I should have been helping him instead. It shouldn't have even been an option not to go to him first." I threw my face back into my hands, but Fell gently pulled my hands down.

He caressed my cheek. The rest of my argument fled my mind as he leaned forward, his lips brushing mine. As he deepened the kiss, I leaned into him, wrapping my arms around his neck. I needed the escape and didn't surface until he pulled back. His familiar twilight gaze locked onto me, and I saw opal light dancing between us alongside his purple and blue. Gently, he disentangled my arms. He sat with his back resting on the wall and pulled me against him.

"Kena," he started, "none of us can look back at our lives without identifying mistakes. I certainly can't. They're unavoidable. But you can't get stuck there. I want you to succeed, for *us* to succeed. Still, I also want you to know that, even if we don't, I will love you to whatever end life brings us."

He'd said it. He'd actually said it. After all the chaos that had been our short time spent Connected, I hadn't imagined romance had been the first thing on his mind. My own feelings were confused. I cared deeply for him, and I felt the beginnings of love. But with everything else that had happened, wave after wave of new tragedies and secrets exposed, I didn't have it in me to commit to that just yet. So I just snuggled further into him instead. He ran a hand through my hair, twisting his fingers through it as he continued.

"You are caring, protective, intelligent. You pull me out of my solitude, and yet I feel calmer with you than in the silence of the forest. I can only hope to do the same for you."

"You do," I assured him.

"I know this is hard. You and the other Earthers have been asked to handle more than any individual should be tasked with, and there's no way to stop the things in motion now. But you don't have to take everything on by yourself. Consider what Warrick said. He's a perfect example of learning from mistakes. He admitted in his message to you that the separation of the Societies is part of why the Spear was able to act against them without being caught sooner. Even the Spear, for all the evil they've done, can teach us something. You're on the right track, aligning the Societals. Now you need to let them share the burden, and work together."

I sat up, my eyes settling on him again.

"You mean, rely more on the rest of the group?"

"Exactly. You don't have to do everything just because you're leading. I think of it more as a quality than a position. You have the Rovers and Dagan here, who are capable of great endurance when the rest of us might lag. You have the Crew, willing to rush in, no matter the risk. Just to name a few. But, more specific than that, utilize the talents of the people around you."

I chewed my lip. I had thought about it. But it felt so selfish.

"Am I any better than the Spear if I *use* the others, though?" I asked.

"I think a lot of that lies in your motivation and what you hope to gain. Their leaders want control, and power. They don't mind throwing lives away to get it. Ours, or that of their own soldiers. You are trying to minimize loss of life, to save the Societies, and you're doing it for the good of everyone, not just yourself. And all of us here want to help with that. You're not forcing anyone."

It still wasn't ideal, but it was better.

"That, and relying on yourself would be both selfish and doomed to fail," he continued. "Vanya and Hok no doubt told all the new Riftians when they began training that no one is a master of every weapon. That's true. And no one is a master of every skill. Even if you don't want to ask anything of the others, you *cannot* do this by yourself. You know I think highly of you, but it's not meant as an insult to say that others outpace us both in various areas. Dex and Hok have more sheer mass and power. Acaius's unique wings allow him to take on multiple adversaries at once, and he's trained to use them to his advantage. Your friend Sarah, from what you say, has gone from a timid girl to the most respected woman on Rover. These are all feats you or I can't hope to achieve. Silas has a mind for strategy. Your uncle does, too, regardless of your feelings about him. Digit's skills with technology have saved us multiple times."

As he listed each one, I started to feel a small spark of hope. We had more at our disposal than I'd considered, because I hadn't been fully willing to accept putting everyone at risk. He was right, though. My friends and acquaintances were talented, and strong. And they were capable of making these decisions for themselves.

"Cassius and Cassia are not only two of the toughest individuals I've come across, but they're both more intelligent than anyone the Spear has. Did you know they each speak seven of your Earther languages? They're calculating, too, and they think before they act. Many times that's just what we need. And for the times we don't, Hale and Nix are more than ready to enter the fray with bravery that's unmatched in most of the other Societies. They all want to help, Kena. Then there's Ama, and we both know she'll place herself as the final voice on any matter she pleases."

"And you? What are you in charge of?" I actually managed a smile.

"Would it be too ridiculous if I said, keeping you safe?" he asked. I rolled my eyes but appreciated it all the same.

"In all seriousness, I do think supporting you is important. All the help you have aside, there's a lot of pressure on you, and I'll alleviate what I can. Looking at it objectively, my forest walking skills can translate easily into stealth. I can be on someone before they know I'm there, which several of the Canopy who are gifted at camouflage can do as well, Nien included." I scowled as he mentioned the instructor, and he kept right on talking, glossing over it. "I like to think that, similar to you, I'm a fairly keen observer, even if the Spear did get the drop on us. I can think on my feet, which I anticipate is a skill we'll continue to need. I'm admittedly not as emotional as many of the others, but hopefully keeping a level head benefits us all."

It did, and I liked his more aloof exterior. It made the side of him I got to see feel even more like a rare gift.

"I'm a skilled fighter, although I'm not vain enough to say I'm the best here, by a long shot. Still, I think if we combine our skills we'll be all right. Also, I have experienced great loss. I know what it's like to feel that things will never get better. I know the cost. And I'm willing to make the decisions needed in the future regardless."

Now *that* was a new perspective. He'd lost his sister, and I'd lost my dad. Neither of us had been able to prevent it. And no matter what we did, no matter how many skills we utilized, and no matter how much I wanted to avoid it, I knew we would lose more people. And I believed Fell. If he had to sacrifice a friend of his, or one of mine, for the good of the others, he would. And what I realized that others likely didn't was that it would hurt him. Deeply. And still I knew he would do it.

"What about me? If winning this somehow put us in a position where I was the cost, could you do that?" I looked into his eyes and saw opal light from my own shining on his cheeks.

"Don't ask it of me." He shook his head.

"That's not an answer. I don't want to lose you. Despite our short time together, I can hardly imagine it, and when I try, I feel despair. But that doesn't mean it won't happen. I need to know. If all of this, saving the others and the Societies, costs me, would you do it? If you had the option?" I didn't voice out loud the reason I asked, but I knew the tightrope I was walking as I moved further in my projection with Ama. I had told Juliard I wasn't him or my father, and that was true. But I had the ability to be both of them, and worse.

"Yes, if that's what you're asking of me, even though I would regret it for the rest of my life."

It was the answer I needed. I wasn't sure I was strong enough to make the same decision.

The silence after his answer stretched.

"Well, I suppose we should go join the others in the library." I pushed myself up and took a step toward the door. Fell reached out and grabbed my hand.

"Stay here. With me." It was phrased as an order, but his tone told me it was a question. "The door is locked from the outside. There's blankets in here, just like everywhere else, and we're the only ones in the office."

I felt my marks waver as I registered, or at least thought I did, the secondary meaning to his request. I pulled my hand out of his and wandered around Warrick's shelves, buying myself time as I ran my hands over some of the knick-knacks.

"If I stayed ... " I stood and paced.

I hadn't finished my own question, either, but it didn't seem to matter.

Fell's marks grew near-blindingly bright as he stalked closer. And that was the word for it; he looked almost predatory as he closed in on me, and I felt myself having to actually work to breathe steadily.

I didn't pull away as he drew me toward him again; instead, I leaned into his kiss. I let him pull me down onto the blankets.

CHAPTER 15

I was surprised the following morning when I opened my eyes and felt rested. A large arm was draped over me, and Fell's marks hummed with a soft glow as he slept. I'd been granted a reprieve from my problems for one night, and I fought the urge to stay with him and keep the rest of the world locked out of the office.

I wasn't looking forward to my first order of business for the morning, but I wanted it done before training began with the rest of the group, which meant an early start. I tried to escape Fell's arms without waking him, although I should have known the effort would prove fruitless.

"Leaving so early?" Light hit my face as one of his eyes opened. He looked different, softer, when he first woke up.

"I have to talk to him," I said, reaching for my ocala bodysuit as I began to get dressed.

"I know. Do you want me to come along?" He didn't have to ask who I meant, even though I'd been putting it off.

I declined the offer. As much as Fell comforted me, confronting my uncle was something I needed to do alone.

I wasn't surprised when I swiped out of Warrick's office and found Juliard moving down the adjoining hall from the library, already up working. I shut the door behind myself with another swipe. Juliard spoke with his form still hunched over whatever papers he was reviewing, but at least he stopped.

"Paired yourself off with a Societal already, then? Are you in love with him, this forest walker?"

I struggled for a quick response in the face of his blunt questioning.

"How did you know what he was?"

"I spent enough years in the Rift before going to Earth to remember what a forest walker sounds like, or rather that they sound like nothing at all. No one else could be that silent, but you've avoided my question, niece."

I huffed.

"Quite frankly, it's none of your business. Although if you must know, he and I are ... Connected."

The papers he'd been carrying fell out of Juliard's hands and onto the floor. He looked up at me after a moment with the glowing bronze I had yet to get used to overshadowing his grey eyes. He bought himself time as he bent to pick up the papers, reshuffling them before he responded.

"Is that so? That's rare. I'm sure they've told you as much. And you accepted it, just like that? You've always had fight in you. I would have anticipated you'd balk at something like that getting determined for you."

I couldn't tell if it was meant to be a compliment or a way to drive a wedge between Fell and me. It didn't matter. I had no intention of playing games with my uncle.

"Being placed in the Rift against my will was something I had to *learn* to accept. Being with Fell, wasn't. When he told me what we were, it made sense. I haven't known him that long, but he's the one thing here I am sure about," I said, laying the truth bare for him. "But that's not why I'm here. You promised to share, and I don't think I want to put it off any longer. I don't want to hear any more secrets or lies. I really can't stand it, Juliard."

He set his jaw and flicked his brown hair out of his face. He was already agitated.

"And you're certain that you want the truth? You're right, you deserve it. But only if you're prepared."

"Whether I'm ready or not, this could be my only opportunity. Who knows what will happen when we go for those escape pods. I need to know." I realized I'd moved into a defensive stance, as if readying for a fight.

He nodded, gaze flicking to my feet as if he'd noticed it as well.

"Very well. Know that when you first came up here, I didn't realize I was sending you into danger. After being cut off from the Societies for so long, I had no idea whether the Spear was still active, and I wrongly guessed when all our talks on Earth seemed to be going smoothly that they must have disbanded or dissipated over time. I debated whether or not to tell you the truth before you left, but judged it unlikely you'd uncover it on your own. I even thought maybe I would lie if you did find it, say I was the golden brother. That would have been fruitless, though. Over the years Tiberius and I learned to hide our marks, but I can't change their color."

He twisted his arms, pausing for a few moments as he looked at the glowing marks. I knew if I tried I'd be able to read them, but I wanted to hear it from him first.

"After so many lifetimes, I felt rushed. I convinced myself that with everything else going on, you didn't need one more thing on your plate. I was also using you. I told myself that I wasn't hurting you intentionally; that if Earth was going anyway, Verkent should be involved. I was so curious about what had happened since we'd left. What, if anything, did people know or remember? And yet, for reasons we can get into some other time, I couldn't bring myself to come back. After all this time, I felt like I was owed the information, and I used you to get it. I put you in harm's way to get it."

He'd gone back to staring at his marks but glanced up at me as my opal ones flared. I schooled my expression and wiped the glare off my face. I clamped down my teeth to prevent interrupting him. I needed to hear it, and I knew he'd stop or get sidetracked if I got upset.

"But you want to know about Tiberius, not my excuses. In our time, the Spear was a radical sect within the Societies that wanted to break away and be allowed back to the Ancestors' original planet. They disagreed with how the Coalition operated within the Societies. The Spear's members had built up Lone as more than I believe it was. They thought it was some sort of utopia or haven. They were bitter and resentful about the Choosing system. Your father and the others felt like it was a forced choice. It wasn't until years later that he admitted to me that they'd approached the magistrate at the time and lobbied for the right to leave. They used their masks, of course. Even those of us who knew of them had no idea who was involved. The magistrate denied their request, and the Spear decided to work toward their goals in other ways."

He ran a hand up the back of his neck and sighed. We both knew what *other ways* he was referring to. There was no denying what he'd already told me, and what I'd seen on holofilm with my own eyes. My father had been a loving and caring parent. And he'd been a murderer. A cold, calculating, and unforgiving one.

"I never condoned the group's violent methods, and I still don't. Tiberius let his anger twist his morals. It's part of why I'm so hesitant about the Reader working with you on your projection abilities. They're undeniably powerful, but they have the potential to get out of hand. He and I never had such talents, and look what happened. When your father spoke about it later, decades after we'd finally reconciled, he said years of working toward a goal and being denied by a corrupt system at every turn twisted him into something. Once he found himself trapped with the rest of us on Earth, though, holding onto that level of anger and resentment was hard. He had to work at it. At first, he was convinced his fellow Spear members would find a way to come back for him. He felt that way, even knowing they'd stolen all records of Earth's true location. He knew his followers would have to use the Hub's equipment to blindly scan the stars."

He began to pace the hall, flicking his hair a few more times. He paused again as he stared once more at his arms. My own marks were mere weeks old, really, yet they felt like an ingrained part of me. I wondered what it felt like for him to have them return after they had been hidden for full lifetimes.

"Even I held out hope we'd be rescued. As Tiberius realized that wasn't going to happen, his resentment turned towards his own group. Over time, and I do mean over multiple lifetimes, that anger cooled. That's when I was able to reach him and begin to turn things around. Why we were given the longevity we were, I doubt I'll ever know. I've never met another Societal who had it, until the Reader, that is."

"Did you ever meet anyone else who could do what I can?" I couldn't stop myself from interrupting that time. Juliard raised an eyebrow, chewing his lower lip.

"No. I've never seen anyone do what you can. I met just one, once, who could do things similar to your Reader. Not as powerful, but similar." He paused, as if waiting for another interruption, but I wanted him to get back to my dad. "Your father and I hated each other for many years, but we were all forced to work together to survive without the Hub's resources and with limited numbers. In theory, we all would have Assimilated abilities of Earth once a new generation grew up there, but it didn't happen. Blanks remained Blanks as they grew up. For those of us who had been stranded, no new Assimilated traits took hold, save for our longevity. Some lived long enough to gain the ability to temper some of their traits, as your father and I both could. Until my arrival here I hadn't seen my marks in lifetimes." He gazed down, as if checking to see if they were still there.

"I could go into all kinds of tedious detail regarding our years of arguments that became discussions that finally settled into agreement, but I won't. The important thing for you to know is that your father changed. Truly changed. He was not the same man as the Spear leader when you were born. I can attest to it. In his past he had done terrible things. I can't deny it. Over time, though, he saw our being left on Earth for what it truly was: a second chance. He took it. If anything, over the last few generations he'd grown nostalgic for the Societies. I, on the other hand, started to feel the same bitterness that had led to his founding the Spear so long before. It had been so many years, and we were still on Earth. For what purpose? We knew the Coalition had the technology to find us again, and yet they hadn't." He'd run his hand through his hair so much that it was standing at odd angles. His marks flashed, brightening and dimming like a lightbulb about to go out.

"It was your father's idea to make Verkent official. He thought it would bring us back to our roots. We were the only real Societal members, but we had stayed in touch with descendants of quite a few of the others. We knew which ones had kept their stories alive. The more we met, the more energized your father became. Maybe he had some enhanced or Assimilated ability he'd kept that likened him to the Whispers. Who can say? But he became convinced that in our lifetimes, the Societies would return. He was really living again, while I had grown tired. The more we discussed the Societies, the more frustrated I became about all the secrets and divisions within seemingly aligned groups. I convinced myself the Spear and the situation with Earth never would have happened without such a deceitful system. I may have been right, but it wasn't healthy."

I pictured them, in my mind's eye, as they'd been when I was younger. They'd had spirited discussions. My father, with his idealistic bedtime stories of the wondrous Societies. Juliard, with his insistence that if they returned they'd have something to answer for. Juliard moved closer and laid his palm against my cheek.

"By the time your mother came along, Tiberius was by far the more charming one. Not that he hadn't always been; his charisma is part of what helped him found the Spear in the first place. I was the more cantankerous. She never really got along with me, not that I blame her. Your father fell head over heels in love with her. He tried to tell her the truth about himself. You were little, and he was becoming increasingly convinced that you'd have the opportunity to Assimilate. He was certain of it. He wanted her to be prepared. He wanted her to know all about him, including his sordid past. She didn't take it well. I'll admit I didn't like her from the start, but everything he told her was more than she could handle."

Juliard pulled back as opal light spilled over him.

"Don't give her that kind of credit," I said through clenched teeth. "That still means that in the best-case scenario she willingly left her daughter with either a murderer or an unhinged conspiracy theorist." And yet, if she hadn't, I probably never would have gone to the Hub in the first place.

He nodded.

"She did. You and he were always so close, and alike in so many ways. I think she was convinced that whatever he was, you'd follow in his footsteps, whether she agreed or not."

I smiled at that, before I could help myself. I remembered all the time my father and I had spent together, when I tried to be just like him. Then I remembered seeing his face on that film, completely content as he watched Earthers die around him. I pressed my lips together as they began to quiver, and a single tear slipped down my cheek, the memories soiled. I had a final question I needed to ask. No answer my uncle gave would have satisfied me, but I had to get it out anyway.

"You're basically immortal. Is there any chance, I mean, I can't imagine he'd have faked his own death and hurt me like that, but I wouldn't have imagined a lot of things before now. Is he?"

Juliard shook his head.

"No. He's not alive. It certainly appeared a true illness, but I can't say for certain that Societal sabotage isn't possible. We knew the delegates were watching us before they actually made their presence public on Earth. I don't think he was surprised when one came knocking at our church door. That was years before the rest of the Earthers received a formal greeting. How they located our group I can't say, but there was no hint they recognized either of us. Verkent is a large part of why the Societies opted to come down, not that I volunteered such information to the rest of the task force. After all this time, not much had changed. The Coalition still couldn't agree. They weren't certain whether to reveal themselves to the other Earthers and open their Societies up to Earth participants. I was ready to tell them to get out. All that time they'd left us to our fates, and then arrived with judgment. Your father was the one who pressed for participation."

For some reason, that hurt worse than everything else I'd learned about him. Perhaps because, as my uncle had said, his time as the leader of the Spear had been in another lifetime. If I tried very hard and ignored the truth, I could almost pretend he'd been a different man. And yet, not telling me when the Societals arrived, after our years waiting together, *that* felt like the real betrayal. That was something he'd done to me specifically, and who knew what the outcome would have been if he'd been honest. I realized Juliard was still speaking, and I tried to get back into his train of thought.

"Imagine the risk, if someone had found out who he was. It's possible someone did. Either way, he'd come to a point where he'd decided that what he'd done was worse than the Societals. They limited our choices and controlled them. His war, though, had prevented so many from having one at all. He wanted to be there for you, even though he recognized the complication having him as your father would bring if it ever came to light. When his illness got worse, he told me that it was the consequence of what he'd done all those years before. That's not for me to say, but I'm glad he made peace with it. And I'll be forever thankful that we got you. You know the rest; you all got invited to the Choosing, and we ended up here."

I was more conflicted than I'd been at the start. I knew the man I'd grown up with. If his actions during my lifetime were any indication, he'd spent at least that long trying to repent for what he'd done. He'd been willing to admit that he'd been wrong. Then again, he'd never taken responsibility, and he'd never told me about any of it. Maybe it was an attempt to spare me, or maybe he'd just spared himself. Either way, it didn't erase his guilt.

"I'm still the daughter of a murderer."

"You are," Juliard confirmed in a cold tone, "no mincing words about it. And? That doesn't have any bearing over the person you are, Kena. It doesn't have to."

And yet, I had the same propensity for anger. Ama had called me out on it. I'd seen it unfold in the time we'd been at the Hub. It had been justified. Then again, wasn't that what my father had thought of his own actions? I'd been desperate, and despairing. So had he. I needed to be careful or risk ending up the same way.

"And you? Why push me away once he was gone? You could have told me. You could have prepared me for all this." I heard my voice shake as I worked to hold back more tears.

Juliard sighed.

"I could have. I should have. But with Tiberius gone, and the Coalition cutting off contact, I had every reason to believe they'd decided against our inclusion in the Choosing. And I was suspicious of what happened to your father. For a good several months, I was convinced he *had* been killed. I stupidly thought that if I distanced you, it would create a level of protection for you. I told you, you're not responsible for his crimes, and that's true. Still, I didn't want you to become a target. Or worse, a figurehead for the Spear to try and rally behind if they were still around and realized you existed."

I hadn't even considered that. "Verkent Princess," some of the other Earthers had called me. They'd meant to make fun, but it hadn't bothered me. Still, "Spear Princess" was different. Heir to a murderous empire. I wanted to avoid that association at any cost, and yet I'd set myself up as the leader of a rebellious group and was training to force the will of my enemies.

"Do you know," I mused, needing him to at least hear what it had been like for me to watch the holofilm of Earth's destruction, "when I saw you both on film it was naturally a horrible shock. I never dreamed it was *you*. I was up here thinking that I was descended distantly from the Spear. I didn't even give them your names in my mind, seeing both your faces on screen. I gave them nicknames."

He reached out and grabbed my hand. It had been years since he'd been so affectionate.

"And what were those?" he asked, and I just managed to catch the faint hint of stormy grey in his eyes beneath the bronze.

"I referred to the brothers, to you, by what you wore that day. I called you the Cloak, and I called him the Wolf."

He gave me a smile, but it didn't reach his eyes.

"Is that so? And here you are, neither Cloak nor Wolf."

He was right. I never would have aligned with the Spear, even if my father had shown back up and asked. And the cloak was a piece of Riftian clothing I had eschewed from day one, only wearing one when necessary.

"I'm not sure what I am," I confessed to him quietly, my words so soft I doubt he would have caught them if not for his Riftian hearing. Following the same pattern, I could have named myself Ax or something ridiculous, after my weapon. But it didn't feel like who I was. Nor would I have referred to myself as Reader. That title was saved for Ama, no matter how much I studied under her. "Who am I, Juliard?" I looked back up at my uncle, not really even expecting an answer.

"Someone else entirely, niece. Someone better than both your father and I combined."

He dropped my hand and walked away, headed into some office or another. I didn't reach up to wipe the tear off my cheek until he was out of sight.

CHAPTER 16

I lost myself in training for the rest of the morning, putting my father somewhere in the back of my mind and leaving my feelings to be examined later.

Once everyone had agreed to work together, training had become much more effective. Instead of just trying to best one another, we were teaching one another. Most individuals in the room were divided up into circles, with Societals from different planets taking turns demonstrating planet-specific moves. Some of the more skilled weapons instructors or fighters were walking around from group to group and giving advice on when and how multiple moves could be incorporated together to improve everyone's abilities.

Scrounging for food had presented limited success. Shawd, Cassius, and Cassia had searched the last Spear-free area we knew of earlier in the morning.

"Two more days, three if we stretch," Cassia informed the group about our supply.

That set our timeline. We'd attack the Spear's stronghold in the housing and dining units in two days. If we could beat them and take over the Hub, all the better. Still, we had to assume it might get destroyed regardless, once the Earther ships arrived. If we lost, or even after a victory, we'd make for the pods that would take us to Canopy. From there we'd be able to detain any Spear members with us, and then use the Tundra Doorways to get to everyone on the planets.

"I wouldn't mind personally handling Kidan," Vanya seethed as she slammed her ocala bow into my ax while I practiced a move she'd taught me. She and the other weapons trainers in particular had taken the Riftian king's betrayal particularly hard.

I'd seen Kidan myself at our welcome dinner to the Rift, but I'd never really spoken to him. My animosity toward him was entirely due to what his actions had caused. Particularly the consequences for his fellow Riftians. I slammed my ax hard against another attack from Vanya as I thought of Bayard's sapphire eyes, snuffed out.

"I want to say that I can't believe he managed it. After all, it was right under our noses," Hok added as he took her place in the circle and gestured for me to drop the ax. He wanted me to practice my projection as he swung at me with his sickle swords. "Then again, he's always been a more solitary presence. I'm honestly baffled he could get the Spear members to join together like this. His loner nature works all right on the Rift, when we're independent anyway. But he rarely ever leaves the planet. I don't think he's set foot off it since the last Coalition meeting four years ago. I can't fathom how he recruited all these other Societal members under everyone's noses."

He stopped and stared down to see his own swords pointed at him. I'd been murmuring under my breath during his entire speech, urging him to miss me and let me duck around his blows. Then I'd focused all my energy on getting him to turn his weapons on himself. It was another new success, and a frightening ability I had at my disposal. Hok dropped his arms back to his sides as I released control.

"He's right. I was never particularly fond of Kidan. I think we were both a bit too aloof. But we all worked with him occasionally, given our role with the Blanks. Not to miss-assign fault, but he never struck me as someone capable of managing a network like the Spear," Fell added as he moved around me in the circle. I hadn't managed yet to stop my Connected using projection, but I'd also never put as much effort into it. I just couldn't make myself *want* control over him, deep down.

He stepped out, and I stayed in the center of the circle as Hale took his place, raising a dagger.

"So," I started as Hale ran at me and then instantly diverted as I told him to go elsewhere, "is it possible he's not the real leader of the Spear? Or he's working with someone?"

The idea fascinated me. I put together the pieces of information everyone had shared. I knew firsthand the difficulty of drawing together Societals with a natural mistrust of one another. And in this case the Spear had also pulled in the Earthers to help them accomplish a takeover, the likes of which my father had been unable to achieve. Which meant surely there had been someone who'd pushed for, or at least had been positive about, Earth's involvement. All those signs pointed not to someone sequestered on their own planet, but a leader heavily involved at the Hub. Someone persuasive, because Earthers had been incorporated into the plan regardless of the fact that many of the Spear despised them.

"Kidan's involved. At the very least, he's posing as leader, but maybe there's someone else. Surely it's someone close enough to him for that to work. As for uniting the others, Riftian projection would surely come in handy, even if it wasn't a skill they consciously controlled, like Ama and myself." I asked Nix to spin in a circle as she came at me, and when I released her, she weaved away, looking dizzy.

I continued to work through the question aloud as the next few individuals charged at me, finding it easier and easier to project with my thoughts alone.

"So, maybe someone else besides Kidan. Likely a Riftian. Someone who wanted Earth to be involved, and someone often at the Hub."

"And someone very smart, because they've out-strategized us at every turn," Silas added after I knocked him back with my ax. He'd managed to catch me off guard.

"Yes. They've been two steps ahead," I agreed, then backtracked. "Except when they haven't. They weren't prepared for us in the arena, which tells me they didn't know we were coming. So at least at that point they weren't someone posing as a resistance member. But think of the prison. They had people at the entrance so quickly, it's like they were ready before any alarms went off."

I paused to catch my breath. Several others around the circle did the same.

"What are you saying? That one of us is secretly working with the Spear?" Hok asked.

I shook my head, a stray strand of hair falling into my eyes.

"No. Not one of us that's been in the resistance the whole time. Someone on the periphery. Someone who acted like they were on our side, and has been with us, and yet not with us for everything. Someone we didn't get to until after we arrived at the Hub. And most likely someone who's still here. I doubt anyone involved with the Spear would have agreed to go to Tundra with the menders and wounded even if—"

After several seconds of silence Fell cleared his throat.

"Kena? Even if what?"

"Even if they *were* wounded. Because they'd have to be able to stay and lead the Spear. No. I have to be imagining things. I'm just too used to all the intrigue of the Societies. There's no way." I let my half-formed thoughts hang in the air for the others to puzzle out, and walked out of the circle.

"No way what?" Hale demanded as several of them started to follow me.

I didn't want to answer. Not until I was sure. I couldn't afford to be wrong again.

I sprinted out the library doors, down the narrow hall, and toward the delegate offices. The Rift's office was empty and dark. We'd sectioned off Dagan and Kite's offices as infirmary locations. As I rounded the corner and went through to the sea-Society's old office, I saw cots and blankets spread out across the floor, the desks shoved haphazardly to the perimeter. It was considerably less crowded than when we'd first arrived. Quite a few injured individuals, and several of the menders, had been transferred to Tundra well before we'd destroyed the Doorway.

Not the person I was looking for, though. They'd stubbornly insisted on staying, to help us. Or so they'd said. I didn't want to believe my own intuition, but I needed answers.

"Bayard!" I yelled across the room, not taking time to check in with the mender on duty.

A few individuals jumped as I shouted, sitting up in cots or looking across the room from where they'd been walking. I zeroed in on the delegate easily enough. He turned from a bookshelf on the back wall, his fingers still running across the edges of several leather-bound tomes.

He tilted his head.

"Kena?" The skin around his eyes was still a garish red, the blue light deadened beneath them. His arms lit up, though. He wore a simple, sleeveless tunic instead of his usual garb, revealing much more of the sapphire markings than was typical. "I've just been conversing with the menders here on possible treatments for my vision."

He turned toward me and began stepping forward, one hand out in front of him as he walked. Hok strode past me, gingerly moving his large form over the individuals resting on the floor. He reached the delegate and offered an arm, guiding him to us. I wasted no time as Bayard made it to the entrance.

"I have to be blunt. What do you know about the Spear? Is there any way one of the other delegates could be leading them, along with Kidan?" Regardless of what I thought, I wasn't ready to accuse him directly. I wanted to see how he responded first. He reached out a searching hand, clasping onto my arm as he stepped away from Hok.

"I think I have some information that may be helpful. Perhaps the magistrate's office would be a more quiet place to have this discussion?" He squeezed slightly as he made the suggestion. It took everything in me to prevent the vibrant sheen of my marks from increasing in intensity as I led him past the others and back down the hall.

We reached Warrick's office, and I held up one hand in front of the screen to allow us entrance. I looked at Bayard as the door slid open.

"I'm sorry to drag you in here during your recovery, but this needed to be addressed quickly."

Bayard nodded.

"Yes, I too, regret that we've seemingly run out of time." His hand left my arm, and before I could react, he'd shoved me into the office. I turned and saw him reach into a holster strapped on his back. He pulled out a bent weapon and snapped it open. From my angle, I couldn't quite see what it was, but he took the handle of it and smashed it into the door's panel. I heard the soft escape of air as it slid closed, locking the two of us inside.

"Kena!" I heard Fell scream as something hit the door from the other side. I jumped at the sound of his voice; it was wild. I'd never once witnessed him out of control. After repeating my name several more times his voice faded, and I hoped the others had pulled him back. They'd find a way in, I had every confidence. Especially with Digit in the group. I just had to stall.

"I'm going to take your locking us in the office as a bad sign, just so you know." I tried to steel my voice with a confidence I didn't feel. "I take it you're working with the Spear, then?"

"Working with?" His sapphire marks lit the space around him in a way that was more terrifying than flattering, "I would hope your estimation of me would be higher than that. I'm leading it."

CHAPTER 17

The delegate's smile was cold. It wasn't just the dimming of his formerly illuminated eyes, either. The expression came off a bit unhinged, with no genuine warmth. I was determined to dig for information, and for delay. I had to trust that if I stalled long enough, the others would find a way to reach me.

"But in the arena, when we got here you were with the prisoners onstage. They were going to execute you." My voice trembled, and I tried to steady my hands and temper my marks.

"A rather ingenious plan, I thought. Kidan is a useful ally, but not as intelligent as myself. Too brash. Too headstrong. Would have done well in the Crew, to be honest. Still, he has his uses. Being the face of the Spear, for one. Me, though, I prefer to lead from the background.

My ambitions were greater than his, and I wasn't ready to get found out. So when you all arrived in the arena I had our executioner, Toth, help me disguise myself alongside the other delegates. I'd made sure not to show my face to any of them, so they were none the wiser. The bruises and cuts I had from our fight during the Coalition meeting helped as well, as you all assumed the Spear had hurt me. When your forest walker killed Toth, it turned out to be fortuitous. There went the one witness in the arena who might have given away my real identity."

Bayard had tricked us, all of us. It didn't take much effort to figure out how. I'd felt more strongly pulled to him than any other Riftian, aside from Fell. It wasn't beyond imagining that he had abilities similar to Ama's and had used them to his advantage. Still, something wasn't adding up.

"But your eyes. You fought with us, and you got injured."

He reached up and put a hand on the scarring around his eyes, then dropped it just as quickly. He frowned as he answered.

"An unfortunate inconvenience, to be certain. Not that I don't have the skills to fight well enough without full use of my eyes. Still ... I had intended to place myself in harm's way to throw suspicion off myself, but I didn't take into account Dagan's love of acidic substances. My mistake. I don't often make such an oversight, but I admit your appearance had caught me off guard. Oh, I knew you'd find a way back to the Hub. I never shared Kidan's doubts about the abilities of the resistance. Still, secret Doorways through Tundra! I must admit I'm impressed. I would have assumed those instructors you're so close to would let word slip to me about them. It seems my hold over them wasn't as complete as I believed."

He'd begun to pace, his steps as lithe and graceful as always. Another piece of the puzzle fell into place as he weaved around the edge of the desk without so much as reaching out to feel it.

"You can see."

"I knew I made the right decision with you. Look how much more intelligent you've proven yourself than the others. The glow from my eyes may be gone, but the function is still there, if a bit blurred. Playing up my injuries has made things easier. While you've been so distracted with your fights, your plans, and your training, I've been able to sneak off to Kidan and relay everything I learned here. It's made it that much simpler to stay one step ahead of you all."

"And you have some sort of projection abilities similar to Ama's. You must. Now that I think about it, it makes no sense to have given you the Riftian office all to yourself to recover when there were so many people crowded into Coalition Hall, and yet we did."

He nodded.

"Another excellent deduction. I will admit,"—his grip on the desk next to him tightened, the only tell that he was upset—"my abilities are no match for yours. To be able to actually *control* and *force* rather than merely influence? A valuable skill indeed."

Given what he'd said, I realized he was probably responsible for the Spear's quick response in the prison, maybe even the amount of opposition we'd faced. He'd likely warned them already about our plans for the escape pods, which meant we'd have to move up our timetable. He also knew about Juliard and me, which brought me to my next question.

"You shut us both in here. So, you tell me, how do I play into this?"

He tapped his nose with his finger, then pointed at me.

"Exactly! See, *that's* the kind of thing that supports my feelings about you. We're alike, you and I. Both so sharp. Then again, that makes sense since we're family."

I felt my lips scrunch as I made a face at him.

"Just because you're a Riftian doesn't make you any family of mine. Not after what you've done."

I glared at him, and he scowled back.

"Tsk, Kena, that's not a very kind thing to say, and not at all what I meant. Don't be so obtuse, it doesn't suit you. What *would* Uncle Tiberius say if he could see you here mouthing off to his nephew?"

The words took a moment to sink in, and once they did I took a step back, and then another. My marks shook off and on with light, and I didn't even try to stop them.

"You're lying." The words came out hollow, and I didn't believe them even as I said them. I *felt* it was true.

He smiled.

"You can tell I'm not. My guess is that, given you're another Riftian with pronounced projection-based abilities, you can sense it when I've dropped mine. I wasn't ready to reveal these things before, but now is as good a moment as any. You surprised me in the arena, and I get to return the favor. Honestly, Kena, let's not waste time on this back and forth. I'd wager they'll make their way in here soon enough. Aren't there any questions you'd like answered before we're interrupted and I make my great escape?"

"You mean before you're captured?"

He shrugged and took slow, long steps around the desk toward me. He came to a stop not even a foot away, and I was forced to look up to maintain eye contact.

"My dad never mentioned another sibling," I countered.

"Quite rude of him, really. They did have a sister. She was a truly spectacular Societal. A Kite, actually." He looked past me and smiled. "You should have seen her wings. I've never beheld any that were their equal. Feathers the length of her entire frame. Stunning, truly. Not important for our purposes, though. She didn't get involved in either of her brothers' schemes, and she's long dead. The only important woman in *this* story is my beloved mother. A Riftian of unparalleled projection abilities. Until you or me, I suppose. Long dead too, I'm afraid. She taught me everything she knew, and I expanded on those skills. Sadly, you've already met dear old Dad.

You can imagine my shock when we first discovered Earth's location and found him still alive. Not only that, but he was spearheading, if you'll pardon the pun, an entire conspiracy group dedicated to Societals. All those years, and he'd placed himself at the head of Verkent, self-important as ever."

Bayard shook his head again, letting out a humorless laugh. I felt faint. I looked around the room frantically, dropping myself into Warrick's office chair. That was a poor move defensively; if it turned into a fight I would have done better standing, but I couldn't manage it. I grappled with his words, trying to deny them even as I felt how honest they were.

"Juliard can't be—"

"My father? Yes, I'm afraid so. He left my dear mother Siana at the Rift when he went to prepare Earth's settlement, with plans for her to join later. She's long gone. You know the rest, of course. I've waited quite some time to meet my family. I'd held out hope some descendant had made it, but I didn't dare dream *he'd* still be around. The Reader is the only other one I'd discovered with my longevity. Not that she recalls it. She's not the only one with a long lifespan and gifted skills of projection. While she was working on everyone else, I was working on her. She always was full of herself. It made it that much easier to fool her." Bayard leaned against the desk, not the slightest sign of tension to his posture.

"That woman is wiser than you'll ever be! And my mentor." I scowled at Bayard.

"You put your faith in the wrong people cousin. I'm the one with real power here."

I wanted to cover my ears and block out what he was telling me. But the puzzle pieces were falling into place. The Spear had been so far ahead of the resistance, even with the assistance of the Whispers. If he'd been able to use projection against Ama, he could have used it against any of them. And it would have worked, given they hadn't known to defend against it. I thought back to my own feelings toward the delegate. How I'd been drawn to him from the first time I'd seen him onscreen. And yet, I hadn't told him about the resistance. I hadn't told him about our plans. Had I known, deep down, that he wasn't trustworthy?

I pressed my hands into the chair, shoving myself up to stand and face him.

"Is he working with you? Uncle Juliard?" I demanded.

Bayard grinned.

"Oh, this is priceless. He deserves your trust, and doesn't have it. I *should* be able to trust him, but I can't. I've grown up looking for information on him. The same passion you had for the Societies, I had for my history. I scoured the homes of both brothers, and hoarded my findings. When I became a delegate—a post I've kept for generations, using projection to turn everyone's mind away from my true age—I utilized the library. There's lots of hidden gems in there. I eventually stumbled upon Spear writings. I knew the brothers were involved. I just wasn't certain if they'd been in on it together, or which one had really led the organization."

"Because you didn't have the holofilm. I had the only evidence of who was truly responsible," I guessed.

He nodded.

"Exactly. Then, when we first made contact with Verkent after the last Coalition meeting four years ago, they'd lost their marks. I couldn't even determine for certain if they were the original brothers. I pressed the rest of the delegates to contact Earth officially, to pull you in for participation in the Choosing. I hoped to draw them out, and it worked, even though it took years."

"So this whole setup, Earth being involved at all, has been about your need to settle a personal matter?" It beggared belief, but then again, it explained why we'd been pulled in even though so many Spear members seemed to despise us.

Bayard waved me off.

"Of course not. I'm much more practical than all that. It's simply an added perk. Kidan wants Earth for the numbers. He knows that ridiculous task force member Kaiser and his mercenaries can help. I see the wisdom in that as well. It's a nice way to bring things full circle, don't you think? In the past the Spear tried to simply dispose of Earth, and that was the cause of their demise. This time, we'll *use* Earth to achieve our long-awaited victory." As he spoke, one hand had curled into a fist, and he raised it into the air before slamming it on the desk so hard that the wood cracked.

I began to take measured steps away from him.

"But you don't care about any of that, do you? You wanted the brothers, even if one of them was a murderer."

He pointed at me.

"Yes! *Now* you've got it. We're both disappointed, you see. You, because you wanted Juliard to be the leader of the Spear. Me, for the same reason. For years I'd been determined to build back the Spear; to make it stronger than ever. And when I had control, I determined I would aim for goals never before dreamed of. Not only will I get us back to Lone, but I will be the savior of the Societies. No more non-Assimilators, and plenty of new planets, if people are so desperate for them. All under the control of Lone. Led by gifted Riftians such as myself. No longer hiding away in some secret forest. We'll use their abilities, and their resources, and we'll never again be forced out of our home. We'll have the means to defend it, save it, and even conquer the worlds of others if we so choose. I'm not just trying to run home to some old planet nobody's inhabited for generations. I'm going to rule an empire."

I stared at him, shocked in the face of his fanatical tirade. A man I'd trusted, and respected, had devolved into a homicidal criminal before my eyes. He'd *been* one all along, and I hadn't even suspected. I opened my mouth to speak, and closed it again.

He held a hand out to me, the sapphire marks on his arms seeming to mock the beauty I'd once seen in them.

"You could help, you know. If we—"

"You're out of your mind. You can't possibly think I'd want to help you!"

A sputtering sound emitted from the damaged panel by the door, and lights flickered along the floorboards. It had to be Digit. I looked back up at Bayard and saw him scowling in the direction of the door.

"It seems we're running short on time. I don't suppose there's anything I could say to persuade you to my side? You'd be a powerful force, you know. I'd be happy to give you a planet to run. Earth, if you'd like it. A new world. Take your pick. I will be retaining sole control of Lone and the Rift, but I'd readily pass off most of the others. And I'm even willing to let you keep the forest walker, if he's important to you. All I'd ask in exchange is some instruction on how to imitate your particular projection skills."

I stared at him.

"You're completely mad. Fell's not some object to be traded."

He nodded.

"You're likely right. I doubt he'd agree. He's rather stubborn, that one. Still, there's plenty of other Societals in the solar systems. You don't have to settle. I could train you. Ama has talents, but think of everything I've achieved behind the scenes. You could possess those abilities."

I shook my head as my shock gave way to another emotion. It took a moment for me to place grief.

"I admired you. I trusted you. When you worked with us at weapons training, it's part of what made me want to make the Rift my home." My voice broke as I tried to hold my feelings in check.

"That doesn't have to change. You could live there while I run Lone. Think about it, Kena. Your mother abandoned you. Your father and uncle lied to you, kept secrets, just like everyone in this blasted system. But I'm here, telling you the truth. We're family, after all, and family should support one another." He reached down and grabbed my hand. I jumped but didn't pull it away.

"Does Juliard know?" I asked.

"Dear old Dad? Hardly. I hadn't even Assimilated when he left. I'd wager I look a lot different than the young boy he left behind. And I went out of my way to make him ignore any resemblance when we met. I only planned to reveal myself if he proved useful, and he hasn't. Refusing to cooperate with Kaiser and the other task force members in our takeover. His little stunt in getting away from the Spear and helping this sad, argumentative resistance. No, I've considered myself fatherless for a long time, and I don't mind staying that way. Aside from his long life, he doesn't possess any particular talents. He's of no use to me. You, though. You have the potential to be more than both of them, more than Ama. We could be the family to each other that we should have had all along. I could be a mentor to you, a sibling if you like, or even a father-figure."

I'd been lingering at the edge of an emotional precipice, and that last statement tipped me over.

"My father *was* a mentor to me. He loved me,"—I'd avoided my complicated feelings about the man since finding out his history, but I knew that much—"and he changed. He never would have asked this of me. He was a different person. He would have abhorred what you're doing."

Of that I was certain.

A hiss sounded behind us, and the door shook but didn't open.

"You're not wrong. Uncle Tiberius disagreed with me. I spoke with them both when we first made contact with Verkent, well before we reached out to the rest of Earth. I'm fairly certain your father saw the real me. 'Like calls to like' and all that. I can't say for certain, but he kept me at arm's length. Kept me from meeting you. He spoke about the Coalition and the Societies as though they were something to be admired. What a disappointment. And he tried to poison Juliard and you with the same ridiculous notions. In one conversation with me, Tiberius even threatened to tell the other Societals who he was. He didn't know my identity, but he knew I was a threat. It would have meant imprisonment or death for him, of course, but it also would have turned the others' eyes toward the possibility that the Spear might have lasted as long as its former leader. I couldn't have that."

He'd dropped my hand and gone back to pacing. For the first time since I'd known him, he had lost control of his marks. They lit and dimmed in erratic waves.

"What do you mean?"

While he was all jittery motion, I'd gone still. I knew somewhere down deep that I didn't want to hear whatever he had to say next. Just as surely as I knew I needed to hear it.

He turned and locked eyes with me. At least, I thought he did. I still wasn't certain, with the scars over his gaze.

"Haven't we been over this? Don't be purposefully obtuse. I believe I told you. I needed Tiberius out of my way to move things forward, and so I made sure he was. There are all sorts of Societal concoctions that can mimic Earther illnesses. Really, you should be thanking me. I mean, you said it yourself, Kena, a murderer for a father. And one who couldn't even finish the job he'd set out to accomplish."

I heard my own scream before I realized it had exited my mouth. I launched at him, swinging my ax. His marks settled into an even glow as he spun and met my weapon with his own, which I saw was a double-edged scythe. Our curved blades were stuck on each other as he held pressure on the handle of his weapon.

"Very well, then." He scowled at me through clenched teeth. "You've chosen your side. You'll realize it was the wrong decision soon enough."

I stared down at his weapon, so similar to Juliard's. Although my uncle's was made of a golden metal, and Bayard's was something akin to steel.

"Like father like son, I suppose."

It took everything in me to make any comment that wasn't a grief-filled accusation about my father. But it worked. He glanced down at the weapon, only for a moment.

I grabbed a dagger from the holster at my thigh. I knew he was the better fighter, but I had to try. I managed a shallow slice into his leg as he moved away from the blow.

As he looked up from it, he smirked, swiping his scythe beneath me and knocking me to the floor. I brought my arms up in front of my face, but another blow didn't come.

I looked up to see one of the shelves that surrounded Warrick's desk slide open. Bayard ran through before I'd realized what he was doing. I moved to follow him, but a small knife flew toward me. I dropped underneath it and slid, and heard a thunk as it embedded itself into the desk.

Two more followed, but neither made contact. I chanced another look from behind the desk. Bayard was pulling them from yet another holster under his shirt. Whether it was a secondary weapon of convenience, or he was a dual master with throwing knives, I didn't know. One glanced off the edge of my ax, and I ducked down again. I was able to keep my emotions in check just enough to not run at him and get myself stabbed. But only just.

"This isn't the end of it, Bayard! Before this is over, I will kill you." Before my arrival at the Hub I never would have thought myself capable of such a statement. It was the type of vengeful proclamation I'd only heard in films or books. But as my father's face, and Pim's face, and those of all the injured Societals passed through my mind, I knew I meant it. With every ounce of my being.

I wasted half a second deciding whether or not to roll out from my hiding place and try to use projection on him. But I had no idea whether it would work on someone who had been practicing his own version for so long.

By the time I looked up, the panel had slid back into place. I ran up to the shelf and located the keypad he must have used to open it, tucked behind a book. I swiped my hand over it, but it didn't work. I knew I had no hope of guessing a passcode quickly enough to make a difference. Instead I turned and ran back toward the office door, just as it was pried open and the others tumbled into the room.

CHAPTER 18

The others ran past me and began searching the perimeter of the room. Fell reached me before anyone else, his face stormy and his marks flashing like strikes of lightning as he pulled me into his embrace.

"Never again," he vowed, face buried in my hair. "He will never get an opportunity like that again. He could have killed you."

"But he didn't," I reminded him from where my head rested on his chest.

The forest walker didn't answer. He reached up pulled my face toward his.

The kiss was unlike any of the ones Fell before. It was possessive, desperate, and left me breathless when it ended. I put a hand up to my lips.

"That was—"

"Where did he go, Kena?" Silas demanded, a hand touching my shoulder. He glowered as he gazed around the office. As a friend I was touched that he was protective, but if I'd been his enemy the expression would have been terrifying.

"There's a secret entrance into the office. But it's too late. He's gone." I was answering his question about Bayard, but I thought of my father as I said the last two words.

I directed them to the panel Bayard had passed through. After a few minutes, Digit shook her head.

"He's wiped the passcode out. I could probably restart the whole system and have us input our own, but there's no guarantee of where the passage would let us out, without seeing the blueprints. I'd wager he has plenty of Spear members waiting at the outlet."

"It might be best for us to just block it off," Silas suggested.

The others agreed, and we hefted Warrick's desk in front of the panel, along with an awkwardly tilting pile of items that included a chair and a small statue of a spiraling snake that he'd kept in the office. A tribute to Rover, no doubt.

I was tempted to ask everyone but the Riftians to leave before I shared everything Bayard had revealed. But that went against the alliance I had worked so hard to get them all to agree to, so in the end everyone stayed. We even waited for Hale, Ryshal, and Acaius to go back to the library and fetch the other Societal leaders.

Reactions varied as I filled everyone in. Vanya cursed, slamming a hand so hard on Warrick's desk that the small crack Bayard had formed on its surface widened. Hok, who had always balanced his brutish size with self-control, hefted the office chair as if it weighed nothing and hurled it into a wall. Fell held me tight the entire time, his grip tightening as I revealed more of the details.

"He was a guide to all of us, a mentor," the forest walker said. "I can't believe we were so fooled."

Ama's reaction affected me most. She didn't say a word through my entire explanation, and when I looked across at her, I saw silent tears rolling down her glowing cheeks. Her voice was a mere whisper when she spoke.

"I failed you. I failed us all."

Fell and I moved over to her together, protesting.

"You are the reason we knew about the Spear at all! Without your help and the Whispers, we never would have thought to make another Doorway. We would have been stranded in the Rift and most likely slaughtered if we didn't give in to our enemy. You're not to blame for this." Fell knelt before the Reader and grabbed her shoulders. She nodded absently but looked past him, her eyes locking onto my own.

"He's revealed himself. That means we may have even less time than we thought. We need to secure those pods before Earth gets here. Tell me again, what did he say about his end game here?"

I repeated the story. "That's where it got a bit odd," I added. "He's clearly got a bigger aim than Kidan. He wants to settle whole new worlds, harness the abilities of the existing ones, and repopulate Lone. Unlike the original Spear, he's interested in much more than just remaining there. Still, how could he hope to accomplish it? There aren't any records of how to settle new planets, right? Why make this move now, if that's the goal?"

Ama sighed, but she didn't look away as she spoke.

"There might be an answer to that problem. I can help us figure it out, but I need time."

"That's something we may not have," Silas said as he stepped up behind the Reader.

"He's right." Acaius's dragon wings were half-unfurled behind him as he spoke. "Bayard knows what we have planned. We've lost the element of surprise and with it our chance at winning back the Hub. We're not nearly ready, but I think we need to get everyone prepared to leave. We should make a run for the escape pods. Now."

Ryshal squeezed his husband's hand as the others reacted. Some stared in silence, some agreed, some argued.

"These Societals aren't prepared enough to execute any plan accurately," Hok grumbled from one side.

"Who needs preparation? We need to be bold and make our move while we can!" Karo snapped back.

"So you're fine just throwing us all in the hall to get killed?" Sarah stepped up by Hok's side, taking his hand as her snake hissed at the Crew captain.

I did a double-take, and if I'd had any emotional energy left to expend, I'd have been curious about their situation.

As the snapping and fighting rose to a fever pitch, I dropped Fell's hand and placed my own hands over my ears. I crouched down, needing to drown them out. After what Bayard had admitted, it was overwhelming. I felt myself panting as my heart started to race.

I heard Fell asking if I was okay, but his voice sounded far away. The room that had been spacious before now felt too small. I needed everyone to be quiet. I needed to run. I needed my father. I felt tears sliding down my cheeks as the yelling and bickering continued.

"Everyone just stop fighting!" I screamed as I crouched on the floor, rocking back and forth. As soon as the words left my mouth, my vision began to blacken at the edges. From my crouch I started to sway and lost my balance. I thought I was going to faint, but Fell caught me in his arms and lowered me into a lying position.

I looked around me as the overwhelming noise settled into an eerie silence. Everyone in the room *had* stopped arguing.

"I, um, I think you *made* them," Fell said, his voice soothing.

I lifted my hands in front of me. My marks flickered and my fingers were shaking.

"I'm sorry. I'm so sorry." I repeated the phrase several times, unsure what else to say. I'd never intended to use projection on the others, with the exception of training.

"That felt ... odd," Captain Karo said, holding one arm up in the light of Warrick's office to stare at it.

"Disconcerting," Ryshal agreed, shaking out his bat wings as Acaius put a comforting arm around his shoulder.

It stung, but I deserved worse. And yet no one attacked me.

"Look, we're all on edge. And like it or not, what just happened has moved this timeline up," Silas said. "Digit, can you monitor any cameras and watch for the Spear, see if they're gathering anywhere in particular? In the meantime, the rest of us will go tell the others to get everything packed and finish up what will need to be a lightning-fast round of training." After ending his directions, Silas turned and left without waiting to see if the others followed. Vanya shot me a small smile as she walked out with him.

"Yeah, nothing to see here, people. Move along," Dex added as he shuffled people out, his steps huge with his furred and hooved legs.

The others filed out until only Fell remained. He moved to hold me again, resting his chin on the top of my head. Before he could say anything, I told him the rest of what Bayard had revealed: that Juliard was his father.

Fell stepped back, his eyes meeting mine.

"What are you going to tell your uncle?"

It was the question I'd most dreaded. The truth was, I wasn't sure. I'd complained and chafed against the secrecy among Societals. That very structure was a decent part of what made the Spear possible. I worried about what he might do with the information. I still didn't fully understand his actions. I knew, at least according to him, that he'd had my best interests at heart. That didn't mean I had to agree with how he'd gone about it. Added to that was the complicated relationship he must have had with my father, given their history, and the fact that he'd never mentioned Siana or Bayard to me. Surely the delegate had adopted a new name since his father had left, or Juliard at least would have recognized that.

After lifetimes of fighting against the Spear, I didn't think my uncle would join them. Then again, he'd grown disenchanted with the Coalition as well. It might have been the wisest choice to just leave him out of it entirely. I couldn't, though; not without feeling like a hypocrite. What we'd gone through so far had done away with any doubts I had about the level of force that might be necessary to reclaim our planets. Bayard could easily get killed in the fighting. I'd vowed to do it myself. Didn't my uncle deserve to know before that happened?

"The truth," I said aloud as I came to my own conclusion, "Even though it's the last thing I want to do. Just not until we're off this ship and far away from Bayard." I told myself it was a fair compromise. My uncle would get the truth, but we'd be distanced enough from the Spear that he'd be forced to take time and think about it before taking any action. After that, if he truly wanted to join his son and take his chances with the Spear, I might just help him into a ship.

We started down the hall toward the library, but we hadn't made it three steps before Ama's glow lit the space. She pointed at me.

"You and I need to speak. Now."

My glance went from her to Fell. He shrugged and dipped his chin to the Reader before going on. He'd protect me against the Spear, but not the wily older woman.

A day before, the fighting had felt endless since our arrival. But in this moment of relative calm, I would have given a lot to be out fighting the Spear again. I didn't think I had another serious conversation in me.

As we entered the office once again, I turned, waiting for her to speak. She didn't. Instead we just stared each other down. At least I did. Ama stared up at me with an unblinking gaze and crossed arms.

After a full minute of silence, she sighed. "Well, ask it. What you're thinking."

"Is it wrong, what I can do?" The words spilled out of my mouth.

Ama didn't answer immediately. She placed a finger on her chin and walked a circle, muttering quietly to herself. Then she turned and leveled an orange sunset stare at me.

"That's something you'll have to decide for yourself. What can your morals tolerate? What are you willing to risk? What are you willing to lose? I don't just mean the others, but yourself. Are you willing to go against your personal principles, how you see yourself, if it means saving others? Not everything is an easy choice. Not everything has a truly right answer. This may be one of those times. In fact, I'd say it almost certainly is. After all, I don't claim to be perfect. I've caused plenty of confusion with my own abilities."

I took her hands in mine as I shook my head. I wasn't sure who I needed to convince. Her, or myself.

"That's not the same. You did it to protect yourself. To protect the Societies. And even then, you mainly just turned people's curiosity away. You didn't order them to do anything they wouldn't have done regardless. This is a step further. One I'm not sure I'm willing to take, because I might not come back from it."

I'd given voice to my biggest fear, at least in part. To control someone else. It went beyond any other Societal ability, and it was an invasion.

"You can have a plan in advance, Kena, but that doesn't mean you'll follow it. Think about what we've discussed regarding the feelings that drive a lot of your decisions. You could say right here and now that you're not going to use this ability. You're going to fight them another way. And yet, isn't it situation-dependent? If one of those individuals had a spear to Fell's throat, if he was injured and unable to fight back, if no one else was near, and you were too far to help any other way ... would you use it then?"

"Yes, without hesitation," I answered honestly. I understood the point she was making. I just didn't like it.

"That's your answer, then. You'll use it if the stakes are high enough." She pulled her hands back.

"And when will that be?" I pressed her.

"You'll know." She left the vague answer to hang before switching topics. "But that's not why I pulled you in here. I told you there might be an answer to settlement. There's something that's bothered me since we saw Warrick's message."

"What's that?" I asked.

"What he said about the non-Assimilators being a setup by the Spear." She paced back and forth, one finger tapping her chin. Her marks glowed and dimmed in a cyclical pattern that reminded me of the sun rising and setting.

To learn the Spear had been purposefully preventing people from Assimilating, aside from that being murder, had been almost a relief. If only because it was one mystery solved and a question answered, in a series of worlds that seemed to produce nothing but more secrets.

"I have worried, and hoped, that perhaps settlement was a similar issue," she said, stopping her pacing in front of the desk drawer with Warrick's secret Spear symbol.

"You think the Spear could have been behind that as well?" I turned the idea around in my mind, but she shook her head. Then she sighed.

"Not them. Me."

I felt my brows scrunch down as I stared at her.

"You're not making any sense."

She stepped closer.

"Kena. I'm one of a kind. Well, nearly one of a kind, as we've found out now with your Uncle Juliard. But I'm still the oldest living Societal. And a descendant of original delegates, as well as the only Reader the Rift has ever had. Let's be honest, dear, if there was a secret to settlement I think I'd have been one of the key people in on it, don't you?" Ama never minced words when it came to complimenting herself. Perhaps that was where Fell picked up that trait.

"It would make sense," I allowed, "but you don't know anything about it. No one does. That's why they haven't settled a planet since Earth was cut off and the knowledge was supposedly lost on my former planet. If it existed, surely someone would have found it by now."

She gave a half-smile and wagged her finger.

"Not if someone very old, very powerful, and very knowledgeable had hidden it from them. And perhaps, even hidden it from herself." She looked down at her arms, twisting them back and forth.

"Ama, you can't be saying you think *you're* the one who stole the information."

She waved a hand again, not looking up.

"Stole, hid. Who can say. But I know that whenever the issue of settlement is brought up, there's a pull in my brain. Like a blank space, or something missing. I didn't used to think too much of it. After all, I'm willing to admit that, living this long, my brain may be a bit addled. Then, when the Spear was exposed for what they'd done to the non-Assimilators, I realized it was possible. I searched my texts, but I wasn't able to find anything that mentioned settlement at all. Then I realized: I have notes, journals of all my lifetimes. And there's one missing. The one from the lifetime where your father and uncle fought on Earth. And I thought, perhaps something about that event made me decide to do what I did."

I shook my head.

"No. You wouldn't. Whatever your reasons would have been, and my guess would be preventing another situation like Earth until the Spear had been sorted out. But Ama, I know you. You're compassionate. When non-Assimilators started appearing, and when they started killing them ... you wouldn't have stood by. You didn't know at the time that it was being facilitated by our enemies. Everyone thought it was due to overpopulation somehow. You'd have told them then."

I didn't think I had it in me to have my admiration of one more person in my life dashed to bits.

"Unless I had hidden it so well that even I didn't remember. Kena, I've told you before about the immense power of projection, and now that you've experienced it I think you understand even better the possibilities it opens up. But as I'm sure you've also seen, it's dangerous. It makes you walk a thin line between what can be done, what needs to be done, and what should be done. Using the power to such an extent that it dissuaded not only everyone else, but myself, from realizing I had the knowledge all along would have taken a lot of strength. I may have overdone it without realizing it. In fact, I'm nearly certain I did."

She sat back against the desk and continued to stare at her arms. She had markings on her palms, the backs of her hands, even on her face. More than any other Riftian I'd seen. Not surprising, given her age.

"Ama, if you did do this ... it would be a good thing. At least for us, here, and now. We'd have answers that could help the Societals, or in a worst-case scenario, be bargained to the Spear,"—not that I liked the idea—"but where's your proof?"

"Kena, what do my marks say?" she demanded.

I paused, tilting my head as I tried to catch up to the sudden change of conversation. I stared at them. They were vibrant and numerous, but ...

"I ... don't know. I can't read them. I mean, I'm seeing them but I don't recognize them. I've actually never thought to try and read them before," I admitted.

She nodded, then dropped her hands into her lap.

"Exactly. And neither can I. I have no idea what they say. I haven't known for years. But I do think they hold answers. I haven't been able to undo whatever I did that made me unable to read them, but my particular projection works better when used against others. So, I thought, if I willed them to be readable, *you'd* be able to interpret them."

The full weight of her words struck me like an actual blow. To read the Reader. And not only that, but to potentially unveil something that could save the Societals. The implications were huge. It would mean another way out. Even if the Spear managed to win, if we had the key to settlement we could evacuate the Societals elsewhere and Assimilate somewhere new. Not that I liked that idea, either.

I felt myself shaking my head before I'd even thought it through.

"No. It's too much. Ama, I can't lead the alliance and bear this responsibility. Perhaps, after we make it off the station. But don't ask this of me now."

"I'm sorry Kena, but this wasn't an ask. It's something I did, and something I've already decided must be undone."

I couldn't bring myself to agree, but I didn't protest again. She was right. I'd said I was willing to help the others, whatever the cost.

Orange light filled the room, brighter than anything I'd ever seen. I slammed my eyelids shut, scrunching my face and throwing an arm in front of it. It didn't matter. The intense glare of orange sunset light filtered through. I felt tears stream down my cheeks at the onslaught to my senses.

After several seconds the light began to fade. I kept my eyes closed until I heard Ama cry out. When I first opened them, it took a moment to adjust to the relative dim of the office. Ama stumbled. She'd fallen to the ground by Warrick's desk and was attempting to pull herself back up.

I ran over, closing the distance between us in a few steps. I helped her into a chair, cradling one of her arms as she situated herself. As I moved to let go, I realized I could read it.

She was covered in history, a dizzying amount of information that included stories all the way back to her past on Lone. I wanted to read it all, but I tried to focus on what she'd asked me to find. It had felt overwhelming, but once the opportunity was in front of me, I wasn't able to pass it up. It was as if her projection had dissuaded me from wanting to look, and once whatever she'd done was broken, I realized that of course I wanted to know.

The answer wasn't on her face, or her arms.

"Excuse me, Ama, but I need to see." I saw my own opal marks grow brighter as I hedged around the direct question. Helping Ama, I had seen Societals in various stages of undress, to be able to read marks wherever they were. But with the Reader it felt beyond disrespectful to ask.

"Of course, dear." She wore a cloak, like many Riftians. She removed it and pulled at the edge of her tunic's neckline.

"There!" I shouted as I saw her shoulder. Written on it in markings, from front to back, was our answer.

Generations of uncertainty. Stalled and failed attempts to Assimilate. Lost worlds like Tundra waiting for settlement. And the Reader had the answer all along. At least, something that pointed us to the answer.

"It roughly tells us that you halted settlement. I don't have any details about why or who else may have been involved. That's on the back; as it goes over your shoulder, it does say something about avoiding a catastrophe. Maybe the Spear using the opportunities in the new worlds somehow? Regardless, it's the front that helps us. It says, to bring settlement back to the Societals you will need to entrust your story to a Connected who carries a soul. Well, that doesn't make any sense. It must—"

I stopped, pulling back from the Reader as it clicked into place.

"It means *me*. I'm Connected to Fell, and we both carry that mark, the one that says *soul*. But here?"

"*Story*. My journals! Kena, this is very important. We *must* find my missing journal. That's where I hid whatever the answer to this is." She grabbed my arms and shook me.

I had a good idea of where it might be. But surely it wasn't possible. It made no sense why he would have had it, but then again, he'd done a lot of things that hadn't made sense.

"I think I may already know where it is. Ama, I was given a book with the planet Lone stamped on the cover. It was written in symbols that looked a lot like your markings. Nien had it. But that doesn't make any sense." I hated to suggest it, because I was sick of covert conversations, but it was the only way to get answers. "We need to talk to Nien."

We hadn't even made it to the door of the office when alarms began to blare and the overhead lights shut off.

CHAPTER 19

Blue lights flashed to life on the perimeter of the hallway as we exited the office, blinking in quick succession at our feet.

Ama and I made our way past the offices, Societals joining us as they swarmed from the library. One grey-jumpsuit-clad Clan member we'd rescued from the prison looked pale as he clung to another former prisoner helping him down the hall with his injured hoof.

"What is it?" I followed his gaze to the lights.

"I was one of the key security designers for the Hub. The blue lights signify a safety protocol activated only when there is imminent danger to the Hub, and we have no choice but to abandon it." He looked like he was hobbling as fast as he could go.

"So they're planning to flee, then? What's so bad about that?" Dex asked his fellow Clan member as he caught up to us. The injured Hub worker gulped before answering.

"It was intended for use against an outside threat. The Societies would never leave all their information and traditions vulnerable to others. This protocol allows an hour or so, to give everyone time to evacuate."

"And then?" Dex's eyes narrowed, and I already suspected the answer.

"And then a self-destruct sequence initiates. They're not just trying to escape the Hub. They're going to blow it up."

Dex cursed, alongside several others. I looked around me to see that Fell, Nix, Hale, Silas, and Vanya had caught up to us as well.

"I thought they were going to use the Earther ships! Or the bombs Juliard found!" Hale yelled, his face revealing panic.

"He's right. Weren't they relying on the Earthers to help them destroy the Hub and act as a getaway?" I asked, not breaking my stride as Fell handed me my ax. I'd already slung my bag over my shoulder before Ama and I had fled the office. Nien's book was inside.

"I guess Bayard had a secondary plan," Silas said.

Digit wove her way through the crowd with her shorter frame. She held her tablet aloft, pictures and diagrams that made no sense to me hovering over the screen.

"Look, I hate to be the confirmer of bad news, but the Hub worker is right. Regardless of their original plan, this is what's happening now. And if there was any kind of failsafe sequence in here, they've deleted it. Entirely. I suspect they didn't want us to have a chance to mess with the code." She frowned down at the tablet as though it offended her.

"So we can't stop them. We'll have to change our strategy, then. It just went from rescuing everyone and taking over the ship to evacuating as many people we can, as quickly as we can. At least there's no need to fight over it anymore. The decision's been made for us." Silas's tone was even, his expression unreadable. It was in situations like the one we found ourselves in now that I was most thankful for his former life. His military past had made him hard to connect with at times, yes, but it had also trained him to stay calm in the face of panic. Or maybe that's who Silas had always been, and he'd just been drawn to callings that capitalized on it.

"Does everyone remember the plans?" Captain Karo shouted over the tops of heads as we neared the entrance to Coalition Hall.

Several affirmative yells sounded back. Whatever the others had been working on while I'd met with Ama, I hoped it was good.

I'd missed out on everything, and I'd had limited projection practice. I still didn't want to use it, but I'd already admitted to Ama that I was willing to. I had to commit. It was the only way it would work. That was one thing I was certain of.

As the Coalition Hall doors opened, there were no Spear members to be seen. Typically that would have been a good sign, but in that moment it was just another reminder that we were in the center, while the escape pods were all docked in bays along the hallway that rang like a giant ring around the perimeter of the Hub. Digit had briefed us all on the layout of the station, which felt a bit like a maze if you hadn't had a look at the blueprints.

We made it two hallways over before our first Spear sighting. A group of resistance members containing two Clan, two Crew, and two Dagan peeled off. I watched as they worked in tandem to take our enemies down. The Crew rushed in first, weapons and fists flying. Then the Dagan shot darts while the Spear were distracted. For good measure, the Clan barreled into those still standing.

When we came across the next group of Spear members, by now in the outer ring and close to a docked pod, Vanya and Cassia followed Cassius, Ryshal, Acaius, and Shawd toward them. The Kites spread and folded their wings in turn as Vanya shot between them. Cassia was a blur as she shot through openings in their feathers with her fangs, making quick work of her enemies. The twins split off and moved farther down the hall away from us, as the other Kites began loading the pod. They were better than having to go one at a time through a Doorway, but still held only a handful of people. We'd need a lot of them to ensure all the rescued people and resistance members made it safely off the Hub.

Ama shuffled along next to Hok, Sarah, and a green fairy-winged Kite I heard Sarah call Tibby. The girl was small, but she flitted around easily in the confines of the Hub. I knew she'd helped rescue the children from the Hub and get them to Tundra. With Ama focused on them, the Spear attackers kept missing their shots at the group.

Off to the side, Veronica's blue eyes shone as she worked next to Dex to take someone else down.

Luckily, the docking arrangements along the curved perimeter of the Hub meant the Spear defenders had to spread out their forces. Unfortunately, it meant we did as well. I peeled off with several of the others as we made our way down the outer hall, leaving the closer ships for any wounded who had stayed on the Hub and those not as equipped to fight. Silas and Dex covered several of the others as they made their way into the closest ships, before following us.

As we sped down the hall, another group of Spear blocked our path, large enough to keep us from getting around them; it was made up mostly of Clan and Dagan, although there was a spare Crew member and Canopy member in the crowd as well.

Fell and Juliard reached them first, one going high and the other low. Juliard was stunningly effective with the scythe, but every time he made a slice, it reminded me of the secret I had kept from him about his son.

Hale, Nix, and Digit were weaving between the Riftians and jabbing out with daggers and a short sword. I'd fended off blows as they came but hadn't thrown myself wholeheartedly into the fray. I shook my head after barely managing to parry a blow from a Clan member. I had to focus. I couldn't afford to let my emotions get the best of me in a life-or-death situation, but that was so much easier said than done.

A pained scream drew me back to my senses. Digit grimaced, holding one arm in the other, blood dripping from somewhere on her upper arm all the way down her wrist till it seeped into the bandages on her hand. A muscled and menacing Spear member—Crew, just like her, no less—towered over her with a cutlass.

I dropped the arm holding my ax down to my side.

"Drop it!" I yelled with all the force I could muster, as I closed the few steps between us and threw my other arm out. The Crew member went wide-eyed as the cutlass hit the floor. Digit picked it up with her uninjured hand and then struck the Spear member down.

"Thanks," she gritted out through a clenched jaw as we moved around him.

"You need to get into the next escape ship," I urged her as we came up to one. She started to protest, something about her having the maps. At that point, though, we'd either find and get into the escape pods or we wouldn't. Her schematics couldn't stop what the Spear had already set in motion.

"Only four pods left," she warned me, before her eyes fluttered and she went limp.

"Hale!" I yelled, my head swiveling as I tried to locate my friend.

"Right here." He grabbed me from mere inches away. I glanced over to Digit, and Hale gave a single, swift nod.

"Got it. Let's go, Digit!" he urged the techie as he bent to scoop her up and headed for the nearest ship. Nix joined them, stabbing at a Spear member who tried to follow. More of our group filled the escape pod. Hale's eyes locked onto mine just before the door slid closed and the ship pulled away.

It was such a short moment, and yet it struck me that if things went wrong it could be the last time I ever laid eyes on my best friend.

Somewhere between that ship and the next, the hallway became crowded. If Digit's count was right, the rest of us had three chances left to get off the Hub. And who knew how many of the other ships had been filled with Spear?

We'd long since lost track of the twins. I craned my head around the Spear in the hall but didn't see any Dagan or Clan from our side, either. Our group was mainly the remaining Riftians, along with Sarah and the green-winged Tibby.

As we neared the next docking station, I heard the hiss of doors sliding closed before it detached from the Hub, Spear members presumably inside. That left us two chances.

When we came upon our next opportunity, I saw other resistance members closing in from the other side of the hall. They'd made it all the way around the perimeter from the opposite direction.

Nien was on the front line of the other group, slashing through his Spear opponents with warthog-like tusks. On our side, Fell weaved between our enemies, daggers moving so quickly they were a blur, as Juliard took out anyone who got close to the younger Riftian.

Seeing that Hok and Sarah, along with her snake, were otherwise engaged, I moved in front of Ama. I yelled at a Clan member who had ducked his head to charge at her to stop, but I was growing tired. I gripped my ax with both hands and tightened my hold on it.

Between our groups, we took out the Spear members and began loading the first of the final two ships. Nien, in contrast to his bloody facade, acted the perfect gentleman as he offered Ama a hand to help her into one of the pods. Iduna joined her, the tight-lipped instructor taking a seat next to Juliard.

"That's everyone else," Silas stated. "We need to get ourselves in the last—"

A pained scream echoed through the hall. I turned to see Vanya with an arrow embedded in one shoulder. She sucked in a breath, but managed to lift her own weapon and return fire. Until a second arrow hit her in the thigh. She dropped to one knee as Silas yelled, moving in front of her. He held up his sword and deflected a third arrow as more Spear members ran toward us.

I'd hoped for a showdown with Bayard, but he wasn't there. Instead, Kidan, black marks glowing, stood in the center of the group as they came to a halt in front of us. The Riftian ruler had worn a fur-lined cloak on our planet. At that moment he was garbed in a gaudy red one with white fur at the edges. To his right was the archer, someone from Canopy. He had flickered into existence from seemingly nowhere, and I realized he must have mastered camouflage even better than Nien had. To Kidan's left stood a gelatinous Dagan, and as she grinned I saw the tufted edges of darts held between her spiny teeth. Next to her was a green-scaled Rover, thick crocodilian tail swishing on the floor as he moved.

Only a few of us in the resistance were left in the hall. Just enough to fill the last ship.

"Stafford," I heard Sarah spit out disdainfully at my side as she acknowledged one of her former instructors.

"Serpentina," the scaled Societal acknowledged, although he said it with more sarcasm and less respect than any of his fellow Rovers.

For a moment, everyone waited, as if no one wanted to make the first move. Then Vanya tried to stand again, a pained grunt escaping as she failed and Silas helped lower her back to the floor. I watched as he turned to the Canopy archer responsible. I'd have run if he'd turned the same look on me, and I had known him for years. It felt like I was getting a window into what he had truly been like as a soldier back on Earth.

He moved to launch himself at the archer, and as his adversary took aim, Silas rolled. The archer's shot went wide as Silas closed in on him.

I heard a hiss as Sarah and her snake Charles moved toward the scaled Rover and Kidan. The four of them clashed, her blackened fingertips flashing as she tried to land a blow. Charles launched himself, but Kidan managed to knock the swift viper away with the handle of his sword. Hok reached down and scooped the dazed snake up gently, placing it around his neck.

Several heavily tattooed Crew members and a couple of Clan, all wearing white spears, joined the fray.

"No matter what happens, make it into that last ship," I heard Fell say as he squeezed my hand. Then he was gone, deep in the crowd of Crew members. Juliard trailed after him.

I wanted revenge on Bayard, but Kidan was the next closest thing. I turned my attention to the Dagan first, recalling what Bayard had said about his mistake in underestimating them. She'd pulled back to the perimeter of the hall. I saw her pull a dart from between her teeth and begin to take aim at where Sarah's friend Tibby hung back, behind the rest of us.

"Drop it!" I yelled, charging toward her with one arm out and my ax held in the other. She did. The dart clattered on the floor, kicked to the side by the boots of fighting Crew members.

She scowled at me. Or at least that's what it looked like as her mouth moved around the spiny teeth where she held five more darts.

"Give them to me," I commanded. She reached a hand up and began pulling them from between her teeth. My concentration broke as I heard my uncle's voice.

"I can't hold them!" he yelled. The Crew around him and Fell were too numerous, and a few managed to break past them, headed for Silas as he grappled with the Canopy archer. Neither one held their weapons anymore; I spotted Silas's sword on the floor.

I took two steps toward him.

"Kena!" A green blur moved in my periphery, snatching something out of the air. Tibby landed by my side, handing me a dart that the Dagan had thrown at us.

I stared down at the petite Kite, realizing how close I'd come to resembling my newly discovered cousin with scars around my eyes. We had no time, and everyone was a priority.

"Get Silas's sword and help Vanya!" I yelled at Tibby. She nodded before flitting into action again.

"You. Give me those darts! Now," I instructed the Dagan. She hissed at me through her spiny teeth but did as I asked. As she handed the last one over, she lunged, teeth bared. I felt the spiny edges of her fangs begin to pierce the skin of one arm as I swung my ax around with the other. My weapon connected with her chest and she dropped.

I turned to help Silas. The Canopy archer had him pressed up against a wall, furred arms bulging with muscle as he slammed Silas's head against the metal. Silas's red marks shook as his eyes shuttered open and closed. Then, the Canopy archer let go and dropped to the floor. Silas stared, looking bewildered, until Nien appeared from behind the fallen archer, wiping blood off one tusk.

The instructor stared at me.

"Kena, if Digit's timing was right, we have mere minutes."

"Get in the ship!" I yelled at him as I barreled further into the fighting after Fell and Juliard.

The two were surrounded, Hok and Sarah were trying to get to them. Stafford lay dead on the floor, blackened veins visible between the green scales on his neck.

"We can't reach them!" Hok yelled as he pulled a horned Clan from the edge of the circle and Sarah slashed at his face.

"Move!" I screamed. I aimed the command at the Spear on the edges of the circle. Four of them did as I asked. Hok and Sarah took care of them before they came back to their senses.

In the center of the Spear circle stood Kidan. I broke through just in time to see him kick Fell in the gut. The forest walker dropped, and as he lifted his head I saw one eye blackened, swelling shut over the beautiful twilight glow. When he moved to strike back, the Spear around the circle reached out to pull and trip him, preventing him from rising and taking his typical graceful steps. Juliard was being held in place by several of the Spear, his scythe lying on the floor behind the Riftian king.

Kidan himself was wielding a large sword, similar to what Silas carried. I'd barely interacted with the Riftian ruler, but I hated him in that moment. He represented the Spear, and they had taken all from me that I planned to allow. Several of the Crew members held Fell in place as Kidan approached. Juliard struggled, but it didn't do any good. They were outnumbered.

Kidan lifted the sword.

I threw myself between two Spear members, letting my ax clatter to the floor as I extended both arms.

"Drop it!" I screamed. A sharp pain shot up my legs as my knees collided with the metal floor. I heard a loud, metallic echo as Kidan's sword fell in front of me.

"Let him go." I made my way back to my feet as I spoke, and the Spear members holding Fell did as I asked. As soon as they'd released him, he spun to grab his daggers back from the captors that held them.

I repeated the instruction to those holding Juliard. They glared at me but did as I commanded. My uncle scrambled for his scythe, then turned and sliced through three Spear at once with it before running back to our side of the circle.

I chanced a brief look over my shoulder. Hok and Sarah helped Juliard get past the remaining Spear.

"Get him out!" I yelled at them as they sprinted for the ship. From somewhere in the center of the Hub I heard an echoing boom. If I'd thought the station had been shaken before during our previous fights, it was nothing compared to what the Spear's explosions set off. Tremors moved the floor underneath my feet, growing larger with each wave. I lost my footing, slamming one knee back down into the floor as I struggled to hold control over the Spear members in front of us.

Fell grabbed my arm, and I felt the panic that had consumed me when I saw him being held captive abate as he squeezed it and pulled me up. He, of course, had no trouble keeping his balance, though the Hub was being shaken apart beneath us.

"Kena! Move now!" Juliard yelled from the pod.

I turned and began to sprint toward them with Fell, but a clanging made me look over my shoulder. Kidan had picked up his sword and was barreling after us with the others. It was a race to the ship. Behind them, I saw orange flames creeping up the walls.

Kidan glared at us. I saw his arm pull back, saw him lock eyes with Fell as he moved to throw his sword at the forest walker in a final, desperate bid to stop us.

"Stop!" I screamed, facing him full on. The remaining seven Spear members in the hall came to a halt, but their limbs twitched. I wasn't sure if it was my exhaustion, or their desperation; either way, they were becoming increasingly harder to hold. My body trembled with the effort.

"Kena." I heard Fell call; saw him bend to pick up my ax, as he tugged me back toward the ship. But I knew if I stopped focusing and released the others, they'd come after us.

"You can't win!" Kidan yelled, voice gruff. I wasn't sure whether it was a statement, or he just wanted to convince himself. He scowled, addressing Fell over my shoulder. "You are a waste of Societal talent. Flitting through the trees when we should have been on the front lines, taking what we're owed. And then Connecting yourself to a piece of Deserter trash." Fell started to move toward him, and I had to drop my hold on the others to grab the forest walker and yank him back.

As soon as I did, Kidan smiled, sprinting toward us. His sword was poised to strike.

"Drop it!" I screamed again, and the weapon clattered to the ground. The station continued to shake, and several of the Spear screamed as the hall grew swelteringly hot.

I locked eyes with Kidan as I backed up toward the pod, Fell next to me. I bent to pick up the Riftian leader's sword, holding it out against him as Fell carried my ax.

"You can't leave us here!" Kidan yelled as Fell and I backed up to the ship.

I looked into the blackened, glowing eyes of the Riftian leader, but I didn't really see him. I saw the Spear, and everything they stood for. I knew if I let him go, he'd hurt Fell. He'd already shown me that was his intention. The Societies were all about choices, but at that moment I felt I had only one.

My voice was soft, but I put all the remaining energy I had into the last thing I'd ever say to him.

"Run."

His eyes, and those of the other Spear members with him went wide as they turned and moved. Not toward the ship, but the fire that consumed the Hub. I backed into the pod, but kept my stance firm and my concentration focused on Kidan. I wasn't going to release my control again, because that's how the people I loved got hurt.

I stared after them until they were nothing but shadows in the flames. I stared until there were stars of light flashing in my eyes from the brightness of the fire as it consumed the Hub. I didn't even break my gaze as the door to our pod closed, and we detached and pulled away from the doomed station.

"Kena. You can let go," Fell whispered, placing a hand lightly on my shoulder. When I did, all of my exhaustion hit me at once. I dropped, and Fell lowered me into a seat, buckling me in.

"Everyone hold onto something, this is going to be rough!" Hok yelled as our ship picked up speed.

CHAPTER 20

I leaned against Fell, who had buckled himself into a seat next to me. Everyone was thrown against their restraints as the craft shuddered.

"They're shooting at us!" Tibby wailed, her translucent green wings shaking.

"The Hub doesn't have weaponized transport craft. Even if the other escape ships were all filled with Spear, they can't harm us right now. We're merely feeling debris from the force of the Hub's blast," Nien stated, wiping his tusks clean with his sleeve.

"Oh yeah, because you know everything there is to know about the Spear, right? You could be wrong. They could have taken some of these ships and modified them. You do realize that, don't you? Or are you really so pompous you're still refusing to see how in the dark you all were?" Sarah shot at him from her side of the craft.

Nien straightened his back and stared down his nose at her.

"Think what you like, young lady; your mind clearly isn't going to be changed by anything I have to say." He sat back, and that enraged Sarah even more. With a snarl, she unclipped her restraints and lunged for him. A fast-moving Hok hauled her back to her seat, but it didn't stop her.

"A fat lot of good you Societals were," Sarah continued, her features drawn into a scowl, "Remind me again how many generations you all twiddled your thumbs up here after Earth was cut off? You had all that time to find the Spear, and to prevent this, and did you do it? No! You did nothing! We're the ones getting results."

Hok cleared his throat next to her, but she ignored him as she barreled on.

"I mean, look at Kena! Good job, by the way, sending those worthless Spear to their fiery doom." She smirked at me, and I felt nauseated by the compliment. "She's up here mere months and she's already knocked off one of the Spear's leaders!"

My chest was tight. The ship was suddenly too small to breathe in. I sucked in air, my breaths coming shallow and quick. Fell looked down at me, then between Nien and Sarah.

"We all need to remain calm," Fell instructed. "You can settle this when we hit the surface. Nien, if you want to stay in the Canopy once we're there, it's your decision."

Nien snorted and bared his tusks.

"I'm seeing this through to the end. You all may not like how I handled certain things, but that doesn't mean I'm your enemy." He frowned and leaned back into his seat.

"Are you all right?" Fell whispered into my ear. I managed a small nod.

I managed to take several deep breaths, determined to focus on anything other than what I'd just done. Justified or not, I'd sent people to their death. I had done it on purpose and without remorse. Perhaps I was more like my father than I thought.

To distract myself, I looked around the escape ship. The passenger cabin was high and wide enough to walk around, but only held two facing rows of seats, in a somewhat oval shape with a small shower and restroom at one end and a closet at the other, containing blankets and non-perishable foods. Not that any of that mattered in our predicament.

I said a silent thanks that Canopy was the closest planet to the Hub's orbit and not somewhere like Dagan. At least we'd all be able to move around there. I had no desire to repeat the use of Dagan's oxygen-filtering reeds needed to breathe underwater. Digit had said that the Hub orbited about a three-day distance from the Society, although she'd guessed based on device readouts that the Spear had been steering the station closer. There was no way to know for sure how long the journey would take until we landed.

I stared over at Nien, who was still frowning down at his feet. I'd behaved angrily to him, and I *was* angry, but it wasn't all his fault. In truth, I'd redirected to the instructor my heartbreak and frustration over my father, Pim, and a lot of other things I had lost. Channeling all those emotions toward one scapegoat made them easier to contain, but it wasn't fair. I'd unleashed enough rage at the Spear; I could spare some reconciliation for my allies.

"Why did you give me the book?" I asked. After learning what it likely contained, the whole thing made even less sense than it had before.

He looked up, sweeping a gaze over my glowing marks.

"Because the Whispers told me to. Before you ask, the Reader doesn't know. They warned me that she had bestowed the book upon them, but I wasn't to mention it to her directly. The Whispers predicted there would be a leader from Verkent that went to the Rift. That this person would also become a Reader. They said that individual would excel not only at interpreting marks but many other Assimilated skills, and would be able to wield those abilities in a way that benefited us all. That *saved* us all. I don't know if it's a vision that caused them to give the book to me, or just common sense. They knew the position I held as the Earther educator when you first arrived. I stood the best chance of anyone at finding out whom the book should go to." I studied him while he spoke. His brows and arms were plated, in a way that reminded me of an armadillo. My focus, though, was on the singular yellow sunburst mark he had.

"So, to ensure I fulfilled the vision of the Whispers, you forced me into the Rift. And you didn't warn me about it."

He didn't answer at first, and when I looked up, he met my gaze, then glanced down at his mark where I'd been staring.

"I knew who you were soon after I met you, but *you* didn't see it. From the first day, you commanded the respect of the other Earthers, and you demonstrated great care and concern for them. You were protective over the Verkenters, but the others as well. I had no doubts about who the vision referred to. It wouldn't have mattered whether you'd written down Kite, Canopy or Dagan on your Choice. If you'd gone anywhere but the Rift, we would have been doomed." He folded his hands together as he finished.

The rest of the group in the craft had gone silent. Nien had tricked me. He'd lied to me. But he'd done it all because he truly believed it was the right thing to do. For the greater good. He'd put his faith in the Whispers. And he still seemed to believe in what they'd told him. I wanted to think of myself as more than just a piece of one of their prophecies. But I also wanted to think of myself as less. Less necessary and vital to the success of the resistance.

"Do you have any idea what's in the book?" I asked, retrieving it from my pack and holding it up in front of him. The others pulled against their seat restraints as they stared at the markings across the cover.

"No. I don't know whether it contains anything that would help us, but you're our best chance at figuring that out. When I went to take your decisions to Warrick on the day of the Choosing, I saw what you'd written. It was wrong. It was only then that I realized that I'd been passive, expecting the Whispers' prediction to come about on its own, but it hadn't. And I was the last one who would have a hand on those papers before they were read aloud. I intervened because we needed you, and because I believed in you. I didn't intend to hurt you, but I can't apologize for what I did." His lips were set in a firm line around his tusks.

I hadn't really expected him to. It wasn't as if I regretted ending up in the Rift. And the more I knew about my past, the more my role in our predicament felt almost like overdue penance for what my father had set in motion. Even if I wasn't at fault.

The craft shook several more times before we made it out of the debris field created by the Hub. I'd spent mere weeks there; I couldn't fathom what its loss was like to those who had grown up in its halls as they awaited the Choosing. And I didn't even want to consider how many may have been left inside.

After the last small bits of debris clanged off the outside of the ship and several minutes had gone by in silence, Hok spoke.

"Well, if that's all there's going to be, I vote we all get some sleep." He unbuckled himself and moved to the supply closet to hand out blankets. He passed a first-aid kit over to Silas, where he'd been cradling Vanya, who'd been suffering in near-silence. The arrows hadn't gone in anywhere that would kill her, but I was under no illusions about the pain she must be feeling. She managed not to cry out, but I saw her cringe and heard her hiss each time Silas pressed down on a wound as he cleaned them.

"How are we supposed to get any rest in this thing?" Silas grumbled as he glanced back and forth between Vanya and the walls of the pod. I myself tried very hard not to think of our confined space. I didn't want to risk a panic attack.

"Sleeping pills," Hok said, passing them out to each of us. "Technically there's a way to release a gas in here that could suspend us for the full two months it would take to reach the farthest Society in this system from the Hub, but I don't think we want to do that. I'd like us all wide awake and ready for whatever our landing looks like on Canopy. So, one of these, and then we can discuss things when we're rested."

Everyone accepted the pills from him without question. I meant to take mine, I really did. Instead I found myself sitting with it in my hand, staring at it. But I wasn't really seeing it. I was seeing a wall of flames swallowing up the Spear members I had sent to their doom.

"Kena." A voice broke my concentration. I looked up to see Silas looking at me from across the pod. The others had all fallen asleep, no doubt helped along by the pills.

"You're not going to take yours?" I asked him. Silas shook his head.

"I'd prefer to remain alert. I'll nap at some point, but I've trained myself to go without sleep in dangerous situations."

"Right, because of your ... job." I knew no one named Silas's work on Earth directly. He'd done something dangerous and covert.

He nodded, his crimson marks reflecting on the walls like droplets of blood.

"Yes. For my job. The same job that gave me a solid understanding of what I think you're feeling right now." He raised an eyebrow as he looked at me, and stayed quiet until I responded.

"I've killed others before this. Since we've been at the Hub. This shouldn't be any different," I defended myself, rationalizing the actions out loud as if it might change my own mind. "Kidan never would have let us make it on the ship. And he was going to kill Fell and Juliard. He had to be stopped."

Silas waited a few more moments after I'd finished.

"Yes, he did. And you stopped him. And even if making the decision to do so was simple in the moment, that doesn't mean the aftermath will be."

"What do you mean?" My marks flickered, opal dancing with his red on the walls.

"Do you remember when I lost my leg, and you came to visit me in the hospital? Do you know how that happened?"

I shook my head, feeling compelled to respond even though he was well aware that no one knew the full story.

"I'd been ... somewhere. The location doesn't matter. But I was working with a team. We'd been sent in to rescue children from some very bad individuals. We got them out, too. A few of my team were clear of the facility with the kids, and the rest of us were just sweeping the building to make sure we hadn't missed any of them. Then, we were attacked." He peered at the wall behind me, his gaze focused on where our glows mixed.

"Fighting ensued. We also found one more child. There were four of us left, not counting the kid. I had one of my guys pick the kid up and run. The rest of us held off our attackers. We knew the layout, but they had the advantage of having lived there. We ended up getting stuck, cornered at a dead end of the building. They would have killed us all. I fully believe that. And before they had, they would have tried to get information out of us on where the kids were being taken, and gone after them. All that to say, I knew what I had to do. I ran back toward our attackers, so the rest of my team could escape. We were just supposed to get the kids and get out, but I knew they'd come after us. I couldn't let that happen."

He continued to stare at the wall, and he didn't speak again as he reached up and touched a spot where his crimson light danced against the metal.

"What did you do?" I couldn't help the question.

He turned back to me.

"What I had to. I destroyed the building; brought the whole place down. Doesn't matter how. What does matter is I killed everyone inside, and irreparably damaged part of my leg when I tried to make my way out. My team came back and pulled me from the rubble."

He went silent again, and I tried to fill in the rest of the story.

"Then you got sent home. You stayed in the hospital. I visited you. Eventually you got a prosthetic. Silas, you did what you did to save people. You were a hero."

"Maybe. And I suffered for it. Not the leg, although I'm not going to pretend that wasn't hard to come to terms with. Sometimes in battles, you kill in the moment. But sometimes, you kill for what *could* happen. To prevent something worse from coming. And at least for me, that ate at me. I knew I was in the right. Still, that didn't make it any easier to get over. It didn't stop the nightmares of screams and falling beams from the building as it collapsed. What I'm saying is, I understand. And if you need someone to talk to, I'm here to listen."

I unclipped my harness, moving over to Silas and wrapping my arms around him in a hug.

"Thank you," I whispered. He hugged me back for a few moments before I stepped back, wiping a hand over my eyes.

"I think I'm going to try and get some rest now. You sure you won't as well?" I asked. Silas shook his head as I went back to my seat and strapped myself in.

I swallowed the pill Hok had given me, and as I fell asleep I saw orange in my dreams. First, the sunset marks of Ama as they grew brighter. Then, the retreating back of Kidan moving into the flames as I ordered him to run.

When we woke up, it was impossible to know exactly how much time had passed, although Nien was able to tell us the pills in the ships were similar to those in the infirmary on the Hub.

"They're good for twelve hours, give or take," he informed us.

Unlike the Hub, which hadn't had a view of the outside, the escape pod had a small metal window we could slide open. As we stared out, I couldn't tell anything with certainty. The blackness and vastness of space could not be overstated, and there was nothing to give us a clue as to the time.

After a while, Hok passed out food to everyone. Vanya was still sore, but the wounds weren't showing any sign of infection, which was good. Everyone fidgeted, shifting and slouching as time went on. At times people unclipped themselves to stretch or walk a small path between the two facing rows of seats, but no one spoke much. I was eager to delve into the book, but I didn't want to try without Ama.

I spent a lot of the time worrying. Over the Reader, and Hale, and Digit. Eventually, we took another round of Hok's sleeping pills.

We started the following morning, if it was morning, much the same as before. Then, around the time Hok passed out what I was content to consider breakfast, regardless of the time, it felt as though the pod was speeding up again.

I was thrown back down into my seat as Fell reached over to hastily buckle me back in.

"We've hit the atmosphere," he said as he checked his own belt. I reached across and grabbed at his hand. He squeezed back as the ship accelerated.

"In theory," Nien started, yelling over the noise that accompanied the increase in speed, "this final descent should take a matter of minutes. We ought to slow just before we hit the ground, and land near a river that's due east of Canopy's main village."

"Unless we crash and die," Sarah responded, reaching a hand out to pet her snake as he emerged from a hiding place in her hair. It didn't make me feel any better.

After a while we did slow down, but as the ship landed and the door slid open, I didn't see a river. I stepped out behind the others blinking in the bright sun. That alone was already a bit odd since Canopy had, well, a canopy. The light there wasn't as blocked out as on Rift, but a fully open sky was unexpected.

"We're sitting in the middle of a field," Hok shouted back from where he'd exited the ship.

Across the expansive area of tall grass, other ships landed as well, and I sprinted toward Hale as I saw him step out of one. I hit him full force, and he picked me up in a hug, spinning us both around.

"Digit's all right, but we had to do a pretty gnarly stitching job on her while we were getting out of the debris field," he informed me as he set me down.

"Where are the markers Cassia told us to look out for?" Digit yelled as she ran across the field toward us.

I scanned the periphery, but nothing looked familiar. I saw none of the vibrantly colored trees that had been present on the Canopy tour. Their plants were bright and saturated. I'd expected a jungle of emerald, magenta, and sunburst-colored plants, in a landscape teeming with wildlife.

This field ended at a treeline. Woodlands. They looked more like the forests of the Rift or those on Earth than what I'd seen on my only visit to Canopy.

More and more ships landed around us. As they did, it became clear that plenty of Spear had made it. Some ships were full of them. I scanned the field for Bayard but didn't see his sapphire glow anywhere.

A hand wrapped around my upper arm. I turned to see Juliard staring down at me.

"We should get to the trees. Regroup there."

It wasn't like him to run from a fight, but I didn't argue. We'd failed at saving the Hub or defeating the Spear there. As far as we knew, they had plenty of their own people on the planets themselves, and Earther reinforcements on the way. We needed to gather our own. Which meant finding Canopy's Doorway to Tundra.

Even as Juliard began moving toward the trees, guarding the green-winged Tibby and several other resistance members as he went, I stayed in the field. Something about it was off.

It didn't take long for the Spear members to spot the rest of us as we gathered. Some were glancing around, looking as bewildered as I felt. Even so, they made their way in our direction.

I heard several heavy thumps as Iduna, Ryshal, and Acaius landed next to our group.

"I see you all had the luxury of a Spear-free transport." Acaius flashed a toothy grin, then cast a concerned glance at Ryshal. The bat-winged Societal clutched his side but gave me a reassuring smile.

"Merely a bruised rib or two. Darned Clan Spear and their hard-heads," he joked.

"Kena, we've got company," Sarah said, moving into a defensive stance and baring her blackened talons as the first of the Spear closed in.

Running around them and even mixed in beside them, I saw some more of our own group.

Shawd, the blue and tan winged friend of Cassius, flew over their heads with an unconscious Cassia in his arms. She was missing one of her rounded, grey, feline-like ears entirely. Only the one with the chunk taken out of it remained. Her tail hung off his arm, limp.

Underneath her, a few of her fellow Canopy limped over to us, one with a furred arm in a sling.

"We've got them," Hok yelled. He and Sarah ushered the injured parties toward the trees.

"What in the world?" Hale questioned. I followed his gaze past the others and saw something glinting against the sun. It was Cassius, the gold flecks in his wings catching the light, making him look like an avenging angel. He yelled as he barreled through the line of Spear that pursued Shawd and his sister.

Hale and I ran out to meet him, and I heard grass swishing behind us. I didn't doubt that Fell and Nix had our backs. Although I knew Nix would have been the only one making noise.

We fought off the four Spear that were swinging at Cassius's wings.

"We have to get the rest of them. We'll finish this now!" Cassius yelled, pulling against us as we tugged him toward the trees.

Even with the four of us, it was hard to make any headway. Then, in the distance, I saw chunks of dirt and smoke fly into the air, arcing like a volcanic explosion.

"What in the ..."

"They've brought the bombs."

I looked down to see that Digit, in spite of her injuries, had stayed with us.

"Those orbs, like the one Juliard used to blow the Tundra Doorway. It seems they made a surplus. We should go." She tugged on my arm with her uninjured one. If nothing else, the explosion had jarred Cassius enough to have him running with us instead of pulling against us.

As we made the tree line, dirt and rock rained down on us, and explosions shook the ground in our wake. We didn't stop until we were deep into the trees and the echoing sounds of the blasts had ebbed. Not until we hadn't seen a Spear member for miles.

There was a clearing with a river running through it, the top of the water white as it rushed to who knew where.

A ragtag crowd gathered along its edge.

I looked all around the group as Cassia arrived, supported on each side by her brother and Shawd.

"What happened?" I ran over to her. Cassius glared and shook his head as he set her down. One of the few menders who had stayed with us instead of going to Tundra ran over to tend to her.

"Spear member got her as we were running for the escape pods. He even made it onboard with us, but I took care of him." Cassius glared as he explained, but his hands were gentle as he laid his sister down against a tree trunk so the mender could have a look.

Cassia blinked up at us, at least conscious, and managed a smile.

"I'll be all right. We have more important things to worry about." Cassia waved the mender away as she pressed cloth over a wound.

"What do you mean, what's wrong??" Silas questioned.

"We're not on Canopy. We landed somewhere else." Cassia hissed as the mender pressed another cloth into her side.

Digit shook her head against Cassia's explanation.

"That's not possible; the coordinates were automatically set for—"

"Don't you think I'd recognize my own planet?" Cassia huffed, glaring as she glanced at the surroundings. "I'm telling you, this isn't it."

I looked across the crowd for someone else who could confirm. Nien was only a few Societals away, his yellow mark drawing my eyes to him. He walked to us and sighed.

"She's right. Wherever we are, it's not the Canopy."

I had an idea of what had happened, but I didn't want to panic everyone without being certain.

"I need to see something." I stated, getting up without further explanation. I took off running and heard several voices yell behind me. I saw Fell, with his purplish-blue marks, keeping pace alongside me. Sticking to the cover of the trees, I ran until I'd come back to the edge of the clearing. Spear members milled about in the field, and I saw Hok and Vanya along the edges as well, signaling to any lingering resistance members. There were bodies in the grass.

I hadn't noticed before, but the perimeter of the field was lined in a tall brush that swayed in the breeze. With the smoke still rising from where the Spear's explosives had hit the ground, it looked even more reminiscent of the scene in my head than before.

I turned to Fell.

"I know where we are."

CHAPTER 21

"We can't be on Lone! First of all, it's a wasteland. That's what the Coalition has always maintained. Damaged beyond repair and any records of its location destroyed. Secondly, Societals are absolutely banned. From researching it, let alone landing on it!" Iduna, ever the rigid and regimented Hub instructor, sputtered as she paced. She even pulled at her hair, displacing a few of the heavily gelled grey strands that she kept swept back into a tight bun.

Nien stepped up and placed a plated arm around her shoulders where they met her wings. She took a deep breath as he took over for her.

"She's right. I may have given you all a brief history of it during your pre-Choosing lessons, but I had to obtain special permission to even do that much. It's one of the least discussed topics at the Hub. An embarrassing reminder of the founding of the Societies. No one likes to remember that we only have the planets we do now because the Ancestors destroyed their home." Nien pulled his hand back as Iduna ruffled her feathers.

"We do have one individual here who could say for certain whether or not we are on the planet of the Ancestors," Fell reminded everyone in that calm, reassuring way he had. My marks brightened, steadily and gradually for once, instead of the erratic flares of light that always betrayed negative emotions.

He looked across the clearing, where it was easy enough to spot the glowing, orange-marked individual of whom he spoke.

The crowd parted as they followed his gaze, revealing Ama. She smiled, but it didn't quite reach her sunset eyes. I wondered if the others, or at least those whose Societies had pronounced vision, spotted the single tear that glistened in the orange glow as it made its way down her cheek.

She took a breath, and I may have imagined that I heard shuddering as she drew in air.

"It's true. This is Lone. The place of my birth, and my former home."

Predictably enough for the group, yells and exclamations erupted. One key difference was, instead of sparking the fire, each Society's leaders worked to calm everyone down. Even Captains Karo and Everleigh were waving down their shouting Crew members. Dex glared as he shushed the few Clan that were part of the resistance.

"We cannot afford to draw the attention of the Spear with this kind of racket!" Sarah seethed at her Rovers, Charles hissing his displeasure from where the black swift viper was wrapped around her arm. He flared his hood, the underside glinting emerald.

"Who knows how long it will take them to find us, or when their reinforcements will arrive," Veronica chimed in, blue eyes glinting in her inky countenance. "We're working on limited time. Fell, Kena, do we have any idea how long we have until the Earthers arrive? Or how we plan to get out of here?" The Verkenter was one of few words, but she'd gone straight to the point.

"Digit?" I passed the question of the Earthers off, and the techie strode up to us. She was a mess. One arm hastily bandaged, still bruised. Her skin was a map of scars, Crew tattoos, and the blue circuitry tattoo she'd gotten on Earth before ever hearing about the Societals.

"Sorry, Alliance Queen." She winked at me, managing humor even with everything that had transpired. "I can't help much there. None of us handled the journey in the escape ships quite the same way. Some chose natural sleep, others the pills, and a few ships figured out how to gas themselves but set the controls to have the ship's landing sequence wake them up. We can't say for certain exactly how long we spent on those ships. And if they sent the Earthers here instead of Canopy, they were playing me the whole time. There's no telling when they'll get here, but I'm betting we don't want to be around when they arrive."

She had a valid point. The Spear was clearly using the Earthers for their own gain, but it was likely the Earthers had their own agenda. Aside from Juliard, the task force had been made up of profiteering men and women of power, such as Sarah's parents, and militant types like Kaiser. Neither struck me as the type of individuals that could be reasoned with after already agreeing to traverse space and subdue us in exchange for the technology the Societals promised them. And who knew what, if anything, they were telling the rest of the world's population about the whole thing.

"But how did they even locate this place? I never wrote it down, and to my knowledge any information on it was originally under lock and key by the Coalition," Ama said, frowning. Silas, Dex, and Hok stood behind her, flanking her like oversized bodyguards.

Ryshal had an answer for that one.

"They've been trying to dig up information on Lone since Acaius and I went undercover. They started with Dagan, Rift, and Canopy, since the first Societies settled were suspected to be closer in distance from the Ancestors' home. The Spear didn't have anything like an exact location, but they knew it had to at least be in the same system, given the state of technology at the time the Ancestors first settled new planets. Not all the planets now exist within the same system. That's part of why it took so long to locate Earth again without records." He spread and flexed his bat wings. It struck me once again how overwhelming the Societies could be at times. Earth barely traveled beyond its own orbit, let alone casually hopping across different systems throughout the galaxy.

"That's what they were trying to find, at first, anyway. Their efforts since the meeting have centered around the resistance and handling the other Societies. So maybe they'd already located it, or they were just distracted by everything else going on?" Acaius volunteered.

Juliard sighed. I watched him leaning against his scythe, its edge planted in the grass as he stared at the ground.

"They knew for certain where it was."

"Then what's the problem? Why didn't they just ship themselves off here and leave the rest of us alone?" Karo grumped.

"Crew members," Ryshal muttered under his breath, shaking his head. "Always jumping to conclusions. And most frequently the wrong ones."

I dropped Fell's hand and walked across the grass to Juliard. I placed my hand on his arm.

"How?"

I waited and stared hard at my uncle until he raised his eyes. "Juliard, *how* do you know they're aware of the planet's location, and how did they get that information?"

"Because I gave it to them."

Several of the surrounding leaders started yelling at Juliard, and it was the Riftians who calmed them back down. I wanted to cover my ears to block out both the noise and what he'd just admitted to, but everyone was watching. One way or another, I'd come to be regarded as some kind of leader of the alliance, and I didn't intend to let them down more than I already had. Fell saved me from confronting my uncle alone.

"You gave them this information, even though it's the last thing they needed to feel secure about destroying the Hub. You put all of us, including your niece, in danger. Why?" Fell's voice calmed me, even as he accused Juliard.

Juliard looked at me instead of my Connected as he answered. The edges of his brows turned down, his stare almost pleading as his face wore an expression I'd never seen before.

"You asked me to bring information on settlement up here. We don't have that, and you knew it. To be honest, I'm not really even certain what they wanted. Settlement wasn't something we'd had problems with before Earth got cut off. It wasn't something I remember the Societies having to work at. I know you intended it as a ploy to be able to reach out to me, but it got me thinking. We might need *something* of value to bargain with, especially if the rest of the task force was making their own backroom deals. So I thought of what I did have: the records for Lone. I was set to become the head delegate for Rift just before I changed trajectories and became the leader for Earth's settlement, and I'd already been granted access to the Coalition Hall's library of holofilms."

That library had been both a blessing and a curse since our arrival. Without it, I'd never have seen the truth of Lone's destruction, or been able to play my film of Earth being cut off. And yet it had become the dumping grounds for many of the Societals' secrets and hidden shame.

Juliard grabbed my hand, making me jump as he squeezed it, and continued.

"I found some historical holofilms from just before the first Choosing. Rather dry stuff, if I'm being honest, political information on how and why they were making the decision to forbid the return to Lone and rely on the whole Choosing process. It mentioned a general location of the planet in the talks."

I shook my head, withdrawing my hand.

"And you decided to take it all those years ago for what reason? Historical interest?"

"Yes, but I wasn't the only one who went digging. I told you that your father had tried to approach the magistrate at that time for permission to go back to Lone. He knew they had to have the location stashed somewhere. After being refused, Tiberius didn't leave the delegates' offices straightaway. He took an unauthorized detour through the library and, when that proved fruitless, broke into the magistrate's office. He managed to find actual paper maps and documents, although they'd been heavily damaged. But generations later, when we put both our partial records together, it was enough to pinpoint with near certainty where the Ancestors' planet was."

I pulled back from my uncle, backing into Fell's chest where he'd stepped up behind me. He placed steadying hands on my shoulders, as if he could anticipate my desire to run. Maybe he could. I'd done enough of it in the face of all the bad news that had been raining down. Once again, my family was somehow responsible. I'd heard it said before that the smallest details of the present could have huge impacts on the future. If my father and uncle, or even one of them, had been eliminated. If I'd never existed, it seemed the Societals would have been better off. Kept in the dark by the Coalition, perhaps, but not under threat of violence.

Juliard reached for me, but I recoiled into Fell's arms.

"Your father's version of the Spear was ruthless, but they didn't have the scope of destruction planned that Bayard does now. Tiberius just wanted to teach the Coalition a lesson with Earth, and then retreat to Lone. Anything else was just talk to rile up his followers. And he didn't want anyone to be able to track him here, so he destroyed any other records at the Hub of Lone's location, and kept the only copies. After several generations he was willing to give them to me for safekeeping so he wouldn't be tempted by them again. And I brought them here, to bargain with. To save you."

Perhaps he'd intended the words as a conciliatory gesture, but it just put me more on edge. It added to the responsibility I felt for our predicament. I struggled to find what to say. His willingness to give up a secret he'd kept for so long was more proof of his love for me than anything he'd done before or since. I'd opened my mouth to say as much when Hale shoved past me, pushing Juliard hard in the chest.

"So we're stuck here because *you* told them! This is your fault!"

I'd gotten used to the bickering of the others, but I flinched in the face of my best friend's anger. He waved an accusing finger in my uncle's face.

"As far as I can tell, you've made one bad decision after another since you got stranded on Earth. Maybe you should have stayed there, or with the Spear, if this is all the good you're going to do us," Hale fumed, voice getting louder with each word of his tirade. I'd seen him upset before, but I'd never seen him yell at Juliard.

"I get why you're mad at him. He gave them the location, but yelling at him doesn't help us now." Silas stepped in and pulled on Hale's arm. "The important thing at this point is the predicament it puts us in and what we can do about it. There aren't any Doorways here, which means—"

"We have no way off this planet. They have the Earther ships. They'll either find and kill us all, or strand us here. Either way, they'll take those ships and head for the nearest Society. Once they have control of it, they'll move to the next one. Eventually, they'll find the Doorway to Tundra. And they'll be able to win this entire war they've waged before we ever make it to the nearest planet," I said without looking up. It was harsh. It was blunt. But it was the truth, and they needed to hear it.

Silas sighed and ran a hand up the back of his neck. It was a tell, just like Juliard's hair flipping. Vanya stepped up by him, wrapping her arms around him and wincing with the movements as red seeped through one bandage. Cassius stepped forward to hold her up.

"It would have been idiotic of them to destroy the Hub with nowhere else to go. So, yes, I'd say Kena's summed up their plan pretty well," Dex confirmed, striding up to his friend. Silas nodded next to the horned man.

"We promised to help these people. To save everyone. Most of the menders, all the recovering resistance fighters, they're on Tundra, and they have no idea what's coming," I insisted.

"Even if we made it to the nearest planet, which is either Dagan, Rift, or Canopy, what then? We'd have to traverse it with this huge group, and make it back to the others. And this whole thing relied heavily on somehow beating the Spear *before* Earth arrived. I don't think that will happen," Cassius said from where Vanya leaned against him. He had a valid point. We'd done what we'd set out to do. Rescued the resistance fighters and innocents at the Hub, but for what? We had no way to beat the Spear, but we couldn't afford to give up, either. We had to try.

"Look, I get the frustration directed at me, but this is all a moot point," Juliard insisted, drawing my attention back to him. "What's done is done, and we're here now. Unless we could somehow overpower the Spear and the Earthers, then take their ships, there's no chance of us getting off this planet."

At that news several people slumped. Others leaned against each other, and a few groaned. I doubted anyone had anymore energy to respond than I did. Several sported fresh injuries, a few had actually fallen asleep leaned up against trees. Others sat in the grass, heads down. We'd been at the Hub a matter of days, but it felt like we'd been fighting the Spear for much longer.

"He's right," Fell said, staring out at the crowd. Then he turned his gaze back to me. "Kena, you know I would do anything to help you and the Societals, but without a means off this planet there's really nothing else we can do."

I felt another hand resting on my arm. Ama glanced back and forth between us before she spoke.

"What if there was a way?"

CHAPTER 22

In spite of pressure from many of the Societals gathered, Ama refused to say more. We were able to get everyone to disperse as the sky grew darker. Exhaustion won out over their desire to get the Reader to talk.

I longed to join the others as they started dividing up watch shifts and choosing places to sleep, but I wasn't granted that opportunity.

"Kena, I need you to come with me, and I need you to bring the book," Ama instructed.

An easy ask, given it was in the pack I'd managed to take off the Hub with me. I still had it on my shoulder, and held it up for her to see. I gave my leg a pat, ensuring the ax was dangling at my side as well, then moved to follow her.

"I only need to speak with Kena," Ama stated, pointedly looking at Fell walking at my side. I waited for him to move back toward the others, but instead he took two steps to place himself between me and the Reader.

"Not this time, Ama. Enough of this separation. I may not have her gifts, but I am Connected to Kena. I have sworn to protect her, come what may. And I think I'll have a much easier time accomplishing that if everyone stops trying to sneak off with her."

The older woman blinked up at him, eyes wide. I held my breath as I waited for a snappy comeback, but she just smiled.

"Good. I was waiting on you to reach this point. Seems that some good did come out of Bayard locking her in that office after all."

Ama hummed as she turned and walked away, following the banks of the river.

"That went better than I thought," Fell muttered as he took my hand in his.

I pulled back on his arm, and he turned to look at me. I stood on my tiptoes, and pulled his face down towards mine, savoring the soft feel of his lips on mine.

"What was that for?" he asked when I pulled away.

"Because things keep spinning out of control. I have no idea what's going to happen, but I need you to know that I love you."

No single event had provoked it, although watching Kidan try to kill him had certainly made me face what losing Fell would mean to me. I needed the calm consistency Fell provided. He was always there, and he hadn't let me down. He hadn't hidden away or lied to me about anything. He was a support when I had nothing else solid to lean against. He was a good person.

"I feel the same way," he said, leaning in again. Before our lips met, I heard someone clear their throat.

"As touching as young love is, we are in a bit of a rush here," Ama huffed.

Opal light illuminated the surrounding trees.

"Yes, right. Of course." I mumbled as I took Fell's hand again and followed the Reader.

The sound of rushing water grew louder and louder the farther we moved. When Ama came to a stop, she looked out over the river. It had grown fierce; fast-moving rapids plummeted into sharp rocks that jutted from the banks.

For a few moments, I said nothing as I let her gaze out at it. She closed her eyes, tilting her head up to the night sky, and her marks grew brighter. After several moments they dimmed again, and as she turned back to us I felt comfortable speaking.

"Ama, you said you thought there was a way for us to get off the planet. Is it your journal, along with whatever information you might have on settlement?"

I reached into my pack and pulled out the book in question, its cover stamped with a map of Lone. Nien had told us the planet was said to be riddled with rivers, and so far that had proven true.

Ama reached out a hand, tenderly tracing the lines of the markings of her journal, but she didn't take it.

"No, the answer to us getting off this planet isn't in there, it's in here." She tapped a finger against her temple. "But before I reveal it to the others, I need to make sure we can get you access to this journal. If I don't miss my bet, it should be the same as making my marks readable to you. Fell, dear, if you'll be available to catch me in case the strain causes me to go a bit faint?"

Soundless as always, he moved across the ground and behind the Reader.

"Very well then, let's get on with it." She swept her hand over the book, the orange glow from her marks shining onto the cover.

True to her prediction, she stumbled back as the glow diminished. Her eyelids fluttered open and closed. Fell held her under her shoulders and lowered her to the ground. She waved a hand, her movements making her appear frail.

"Open the book. Can you read it?" Her voice was tense, and I wasn't sure if it was from the strain of what she'd done, or her desperation for the answer.

I held my breath as I cracked the book open. I'd spent hours looking through it before. Silas had tried to help me, but we'd never been able to make any sense of the markings inside. As I exhaled across the page, my breath stirred the paper, and the faintest glint of orange gleamed in the air before fading. It was as if Ama's magic—and I was past refuting her ability as anything but—had left a physical mark.

I stared down at the page and gasped.

"I can read it," I confirmed. I heard her murmuring in relief but couldn't tear myself away from the page. There, written in script I now knew Ama had penned herself, was the beginning of an answer.

I recommended to Juliard that he trade his spot as head delegate of the Rift for head of Earth's settlers. And for what? I've gotten them killed. I was so sure, and so wrong. These people think we're different; more evolved than our Ancestors. The truth is, we aren't. None of us. Despite all the Societal rules and regulations, and all the secrets and charades, we're nearly identical. The same selfish desires, and the same penchant for destruction. Elsewise, how did a group such as the Spear take root? And I know they must be responsible. I'd heard whisperings, though not from the Whispers themselves. I thought them a disgruntled fringe group. I can only hope that with the cessation of Earth's settlement, the Spear has ended as well. In any case, the Coalition refuses to hear any of it.

I cannot allow something like this to happen again, but how to prevent it? My abilities grow stronger by the year, but I cannot make the

Coalition do what I advise. Speaking to them directly won't work. But I may have a way, if I dare to risk it.

The entries weren't dated at the top. She had merely slashed a tall X, curved at the edges, of each new installment. As if by the time of Earth's settlement, she'd long since ceased to monitor the years.

"Well?" she demanded. She had stood but was still balanced against a tree, with a branch bearing most of her weight. Her eyes flashed with light.

"It's the journal you were looking for. Should I read on?" Even with the answer in my hands, it felt like her right to say. After all, they'd been her words and actions.

"Soon. But not yet. Knowing it's the correct journal is enough. My solution to getting off of Lone is tied in a way to the answer I think you'll find in there. I just wanted to confirm my suspicions. Get some sleep. Starting tomorrow, we work our way off this planet. And Kena, I will have to ask much more from you before this is through."

She strode off back toward the group, and I stood, her cryptic words hanging around me like the bars of a prison. I'd already, time and again, confirmed my desire to give whatever it took to save the others. But there had been a finality about her statement.

The sun was barely a glimmer through the leaves when Fell woke me the following morning.

"Ama is gathering all the leaders together," he informed me.

We weren't the last there, but just about. The Crew captains and the Kites clustered together. Cassia leaned against her brother. Veronica represented Dagan, and Sarah stood alongside a couple of Rover bodyguards. Minutes after we arrived, Dex strode up to the group alongside Silas and Vanya. She looked drained, her cheeks pale, but more alert than she'd been since getting injured. Digit and Hale followed the group, chatting noisily about some sea monster or other.

"I'm telling you, I could use those scales to create a near-indestructible casing for holocorders. It could be revolutionary!" Digit said, waving her one good arm.

"Saving the worlds first, *then* technological advances, Digit. Priorities, honestly," Hale huffed, but he smiled at me over her shoulder.

I returned the expression, feeling a pang in my chest at how far our friendship, alongside everything else, had changed. Even after all that had happened, I wouldn't have taken back going to the Societies, and yet, I longed for the ability to simply live in them. The way I had envisioned them to be.

Ama clapped her hands together, a circle of orange light flaring from her marks as she did so. She excelled at the skill of controlling them as much as I stunk at it.

"No use wasting time. We all know, or we're at least aware that we don't know, how much time we have before the Earthers arrive. We need a way off this place and back to Tundra. And from the relative safety of that location, we'll figure out this whole settlement issue without the worry of being bombarded by Earthers and the Spear."

"And how's that going to help us exactly?" Captain Everleigh demanded from her spot in the circle. "What are we supposed to do with that information—spread our already limited numbers further across uninhabited planets? Retreat, abandoning our own Societies, like rats on a sinking ship?"

Ama said nothing but stared the Crew captain down until she looked at her boots.

Acaius stepped forward, his black wings draped behind him like a cloak.

"Everleigh does have a point, esteemed Reader. Not that I think it's a bad thing to figure out, but shouldn't we be working on how to actually fight and win against the Spear?" He gave a slight bow of his head as he finished.

Ama gave a sharp laugh.

"Societals. Honestly. I cannot do *everything* for you dears. I'll let you militant minds come up with the battle plan. I, on the other hand, am offering what I have. Which is quite a lot, thank you very much. Figure out settlement. Barter the knowledge to Earth to get them to leave. Use it, yes, as a retreat or last resort. Sell it to the Spear, if you absolutely must. But take it or leave it, because that's the knowledge I believe I have to impart. That, and the Doorways. And unless I'm sorely mistaken, I don't see anyone else here with half that much."

She scowled, eyes narrowing as she turned a slow circle to face all the leaders around her. One by one, they all dropped their faces as she gazed at them, each one looking sheepish and childlike next to the small but powerful Riftian.

She gave a sharp nod.

"That's what I thought. Now then, if I may proceed?" She raised a brow, the silence growing to awkward lengths.

"Please, Reader, whatever knowledge you can provide we are happy to receive," Silas acknowledged as Vanya and Hok murmured similar statements.

Ama smiled at him.

"As I'm sure you're all well aware, thanks to my apprentice's projection abilities, Riftians can sometimes take Assimilation beyond the realm of what is typically possible. With projection specifically, we can affect the world outside ourselves in varying ways. For most Riftians, we alter your perception of us the slightest bit, although we do it subconsciously. I've worked for years, and it seems Bayard has as well, to successfully hide information and my own existence from people through conscious effort. Kena can temporarily control people's ability to act on their own thoughts. I'm assuming Juliard hid his marks using a similar skill, even if he didn't realize what he was doing."

She swept her hand out to me and my uncle, as the other leaders turned and stared. It wasn't as if it was new information, but I saw opal creep across the grass as my marks glowed under their scrutiny. Ama cleared her throat, and one by one their attention was directed back to her.

"Given the many, many, many years I have had to explore the limits of projection, I've been able to discover a few new tricks. While our solution is something I've only theorized about, I am confident that I'll be able to pull it off. If projection can influence people, why not things? I've drawn and collected power over the years, and with enough of it, I'm fairly certain I can convince something inanimate to simply exist."

Everyone blinked back at her. I looked at Fell, and he shrugged, the movement looking foreign on him in comparison to his usual, fluid motions.

"I'll be able to create the Doorway myself," Ama clarified. Her hands were steepled under her chin as she awaited our response. She tilted her head up as though she'd suggested nothing more exciting than a trip to the grocery store.

"Yourself?" Hok asked, silver marks giving off a vibrant light. They glinted against Sarah's leathery skin where she stood next to him.

Ama nodded.

"Out of thin air?" Vanya questioned, blinking so rapidly that the leafy green light from her eyes looked like it was blipping out bits of Morse code.

She received another nod in response.

"But that's magic!" Dex yelled, arms waving. He stamped a hoof into the grass.

Even after everything else I'd seen, this particular ability held me in disbelief. Most of what the Societals had through Assimilation was just a very fast form of evolution that took them down unique physical paths. What Ama and the Whispers could do already bordered and teetered right on the cusp of mysticism. I'd been able to buy into it strictly as a mental ability. This, though? She'd be utilizing a mental ability to create a physical thing from scratch. My mind barely comprehended it.

"What will constructing this Doorway cost you?" Fell stepped forward, one eyebrow tipped up in question.

Ama pursed her lips, brows knitting downward.

"It will be taxing," she said eventually; her only response. I saw the slightest flicker in her eyes, the most minute shake in her hands as she answered. She was holding something back.

"Could it hurt you?" He pressed the issue. Her frown deepened.

"Anything's possible, but really, dear, I'm insulted you think so little of my abilities. I'm quite a bit tougher than I look." She smirked. Fell paced, and my guess was that he was trying to come up with another response that wouldn't set Ama off on one of her more vindictive tangents.

Hok spared him the opportunity.

"Could it hurt the rest of us? Doorways are created encased inside tunnels for a reason. They're volatile. What you're suggesting, or at least what I think you're suggesting, is just a freestanding Doorway. What would that mean for the rest of us if the process goes wrong?"

Ama turned a beaming gaze up towards Hok, patting his arm as her orange eyes gleamed.

"Now, *that's* a fair question! In truth, if the process isn't completed with absolute perfection, there could be disastrous consequences."

"Such as?" Vanya stepped up next to her fellow weapons specialist, green eyes gleaming.

Ama shrugged.

"The destruction of Lone and everyone on it."

Gasps and protests rang out, and I recognized Cassia's voice among them. The saber-toothed woman grew louder as she strode forward. She ducked out from beneath her brother's wing, a steel-grey tail flicking in agitation in her wake. Her gaze held fire, but Ama looked right past her to finish answering Hok's question.

"But I wouldn't suggest it if it wasn't our best option, nor would I put this idea forward if I weren't firmly convinced I could accomplish such a task."

"Be that as it may," Cassia cut in before Hok could speak over her, "this is not a decision that can be made by any one individual. *Or* any one Society. This must be a vote, where all are represented." She leveled a gaze at the gathered Riftians.

"That idea has merit. I agree that we put it up for a vote." Hok dipped his head at a slack-jawed Cassia.

"It is settled, then. We'll vote," Fell stated. The other Riftians, including Juliard, inclined their heads toward him.

As I watched their response to Fell, I realized that if we managed to win, and salvaged some form of the Coalition, the Rift needed new leaders. Not a Queen of the Alliance, but real ones. A head delegate and a king. Fell and Silas struck me as good options.

As the group broke out in whispered discussions, Ama turned on her heel and stormed off.

CHAPTER 23

I gave Fell's hand a squeeze before slipping into the trees after the
Reader, trying to keep my steps even more silent than Fell's. At no
particular place—at least, I saw no defining landmarks—Ama came
to a stop. She dropped onto a fallen, moss-covered log as if she was
too weighed down to stand a moment longer. She ran her hands over
the soft greenery while grumbling to herself.

"A waste of time," Ama grumped. A small, toothy mammal I'd
never seen before wandered out of the trees. It was no bigger than
a squirrel, with soft white fur. Ama just scratched it behind the ears
as though it were a beloved pet. She sighed and bent her arms as she
pushed off the log with a huff. The movement looked more effortful
than normal.

"How does it feel, being back here again?" I asked.

She just smiled. The same sad smile she'd been wearing since we'd landed on her former home.

"To be honest, relieving. And here I thought it would be strange. Seems even I can't predict everything. Well,"—she rubbed her hands together—"no sense in wasting time. I've a few things to get organized and then we can begin." I was doubting more and more whether this process was as simple or safe as Ama had touted. I believed it was dangerous to her, and that she knew it.

She leveled a look straight at me.

"Kena. There's a few things I need you to do for me, if creating this Doorway doesn't end well."

My shoulders tensed, and even though I'd been the one to follow her, I felt a strong urge to turn and go back to the group.

"Ama, they haven't even voted on whether to let you attempt the Doorway. Shouldn't we wait until—"

She laughed.

"Voting. As if their decision could stand in the way of their needs. Hear me in this, Kena. I have seen what happens when those with power or control fail to consider the needs of those around them, and the planets they call home. That being said, I've also seen the Coalition get so tied up in every single voice having so much opportunity to speak that nothing gets done. Am I taking a decision into my own hands that will profoundly affect us all? Yes. Am I going to be stopped by those with no knowledge of the abilities I speak of, when their only alternative is to die on this planet and let the Spear win? No. I will do what I must, and I will accept the consequences."

I hated hearing Ama talk as if she was certain she wasn't going to make it through the process, and it must have shown on my face. She shook an admonishing finger at me.

"Don't go crying over me yet. I have no intention of dying unless absolutely necessary. All these centuries, and I'm finally seeing another worlds-changing event. I'd like to see what happens next. That being said, this is a situation where it seems wise to be prudent. It would be irresponsible for me to go off all half-cocked and end up dead with no preparations in place."

"That's not the only thing, Ama. Let's say you're right. How do you know, when you're making a decision, whether to give other people a say in it?"

She walked over, grabbing my arms and pulling them toward her.

"You're not asking me for me. You're asking me for you. Kena, do you know what your new marks say? Have you taken any time to try and interpret them yourself?"

I hadn't, but I should have. I shook my head. "I know the one that was incomplete says *soul* and that it matches Fell's."

"Exactly. Soul. Yours. It may be Connected to him, but it belongs to you. And the rest of it,"—she started to circle me, checking all the marks that were revealed by the bodysuit she'd had made for me—"just tells me what kind of soul you have. One that is protective, compassionate, and one that has depth. But also, one that is emotional, fierce, and capable. I know you've had so much thrown at you, but you *must* be willing to choose who you want to be. And stand by it. No matter what the others have to say about it."

I felt a tear make its way down my cheek as I whispered an affirmative response.

Ama tugged me down towards her and wrapped me in a hug.

"Now then, on to my business."

I did my best to look cheerful for her, but I couldn't muster up anything to say. Luckily, I didn't have to.

"While ideally we should have spent more time on it, you're doing remarkably well as a Reader. Especially given I've never properly trained one before." She chuckled at her own joke. "If necessary, I suspect you'll be able to muddle through, like I did, until you get the hang of it. Part of being a Reader is just learning to read the *people* who bear the marks, as well as the marks themselves, and you've got a natural talent for that." She paused, glancing away. "Yes. I think you'll be fine there. Now, of course, if the worst happens I'll be leaving you my house and all the contents. Books, herbs, and the like. That should also help you along."

I stared at her.

"You're giving me your house?" I sputtered.

She waved a hand as if it were nothing.

"Only if this ends badly. Don't feel obligated to live in it if things come to that. I understand it may not feel like yours at first. That will take time. You're welcome to utilize it for study and readings only, if that suits you better. Make sure you look after the chimes, though. You've got to make sure the tree is kept trimmed in such a way that they have an open path to the sky and sunlight, or they don't sing quite right. And of course, clean them now and again. I've also taken up the habit of feeding some of the local birds. Fell has been on me for that, but phooey on him. I enjoy it. You'll need to get feed for them occasionally. Samell and the other arborists have been providing me with that."

I stared at her, dumbstruck, as she casually willed me the majority of her worldly possessions while worrying more about the chimes and the birds she kept up with than her own demise. She took both my hands in hers and gave them a small shake, drawing my attention back to her. My marks lit like a lantern.

"This next part is very important. I'm entrusting you not only with the house, but essentially as an executor of some of the items within. I'm certainly hoping not to die, but I'm not discounting the possibility. If anything, my long life has made me more aware of mortality, not less. Watching those around you slowly grow old and wither draws into even sharper focus that death afflicts at least ninety-nine percent of us. I imagine I won't remain the exception forever. If I manage to make it through this process with the

Doorway, there's still plenty of opportunities in this war for something to happen to me. I've got a few packages and things set aside in my house, off the bedroom. They're clearly marked with names for a few choice individuals, Fell included. I'd like you to make sure they're delivered when this is all over, if necessary." She squeezed my hands tighter, eyes boring into mine with a relentless, beseeching stare.

I swallowed my fear down. I buried all my conflicting feelings over what she intended to do, and whether she even should.

"Of course, Ama."

"Good." She turned and shouted toward the woods. "You can stop sulking behind those branches and come out now!"

Fell stepped out from behind a tree, where he's been hidden in the shadows.

"I wanted to give you privacy, but I had to keep an eye on Kena. And you as well."

"Nonsense. I'm perfectly capable of looking after myself. Though I have to say, I am very pleased to see you both getting on so well. Don't tell the others, but you are my favorite couple in the Societies." Ama walked over as she spoke and picked up Fell's hand, patting it. His own marks sparked to life, just like mine had. As they illuminated his face, I noticed his eyes were shining with unshed tears. Either Ama didn't see them, or she chose to ignore them.

"Ama, I don't think it's a secret that you play favorites," Fell teased.

She threw up her hands.

"Can't an old lady have her preferences?" She sounded annoyed, but her grin gave her away. My heart tugged painfully in my chest, and my throat hurt with the effort of forcing tears down.

Nothing has even happened yet. She might be fine. I tried to convince myself.

There was a rustling of leaves and we all three turned toward the noise. I stepped in front of Ama, raising my ax. Fell moved next to me, so quick that I didn't even see him reach for the daggers he held in his hands.

Silas and Dex ran from the trees, palms up in surrender.

"Whoa, you Riftians don't mess around. We come in peace!" Dex said, shaking a couple of leaves from where they'd caught on his horns.

"Are they done voting, then?" Ama asked, stepping from behind us.

Silas frowned.

"Not exactly. For what it's worth, I do think you would have won. But it doesn't matter right now. We have a problem."

He led our group all the way past the others and through the trees, explaining as he went.

"We've had several resistance members monitoring the field where we all landed, just in case. Wanted to make sure the Spear didn't get the jump on us again. Then, well, you can see for yourself."

We'd made it to the field where the escape ships had touched down.

The brush and grass waved wildly in front of us, and not because of any natural breezes on Lone. All around the massive field, ships were touching down. Larger at least a dozen times over than the escape pods.

"Unlike the emergency transports that we used to get here, those *are* armed," Hok informed us from where he hid in the brush. The others had staked out spots in small groups as close to the edge as they dared to get.

"How do you know?" Silas threw back, his voice just above a whisper.

Vanya touched his arm, answering instead.

"They asked us for our input on the ships years ago. I think they asked instructors from every Society. Just because most of us eschew use of advanced combat doesn't mean we don't have the capabilities. These ships—they used to keep one anchored near the Hub, and another on each of the planets. I didn't realize they were the ones being used for the Earthers. They were a failsafe." She kept her eyes locked on the ships in question as she spoke.

"Against what? I thought the Societals were supposedly a peaceful group, their killing of non-Assimilators aside, of course," Hale groused from one group over, his voice rising just enough that I cast a worried glance out across the field. Not that anyone was likely to hear us over the noise of the massive transport vessels landing.

"Outside threats. We've never come across any that I know of, but that doesn't mean they aren't out there. The Coalition garnered support for the project back when Earth was first cut off. A scare tactic. You know, the whole idea that you all might show up one day, ready to destroy us. Seems we missed the mark on that one." Hok let out a humorless laugh. Sarah grabbed his arm and squeezed.

"They've been periodically updating and improving upon the designs ever since," Vanya finished.

"Some of the task force is here," the Sarah said, eyes wide.

I crept closer to the edge of the trees, as far as I dared. It reminded me of when I'd first broken into the Hub's library and found the holofilm of Lone. The individual in that film had crept through the brush and ended up dead in the dirt. Still, I risked it.

I craned my neck out above the grass, and I saw she was right. I knew very few individuals on the task force personally, although I'd met some of them when Juliard had been on it.

"Dawes, Herald, Smith," Juliard listed a few individuals I didn't even remember meeting while he pointed out the Earthers around the field.

"I note dear old Dad seems to have avoided this particular trip. Figures. Sending other people to do his dirty work for him," Sarah said, a frown on her face. "I know that guy, though." She pointed to a tall individual who looked ridiculous walking around the field in a well-tailored navy suit, of all things.

"Derek's dad," Cassia supplied. "Our father had dealings with him as well." I knew there was some history with the twins' father and Derek's family, but they'd been tightlipped about it. That, or I and the others hadn't pressed enough.

"Son of a—look who's with him!" Cassius exclaimed, grabbing his sister and shaking her arm before dropping it when she winced. "Sorry, sis! Forgot the injuries."

Walking next to the man, no Assimilated features in sight, were Earther teens Derek and Mancio. They'd been mouthy and rude to Societals and the rest of the Earthers alike before the Choosing, but I'd thought they'd been stuck on Clan.

"Those little jerks," Dex seethed. "Wait, do you guys think? ... Remember how Warrick said the non-Assimilators were actually the result of some substance being given to people? Could those two have been given it on purpose, and that's why they're standing out there looking like Blanks?"

Silas cast a side-eyed glance at his friend.

"I'd be willing to bet serious money on that."

"And there's the man himself," Juliard pointed out.

Kaiser stepped out from one of the ships and joined the others in the field. He had been part of Earth's task force for reasons I couldn't fathom. He was staunchly anti-Societal from the beginning, although it seemed everyone had a price. He looked the same as he had on Earth. Close-cropped hair that made him appear militant, cargo pants, tight-fitted athletic shirt. Guns, multiple, slung across his chest and in holsters on various areas of his body. Muscled, but nowhere in the realm of Dex or Hok, who I would have loved to see beat him up.

Moments later, a tall, graceful individual followed him, glowing blue.

I glared.

"Bayard."

I didn't realize I'd moved until Fell yanked me back. I felt my eyes go wide as I collided with him.

Sarah's serpent stuck his head out from her hair and hissed at her. She nodded as if she understood it.

"Right. We have company," she said.

I glanced back and saw that several Spear members were looking toward the perimeter of the field, headed our direction. Quickly and as quietly as possible, we retreated back into the trees.

Once we'd come to a stop, Ama waved a glowing arm back in the direction of the ships.

"We're out of time. You need to let me create the Doorway. Now."

"Or," Sarah countered, a grin on her face, "we fight."

CHAPTER 24

Several of those around the group agreed with the Serpentina, including me.

"Yes. We take them out now. They're planning on using the Earthers as an army. We prevent that, and we prevent any further conflict."

While some of the others debated, Silas pulled me aside.

"Tactically, it's not the worst plan. Digit and Hok are guessing each of those ships can hold hundreds of people, and there's a dozen of them. Which gives us a rough ratio. They outnumber us ten to one, at least. That being said, if we could pull it off, it would save innumerable lives back on the Societal planets."

"And then what? You'd still need the Doorway. Unless you're planning to pilot those things through space to each planet, while holding the Spear members and Earthers captive, and hoping they don't break out along the way," Ama argued back.

"Not necessarily. We strand them here. It's what they wanted anyway, right? We take the ships, take the tech, and leave them on Lone," Silas responded, arms crossed over his chest.

Ama pursed her lips like she'd tasted something sour. I doubted she liked the idea of leaving her former home to the Spear at all, but I was all for it if it meant she didn't have to risk herself for the sake of the rest of us.

"So how do we do it?" I asked.

Digit spoke up.

"If you two,"—she pointed at Hok and Vanya—"and anyone else here who provided input on the ships' weaponry can give me some information, we might be able to do it. Give me a good idea of what kind of firepower we're talking about, and anything you know about the layout of the ships. Then, if we can get on unnoticed, I can try and disable their firing systems. It won't do anything for our numbers on the ground, but it takes away one of their best advantages against us."

It was our last shot at the Spear if we wanted to keep them off the other planets. We decided to go in at night, when we hoped that most of our enemy would be asleep. We determined that Fell, Nien, and Cassia would help Digit get to the ships. Fell because he moved so quietly, and the other two because they'd mastered camouflage and could get in without being seen.

Acaius and Ryshal, with the darkest wings, would circle overhead to monitor and try to warn them of any threats, with the other Kites joining as light set in.

The rest of us would split off and follow as Digit disabled the weapons on each ship. As distasteful as it was, we hoped to kill or detain the Earthers and Spear on each vessel systematically, thereby gaining control over the ships for ourselves. Captains Karo and Everleigh had explained that each vessel's system had the ability to lock off whole portions of the ship. It had been their planet's contribution to the structures.

"Something you have to consider when you live your life on ships, in case anyone gets out of control," Karo shared.

As the night deepened, our only snag was that one ship, larger than the others, was sitting at the opposite edge of the field from us. We'd seen Kaiser, Bayard, and the other Earth task force members go inside. They'd been accompanied by a variety of Spear from each Society, who I'd guessed were Bayard's seconds in command.

"We either take that one out first and risk being seen by every other ship we pass, or we save it for last, or we go with our original plan knowing the final ship will be the toughest," Silas said, shaking his head as his deep red marks illuminated the darkness. "If Ama's recall of things is correct, it should be getting light within the next couple hours. We need to move."

"I'll start with the closest, and trust the rest of you to handle whatever I can't get to," Digit stated.

We divided up, and Digit made her way toward the first ship with her entourage. As planned, the rest of us waited several minutes to follow. I kept my ears open for any shouts that signaled they'd been discovered, or any Spear guards wandering the field.

Vanya and Sarah spotted several of the latter but managed to take care of them and leave them hidden in the brush before they could shout out a warning.

"They've been in too long." Silas sounded agitated with his eyes locked on the first ship. "We should go in after them."

Dex placed a hand on his friend's shoulder.

"Give them a minute longer."

As he finished speaking, Nien, Digit, Cassia, and Fell came sprinting from the first ship out a side door. The vessel gave off a soft whirring sound as the limited lights that dotted its exterior powered down.

Digit was panting as she jogged up.

"I managed to shut down the whole system! They'll be stuck inside the ship until they can figure out how to reboot it or bash their way out. And if they go the second route, they'll be rendering the thing inoperable for the Spear's purposes. Can't fly a ship through space with a giant gaping hole." She grinned as Cassia clapped her on the back.

Nien stared at the techie.

"She's amazing!" he gushed.

It was true; without Digit we'd never have come as far as we had. We followed them to the second of the twelve ships. Nien and Cassia disappeared as we got close. They got through the first four without incident. They were inside the fifth when problems arose.

Light spilled onto the meadow as a large cargo door of that particular vessel creaked open. I cast a panicked glance at the final ship, the one with Bayard in it. But no one came out. Hopefully whatever was going on inside shielded any noise we made.

Several of us ran to the smaller ship. The door gave another squeal as it froze, partway open.

"We need to get up there!" I whispered to the others. It was too far off the ground without the door being opened further so we could access the ramp.

"Leave it to us!" Ryshal swooped down, and grabbed me under my arms; he carried me over and then dropped me into the cargo bay.

Acaius followed with Sarah, and soon enough the Kites had us inside. Luck was on our side, and they'd set us down behind a pile of wooden crates, stacked high. Each was labeled as to what weapon lay within. Hok pried open the lid of the nearest one and pulled out some gun I didn't recognize.

"Not good," Silas said, frowning down at the thing. He grabbed it and tossed one to Dex as well.

Vanya turned her lip up at the crate.

"This is despicable. It's … cheating, is what it is." Vanya sputtered as if she was more offended by the advanced weaponry than anything else the Spear had done. Then again, it did go against the Societal code and how they engaged one another.

"They're not trying to play fair. They're trying to win," Silas stated as he hefted another gun out of the box and handed it to a bewildered-looking Hok. "Don't use this unless absolutely necessary. It will be loud, and it'll throw you backwards if you're not careful."

There were Earthers milling around our area of the ship. Vanya took out several with her bow before we'd even left the cover of the crates. We handled the rest. Most of the occupants as we passed through the ship were asleep, as we'd hoped. Silas signaled with a hand and we followed him up a metal staircase and through a door further into the vessel. It was so large, I worried it would take us forever to find the others, but on the second floor we found Digit typing away on a massive keyboard that spanned the length of a small room.

"We may have made a slight error!" she said as she spared us a brief glance.

"What kind of error?" Silas questioned.

"This kind," Fell said, leading him back out the door. The hall leading up to where they'd been working was littered with a trail of a dozen or so Spear and Earther individuals. "I think they guard in groups, and they make rounds. We were just lucky enough to miss them on the first few ships. Digit locked down most of the rest of the ship, but we can't be certain these guys didn't alert someone on one of the others. We need to move even faster."

By the time we'd returned to the room with the keyboard, Digit had wrapped up her work. She wiped her brow.

"You know, this would be hard enough with two good hands," she said.

"You're doing great," Cassia encouraged her.

We made our way back down the metallic halls, doing our best to keep our steps quiet. Fell was, of course, better at it than the rest of us.

"We have to get out before the lockdown sequence finishes," Digit warned us, "or we'll be stuck in here with them."

That sounded like one of several bad scenarios we might find ourselves in before the night was out. We managed to make it out just before the cargo bay door shut. The lights on the outside of the ship powered down as we made our way out and around the front of the ship, moving toward our sixth target.

"Well, well, well. It seems that distress signal wasn't a false alarm after all."

Kaiser stood in front of us, muscled arms folded. Fanned out in a line behind him were several other Earthers. A few were heavily armed. Behind them stood a line of Spear members. I looked at every member of the group, but none of them were glowing with sapphire marks. No Bayard.

"Yuck, I can't believe you all *actually* went through with this process. You've turned yourselves into total freaks. It's disgusting." Derek stepped out from behind one of the larger Earthers.

I doubted that I was the only one who longed to punch the teen in the face at that moment. He'd whined and insulted and bullied everyone during the pre-Choosing process. He probably had gone running to his father with all sorts of useful information on the Societies. And despite my distaste for him, I'd tried to protect him.

"Why don't you come a little closer and say that again. I don't think I heard you the first time." Sarah stepped out to the front of the group; her snake Charles hissed and showed his fangs. The Serpentina bared talons at the boy.

He grimaced.

"Ew. Sarah, really? And to think, my father and yours once thought it would be a good idea if we got married. Well, you can take that possibility off the table. No one with any class would touch you now."

Cassia and Cassius flanked the Serpentina. Cassius spread his wings out and glared at the arrogant teen.

"Your family is the one with no class. By all means, bring Daddy out here. We'd love to reacquaint ourselves," Cassius said before flashing the teen a toothy smile.

Derek paled and took a step back. But then a few Earthers next to him snickered. I could imagine what they thought of the pampered teen, only brave enough to swap insults when he had an entire guard at his back. Derek glowered and marched toward us a few steps, although not out of the relative safety of his comrades' perimeter.

"You two will be dealt with, soon enough. And I stand by what I said. Sarah made her *Choice*." He spat the last word and made quotation marks in the air, mocking the Societal system. "The wrong one, obviously. Don't think your dad's going to want you back now. Although he requested I deliver you to him, so I guess we'll go ahead and take you anyway."

Sarah paled a bit as Derek spoke, her glower falling away at the mention of her father. She looked less like a Serpentina and more like the scared teen she'd been on her arrival at the Hub. Derek continued to mock her.

"It's a rather boring and long trip, I'm afraid. We'll have to find some way for you to pass the time. *I'm* no longer interested, of course, but I'm sure some of these Spear allies of ours would be more than happy to let you entertain them on the way home."

I heard a roar and saw Hok sprinting past the others toward the teen. Derek squealed, the sound satisfying as he turned and fled.

Shots rang out, and both groups charged one another.

CHAPTER 25

Hok ducked and rolled, somehow managing to miss the spray of bullets that rained over him. He plowed through two of the armed Earthers and kept sprinting at Derek's retreating back.

"Cease fire!" Kaiser yelled at the other Earthers, and they lowered their weapons as he pointed to me. "Bayard needs that girl alive. Says we've got to study some ridiculous ability she's got. You can't kill her."

Several of the gun-wielding militants glared at me across the field, and I could only guess Bayard had provided them with ample information on how to identify me. Kaiser had said something similar, months ago. He'd spoken about studying the Societals. It had made me nervous at the time, but standing across the field from him, I felt only fury.

The nerve of Bayard, to think he could control my life. To attempt to steal something that belonged to me. And that's what my ability felt like, something that was *mine*. As much a part of me as my heart, and I had no intention of letting him take anything more than he already had.

"No," I said, stepping out toward our opponents. "No!" I yelled it louder the second time, as I ran across the field. "If Bayard wants something from me, he can come and claim it himself!"

I spotted Fell's marks as he ran beside me.

"Get Digit to the next ship! Please!" I shouted to him. He frowned, but veered off.

Spear members, Earthers, and resistance members were fighting each other across the field. No more shots rang out near us, which told me Bayard must have been serious about his orders regarding my safety.

The Societals weren't shooting, either, although I saw Silas had found a better use for the weapons. He flipped the large gun he carried around like a bat and slammed it into one of the other Earthers who had lunged out toward Vanya while she shot down his comrades.

I went straight for Kaiser, who, in spite of all his bravado, turned and sprinted back toward the main ship.

I followed him, cutting down Spear and Earthers alike.

I crossed paths with Sarah and Hok. Derek was hiding behind two others, an Earther and a Clan member. The latter rolled their eyes as the teen whimpered behind them, face bruised where I assumed Hok had punched him.

"You'll regret this!" Derek yelled from his relatively safe position behind the two larger men. His bodyguards surged forward.

"Stop!" I yelled, arm out.

"Thanks for the assist, Queeny." Sarah smirked at me as Charles dove from her arm toward the Clan member. Hok took care of the Earther.

Sarah stalked over to the cringing teen.

"If I were you," she seethed, staring him down, "I would march my sorry butt back to that ship like the coward you are, and stay there. Someone from our side will be by to lock you in momentarily."

She flipped her hair and turned. Hok reached for her hand. I stood in front of the teen as they began to walk away, but Derek couldn't leave well enough alone.

"You're trash—you know that, right?" he yelled at her retreating back. "Even your own father knew it. That's why he was trying to sell you off to my family. He didn't want to have to deal with you anymore. So go ahead and shack up with this beefed-up freak of nature if you want, but one way or another they *will* drag you back home on one of these ships. And that *thing* you're holding hands with will be dead in the dirt."

Faster than I could react, Sarah had sprinted back past me and grabbed Derek by the collar of his shirt. Rovers weren't the strongest of the Societals, but they were tough. She lifted him up until his toes dragged on the ground. Charles slithered down her arm and onto the teen as he cringed.

Sarah smiled, the expression feral against the glare in her eyes.

"You know something? I don't think I like the way you're talking to me. Or the way you're talking about Hok. But I don't expect anything less from the type of individuals my father hangs around with. Do say hi to him next time you're around, won't you?" She slid her hand back from the edge of his shirt, and he kicked and struggled as she moved to set him down. One of her nails slipped and nicked him under his chin. A single drop of blood dripped out as black veins spread from the spot. She dropped him.

"Oops, guess he won't be telling Dad anything, after all."

I had no way of knowing if it had been accidental due to Derek's struggle, or purposeful. And I wasn't sure it mattered. I was determined on my own revenge. And I was sure Sarah had her reasons for wanting hers. Hok offered her his hand, and they moved past me to one of the other ships.

I saw Fell and Digit emerging from the side of one. I did a count in my head.

Seven down. Five to go.

Several more Spear members and Earthers had flooded the field, but it looked as if Digit had managed to keep the majority of them locked away.

I scanned the crowd and spotted Kaiser shooting at Acaius, who dove and weaved, barely missing being struck. It seemed the no-killing rule only applied if I was in range. I ran toward them.

"Put it down!" I yelled as soon as I got close. Kaiser dropped the handgun.

"Unnatural!" he seethed. His eyes narrowed as he glared at me. I stepped in front of him, and he bared his teeth back at me. His legs shook as he fought against my projection.

"You think Bayard cares about salvaging lives? We *will* win. And when we do, I'll make sure these planets and all the oddities that inhabit them will burn."

"You won't get the chance," I swore. "Take off the rest of your guns." I saw his pupils dilate as he began removing each and every one, and I questioned whether he felt fear, or just indignation. Ryshal and Acaius had landed beside me and collected each one of the discarded weapons.

Kaiser's gaze followed the Kites' movements.

"Bayard told me about you, you know. I can promise you, *girl,* you'll live to regret this. That abomination you've attached yourself to? The forest dancer, or whatever Bayard called him? I may have to keep my hands off you, but he's not off-limits. I'll kill him, slowly. And there will be nothing you can do."

"Quiet!" I screamed and he slammed his mouth shut, as I tried to balance my control. His words were poison, even if the others thought he could be useful. And I'd already seen what happened when I let Spear members get anywhere close to those I loved. I wasn't going to repeat my mistake back at the Hub prison.

"Wait," I said as Kaiser moved to hand over his final handgun. "Turn it around."

"Kena," Ryshal cautioned as the Earther pointed the weapon at himself. "He's not a threat right now."

"You don't think so?" I cast a side-eyed glance at my friend.

I released Kaiser. The moment I did, he aimed the gun at Ryshal.

"Stop!" I yelled before he could pull the trigger. His finger hovered over it.

"I don't need your help," Kaiser spat out toward my feet. "I could wipe the floor with you! Make no mistake—that blue, glowing freak may think he's in charge here. But we have the tech now, and I will use it to wipe you all off the map. We'll take care of your sad little resistance, and then we'll visit your homes. Dropping bodies as a warning to all the rest of these monstrosities. And don't even think of retreating back to Earth. We've made sure that option's off the table."

I'd been about to make him shut his mouth again.

"What do you mean?"

"I mean that some of those other task force suits made sure to run a smear campaign against you all before we left Earth. Painted the whole lot of you as loonies and traitors. They let everyone know the Societals are dangerous. That they'll take our people and brainwash them, turn them into something unnatural. We've been broadcasting that information for weeks. We couldn't have you viewed in a favorable light during all this."

I glanced down and saw the gun still pointed at Ryshal.

"Turn it back around." He did, glaring the entire time.

Kaiser's finger flexed and had started to press the trigger just as the gun was kicked from his hands. In my shock, I let my control over him go as well, and Kaiser scrambled toward Ryshal and Acaius, who held the remainder of his weapons. They took off into the air, circling above.

"Hello, cousin." Bayard smiled at me from where he'd placed himself between me and Kaiser.

He whipped out his scythe, clicking it open and spinning it. I didn't reach for my ax.

"Drop it!" I yelled, focusing all my anger and energy on him. But his spinning only slowed down, fingers twitching but not losing his grip as the weapon wobbled in his hands.

"Now, Kena," he said with labored breath, "I would think you'd know better than to try your little trick on me. Make no mistake, I've been practicing projection much longer than you. And I dare say I'm better at defending against it, no matter what form it takes. How do you think I've gotten around the Reader all these years?"

I saw the speech for what it was: a distraction. Even so, I barely had time to pull out my ax as the scythe slammed down and connected with it.

We moved back and forth, dodging and slashing. In the past I'd never have judged myself his equal. And I still wasn't. But I managed to hold my ground just enough to avoid getting hit. It probably helped that I knew he wanted to collect me, not kill me. Keeping me alive required more finesse on his end.

Ryshal dove toward us, reaching for Bayard's scythe. Bayard swept it upwards, and tore the edge of one of Ryshal's wings. He didn't damage it enough for Ryshal to fall, but the Kite wobbled in the air and Acaius flew over to keep him steady.

"It's okay! Take him to the others!" I yelled as I traded blows with Bayard.

As they flew away, I saw Digit and Fell, and I assumed a camouflaged Nien and Cassia, running between ships nine and ten. More and more opponents were spilling onto the field, but the more they were able to keep locked in, the better for us. Every individual counted.

I was impressed I'd managed even a few minutes fighting against Bayard, but any excitement I had about that ebbed as the minutes dragged on. I felt my moves slowing as my energy waned. Bayard managed a strike on my arm. I looked down, panicked for a moment that he'd cut the mark I shared with Fell, but the wound was below it. The injury wasn't going to kill me, but I suspected I'd need stitches. My loss of focus while looking at the mark cost me another blow, this one a light scrape across my face.

"You can't win, cousin. I'm the superior fighter. And the superior Riftian." Bayard smirked and spun the scythe in a circle in front of me, as if proving his point.

"Only one of those things is true," I huffed, raising my ax back up to meet him.

After what felt like hours, but had probably only been another handful of minutes, he wore me down. Moving with the same grace I had previously admired about him, he spun and kicked out, sending me off-balance. Then he swiped one side of the scythe down, using the middle of the weapon to knock my legs out from under me. I slammed into the dirt, and I tasted blood as I bit into my tongue.

He lifted his weapon up, and for a moment I wasn't sure if he'd capture me or take my head. I was too tired to even try to control him. As the blade whisked through the air, a golden gleam caught my eye.

I heard the metallic sound of two weapons colliding as Juliard's scythe made contact with Bayard's.

The delegate's eyes went wide as Juliard fought against him, forcing him back.

"Not my niece, you filth. No one hurts this family!" Juliard yelled as he rained blows down, which Bayard barely managed to block.

Even to someone as cold as Bayard, the words had to sting, given the truth of their relationship. I pressed my hands into the grass and pushed myself up, grabbing my ax. As I stood, Juliard slid his scythe under Bayard's in a move I hadn't witnessed before. He hooked the blade around the handle of the delegate's weapon and wrenched it from his hands. Then, Juliard grabbed his opponent's scythe and threw it back to me.

He lifted his own golden weapon above his head and swung at Bayard. I lunged forward before he could make contact.

"Juliard, no!" I threw an arm out and my uncle came to halt, the scythe swinging but falling short of Bayard by several inches as I forced him to freeze in place. I'd almost been too late.

Bayard's face betrayed multiple emotions in succession. His eyes went wide at the near miss; then he scowled at his father before plastering a smile on his face.

"Much obliged, Kena," he said, before turning on his heel and sprinting away, almost as quiet as Fell when he ran.

I released Juliard, and he rounded on me.

"What was that? We could have taken care of him and brought this whole thing to a close! If you hadn't—"

"Another leader would have risen up, and it likely would have been Kaiser." It was a poor excuse, and Juliard frowned at me in response.

Fell, Digit, Vanya, and Nien strode up. Fell grabbed my arm.

"We got ten of the twelve ships locked down. I'm not sure for how long. Digit said it depends on if they reboot them or break out of them. Either way, we need to go."

I looked around the field. There were bodies. More Earther and Spear ones than ours, but every loss hit us harder, with our smaller numbers. Our opponents had retreated to their remaining unlocked ships for the moment. I looked up at Fell as our group moved toward the trees.

"I almost had Kaiser, but Bayard stepped in and—"

"And I would have had him if my niece hadn't saved him, for who knows what reason!" Juliard ranted as he ran next to us. "I vote we turn around. We could take care of this right n—"

Thundering shots rang out, cutting off Juliard's tirade.

The Spear were choosing to put their two working ships to use.

"Scatter!" Dex yelled to us as he and Silas waved everyone over to the trees.

Bullets pelted the ground near our feet as we ran for the tress.

CHAPTER 26

I ran as I never had in my life, my lungs heaving as I struggled to keep up with Fell, who I suspected had slowed his own pace for me. I saw one of the others fall, a Crew member I didn't know, although surely Nix and Hale did. We moved without letting up until we made it back to the encampment. Everyone was instructed to pack up and move again.

"We're out of options. I'm making us a Doorway," Ama stated as everyone else grabbed their things in haste and cleared away our campsite. Not a single person argued.

"Then we'd better get on with it," Karo said, the Crew around him nodding.

Ama sneered at him.

"Not here. Not now. They'll be combing these woods to eliminate us, just like we tried with them. No, we're not going to set up that Doorway until we're somewhere secure, where I am confident the Spear won't just stumble onto it and land themselves an easy pathway to the Tundra and the others. Get your gear and someone tell me when we're all ready to do what we should have done to begin with." She stomped off, following the river.

I threw my arms up, casting a glance at Fell.

"Why is she always doing things like that? Mysterious statements and wandering in and out of places!"

Fell tried to hide his grin behind a hand.

"What?" I demanded.

"You realize she's not the first one to go storming off into the woods, or elsewhere for that matter, alone? You two are much more alike than even you realize."

"And maybe that's not a good thing," I grumbled as I walked off to the edge of the group to gather my thoughts.

I dropped my arms and let out a breath.

"Rough day, right?"

I looked up and was a bit surprised to find Dex walking toward me. He'd always been perfectly pleasant, but I hadn't really known him well before we'd left Earth. He had joined Verkent during the time I'd been avoiding it, pulled in by Silas.

"Listen," he started, "I know what you did on the Hub. To Kidan and the other Spear members. And I know what you did in that field just now, letting Bayard and Kaiser go."

"That's not—"

He held up a hand.

"I'm not saying I judge you. For either. And before you get worried about who blabbed on you for the first thing, the answer is Sarah. She's quite impressed."

That was just what I needed, a publicity campaign that painted me as a cold-hearted killer.

"I didn't just let Bayard and Kaiser go. For the record," I mentioned. That was another thing I didn't need getting around the group.

"Kena, do you know what happened back on Clan when they saw the Spear attack during the Coalition meeting?"

I shook my head.

"I'm told that they cheered. Most of them, anyway. Pounded the stone tables with tankards and stomped their hooves in appreciation as the Spear announced their plans. As they killed delegates and sparked this whole conflict. In my time with them, I learned to appreciate a lot of things about Clan members. They're practical. They're straightforward. And they're hard workers. But they're also at odds with the other Societies. Although I guess that's true of them all, now that I think of it. My point is, many of them celebrated. But none of the other Societies did."

He leaned toward me, an unblinking stare boring into me. I gathered I was meant to take something important from the message.

"Dex, I'm sorry, but I don't know what you're getting at." I sighed, shoulders slumping.

He reached out and took my hand.

"Only this. The small contingent on Clan who didn't agree with the Spear had to risk their lives to sneak off to the Tundra Doorway and find the rest of the resistance. But again, that situation only happened on *one* planet. On all the others, there are tons of Societals just waiting. They likely don't know the Hub's been destroyed. They don't know if their leaders are dead. They don't know if the Spear will come for them. It may seem like the Spear's fighters outnumber us, and they do. Especially now that they've got the Earthers. But it doesn't matter. On our side, we have not just the desire, but the *need* to win. It's the only way to save all those other people. The Spear has a lot of fighters. On our side of things, those willing to stand up are few, but those who need protection are many. What do we do about that? Do we just let them fall? Or do we put every ounce of effort we have, every ability, even if it's frightening, into the goal of saving them?"

I found myself speechless as I took in his words. Dex stared a few more seconds, then dropped my hand and stretched.

"Well, I'm going to go grab my pack. Just thought I'd mention that." He walked back toward the others.

He was right. I'd killed Kidan, but I'd spared Bayard and Kaiser. I couldn't afford to be selfish. Even if it meant hurting my uncle. Even if it meant letting the others put themselves at risk for a cause they believed in just as much as I did.

I left the others to gather things, with Hale promising to make sure all my things were accounted for. I went after the Reader. She didn't acknowledge me when I first found her. She just stared out at the river. The rapids slammed against the rocks in their path, as though trying to force them out of the way. White-tipped waves crashed against the shore.

"On the surface, it looks like mindless rage, this river. But if you look deeper, there is a purpose for every turn. Every ebb and flow. Every drop has a destination," Ama said, eyes and marks casting a soft, sunset glow onto the dark blue waters.

"I'm beginning to see what you meant by rage, but I still haven't figured out how to control it." I clenched my fists, dropping them on my thighs. Without even glancing over at me, Ama moved like a viper, swatting one of my hands with her palm. It stung, but only a bit.

"Does nobody listen to me? It's not about mere *control*. It's about purpose, and motivation. You are not trying to force it away from you, and you are not trying to tamp it down. You should be trying to acknowledge and accept your emotions as a part of who you are. Then you will see progress." Her orange eyes glinted against the dawning light.

"I don't know what you mean by progress, either," I responded, shaking my sore hand. She just smirked.

"You will. Some of this you have to figure out yourself, you know. But I don't mind telling you what I see. Not what marks will tell me. But what *I*, Ama, see in *you*, Kena."

"Aren't they one and the same?" I questioned.

"For someone as unbelievably wise as me? Yes. To most people who would look upon your marks, no." I couldn't help laughing, her unfailing confidence in herself breaking at least some of the tension.

"You are stronger than you give yourself credit for. You analyze all sides of an issue, but that gets in your way. You get so caught up in your thoughts that you forget to act. Forget to let go and trust your feelings. Too many conflicting desires. Wanting to support others, not wanting to get in the way. Wanting to be honest, but not wanting to take up too much space."

I frowned as she mentioned the very contradictions I'd just been mulling over.

"Am I anything like you?" I asked.

"In some ways, yes." She smiled over at me. "In others, not at all. But that's part of what I like about you." She winked.

"Ama, Bayard being related to me was a shock. Then he drew these parallels between himself, my father, my uncle, and ... you. I wondered if, maybe—"

"Maybe I'm a long-lost grandma or something?" She raised a brow. "No, I'm afraid not. Although I would claim you as a relation in a heartbeat. I can assure you that even when I withdrew from the others, I kept track of my family. And I am sad to say they died out generations ago."

I murmured an apology, but she took my hands in hers and shook her head.

"It's all right. That's just the way of things over that long a span of years. If anything, I'm a bit glad you're not, if only because it shows some of these abilities aren't about lineages. They're about people. It should comfort you as well, since I know how terrified you've been of becoming your relatives."

"Yes, and I could have tried to become you," I teased. She just laughed.

"That would have been a terrible goal as well. We all have our own accomplishments, and our own regrets. No use taking on those of other people as well. You will have your own heroic feats; you already have. And your own failures; you've experienced those as well. Own and learn from both. But don't add the responsibility of the dead, or the living, to your shoulders. It's too heavy for anyone to carry."

I followed her as she walked farther down the bank, settling under a tree as she watched the waters.

"Ama," I started, "that's why I sought you out. I wanted to say, I support you. Whatever you think you need to do, whatever has to happen for this Doorway. I think you should do it, if you want to. And I appreciate it. I know you're offering it because of how much you care about the Societies, and it's your choice to make. I just ... wanted you to know that."

I stood beside her while she continued to watch the rapids crash and cascade. After another few moments, she spoke again.

"They had said this planet was totally unlivable. That it always would be. But just look at what happens without our interference. It thrived. You know, we Societals muck up all sorts of things. Take our decision to leave this place. We made such a big deal of the first Choosing. Of having only one choice. But that's never *really* true, nor has it been. We always have choices, and we can always go back and do our best to mend the ones we made wrong. That doesn't mean we get to make them over; just that we don't have to leave them as they are."

She left me staring out at the water. I knew what she meant, or at least what she said had meant to me. That I had choices left. And I knew I wanted to make the ones that protected those I cared for. Everyone deserved to make their own. I needed to talk to Juliard.

CHAPTER 27

There was only one thing that still needed to be done before I felt comfortable leaving behind the landscape of Lone. I had to tell Juliard the truth. Just thinking of it made me feel like my stomach was twisting in on itself, but the longer I waited, the worse I felt.

Or maybe it was one of those situations where you already feel so bad, seeking out a different pain to relieve the first seems almost preferable to dealing with it directly. Like pressing on a toothache.

I found my uncle in the woods, training next to one of Lone's many rivers. I stood for several minutes, watching from behind some branches as he swiped out with his scythe, lunging and twisting as he sliced single leaves or the tiniest buds off of twigs with precision.

Almost as if his return to the Societies had invigorated him, he looked younger than he had in years. I still missed the stormy grey of his eyes, but that was likely because I associated them with a father whose memory was also tainted.

His defensive feelings against the Coalition aside, Juliard appeared more alive on Lone than he had anywhere else. I sighed as I managed to convince myself to move forward. The small exhale caught his attention, and Juliard turned toward me, scythe out. It was a unique weapon, the gleaming gold causing it to stand out. Another testament, even if accidental, to his fallen brother.

"Niece," he said as he pulled the weapon back, planting the edge of it in the grass, "are we having trouble getting everyone coordinated and ready to move?" His brows drew down. He was always one complication away from getting involved and taking charge.

I shook my head, and then swept a straw-blonde piece of hair back behind one ear.

"No. I needed to speak with you. Alone. *Before* we leave."

"About your father." It was a statement, not a question. I almost, *almost,* said yes. I only just stopped myself.

"About your son."

He'd been standing still before, but he became completely motionless at that statement.

"I have not had a son in many lifetimes." He whispered. "I had a wife once, and a son. I've no idea how you found out about them. But they've been dead for many years now." He didn't so much as flick his hair back, but I caught his marks flickering. I tried to keep my gaze on his face and not let him catch me staring at them.

I'd gone to find him because I was determined to tell him the truth, and so I did. He didn't so much as shift his stance while I relayed everything Bayard had told me. Not when I told him he still had a son. Not when I told him Bayard, his son, had murdered his brother. Not even when I told him that he'd tried to get me to join the Spear.

"So that's why you stopped me," was all he said.

I kept my eye trained on Juliard's scythe as I spoke. Deep down, I couldn't envision him attacking, and yet I didn't feel quite safe enough to take my eyes off it. Or to have come to the clearing without my ax, which was slung in its holster at my thigh.

"Do you remember how I said I was supposed to be the head delegate for the Rift before deciding to go to Earth instead? It was the Reader who dissuaded me. The week before I was set to begin my tenure in the position, I gained new markings. The ones on my left shoulder and down the upper half of that arm, if you care to interpret them yourself." I didn't doubt him, and I didn't tell him I'd already learned the information from Ama's journal. "She got so excited and pushy when she saw them—you know how she is. Insistent that I heed them. They told her of a distant world. I'd already had marks that spoke of a position of leadership, which is part of what had made me pursue the position of delegate in the first place. After a few days of thinking it over, I gave up my spot and instead worked at becoming the head of the settlers for Earth."

I wasn't sure what he was getting at. Except that Bayard had almost literally followed in his father's footsteps, actually becoming head delegate. And then, in a much more murderous manner, attempting to reclaim if not newly settle a planet. Not that I wanted to draw attention to any similarities my uncle didn't already see for himself.

"Do you think Ama was wrong then? That you should have stayed and become head delegate after all?" I questioned. I knew better than most how insistent the Reader was, but I wasn't about to let him badmouth her or her judgment.

"She was right," Juliard said, at last moving as he stamped the edge of his scythe decisively on the grass a few times. "Oh, I'm not happy with how everything played out with Tiberius. But if I hadn't gone, he'd have succeeded. I didn't want to fight with my brother, but if I hadn't, all would have been lost. Including any chance to save your father." He looked at the ground where the handle of his scythe had worn away the green and left a muddy circle.

"What are you saying?"

"Nothing more than the ramblings of a truly ancient man, most likely." The hair flicking made an appearance, hickory locks flopping across his forehead. His hands tensed on his scythe as well. "Merely that we sometimes have to make great sacrifices for the greater good. As I did on Earth. As you might, if you continue down this path. The Reader pushed me toward what I needed. What exactly did she see in your first markings that convinced her to have you apprentice with her?"

I'd just told him his son was still alive. That he was a murderer. That he was trying to end the Societal way of life as we knew it, and he was focused on Ama. I pondered for a moment whether to let him stray off topic or bring the focus back to Bayard. In the end, I relented. Who was I to say how he should respond to the news, or grieve over the upbringing his son never had? I certainly hadn't responded perfectly to the bad things that had happened recently.

"She never said," I responded with honesty, "merely that she trusted her own judgment in the matter."

He laughed, throwing his head back.

"Yes, that sounds like her. Do you know, I think she's secretly been running most of the Rift for years. Even the whole ceremony in the Twilight Grove is something she cooked up, if I make my guess right. After all, it's just another event full of markings and interpretations. Her chance to give people the symbols she thought they ought to have, but didn't Assimilate themselves."

That hadn't been the case with me. She'd given me the incomplete marking already on my skin, which had turned into *soul*. The one I shared with Fell.

Juliard glanced up and down at my attire. I wore the full bodysuit, boots, bracers, and holsters that were part of the clothes Ama had the makers create for me out of the deep black ocala from the Twilight Grove. They were all stamped with the half-mark. Just the thought made me long to end the conversation and get back to Fell. Even amid all the turmoil, the more time I spent near the forest walker, the less I was able to imagine ever being away from him.

"What did she give you?" I asked, glancing at the scythe and his clothes, even though nothing he wore was made of the precious, near-indestructible material the makers used.

"Two things." He held up two fingers in support of his response. Then he reached a hand into the collar of his shirt and withdrew what appeared to be a leather cord. At the end was a small ocala pouch. Smaller than a closed fist. On it, two overlapping symbols were stamped.

I leaned in for a closer look, and he held it out obligingly. The first symbol stood for something like leader or leadership. I suspected I was years away from distinguishing such similar things in the way Ama had always been able to. I still just read the symbols; she was the one who understood the true power of meaning behind them. The second symbol, imposed over the first, was interesting. It stood for sacrifice.

"Sacrifice was not something I was ever as good at as I tried to be, I'm afraid," Juliard said as he placed the pouch back under his shirt.

"Really, aren't they one and the same? If there's anything I'm learning from watching you, and Warrick, and B—" I barely stopped myself. "And the others from the Societies, it's that leadership, good leadership, cannot exist without sacrifice. Before Sarah became de facto leader of the Rovers, she said their ruler Sorvay won by combat, and he's not here only because he got injured defending them. And she's had to kill to protect her people. That's a sacrifice of innocence, if nothing else."

He nodded, placing a hand on his chin as I rambled.

"Every once in a while, I make the mistake of forgetting how wise you are, niece. You're right, of course. And some sacrifices are bigger than others. I *do* regret not letting you in on what was going on, back before your father passed. That being said, we both know I'm not one for oversharing. I need some time to sit with the news you've brought to me. You can come get me when everyone else is prepared to leave."

I nodded as he picked up his scythe and went back to his training moves.

"We can talk about it on Tundra, then," I offered.

"All right," he said simply, not even glancing up.

"Juliard? What was the second item Ama gave you?"

He paused then, although he continued to look down the edge of his scythe, where he held it out in a swiping motion toward some invisible foe.

"Another matter I'd prefer to keep private for now, I'm afraid. Although I'll say it's something that never made sense to me. Not until very recently." With that, he went back to his motions, and I left him in the woods.

CHAPTER 28

We walked through the day, following the edge of the rivers. A few times, Ama had us stop and cross over where rocks formed something akin to bridges.

"How much longer are we going to spend on a nature hike when we should be either fighting or going to Tundra?" Karo grumped at one point. I turned to snap at him, but Captain Everleigh beat me to it.

"We had our chance, and we failed to get the job done. So we follow the Reader's plan. And we do it with respect. *She's* the captain here."

Some time after we'd stopped to rest and eat, I told the others what Kaiser had said about turning the Earthers against us.

"But surely he's bluffing, right? They couldn't launch a planet-wide smear campaign, could they?" Hale questioned as he shoved half a fruit into his face, green juice dripping down his chin. It was lucky for us Ama still remembered which plants on Lone were edible.

"They could and they would," Sarah assured us from where she walked hand in hand with Hok. If I'd had any doubts about their relationship, the way they'd been making out when we stopped for breakfast had put a stop to that.

"She's right," Dex said. "Silas and I managed to do a bit of recon on the main ship while everyone was fighting. Several of the soldiers in there were discussing it. What a brilliant scheme it was, and all that."

Silas nodded.

"It makes sense. We come off as dangerous and crazy. So do the Societals, for that matter. That way, no matter what, the task force looks like the good guys to everyone on Earth. Best-case scenario, they come home with all kinds of new technology. Maybe even a second planet. But even if they go back with their tail tucked between their legs, they can point to us as the supposed aggressors and still get sympathy. Not a bad plan, and honestly not even that original."

"They've out-conspiracied our conspiracy theorist group," Hale declared.

The light was beginning to fade from the sky again when Ama pointed to a large, flat-topped rock outcropping that overlooked yet another branch of the river.

"There."

She led us upward, and I saw that the rocks provided a bit of a shield if looked at from below. There was plenty of space to have everyone spread out on the wide stones that dotted the hill. The path from the river was lined with trees, like a natural path.

I was taking in the beauty of it when I heard a clap. Ama rubbed her hands together, staring out at the water.

"Well, no point in putting this off any longer. I'm fairly certain you'll all be safe, assuming this is done correctly. Still ... you might want to stay back, at least to the water's edge." She strode toward the center of the rock with her back straight and her head held high.

"Now? Shouldn't we rest first? Or maybe have a meal, or something?" I rambled. If she succeeded, at any cost, it was very likely she was saving us all. But if she didn't, I worried for her. I knew firsthand the physical toll that projection took, and what she'd suggested had to come with a massive physical cost.

"No more breaks. No more delays. Now," Ama insisted. She gestured me over as the others started to move back toward the water, forming a perimeter around her at the bottom of the hill. "It will be all right, Kena." She put one hand under my chin, and since I stood on a step below her, she actually had to lift my face to stare into my eyes.

"Okay," I managed before backing away. Fell held my hand as we moved down the steps.

Once everyone was at what the Reader deemed a safe distance, Ama closed her eyes and held her arms, palms out, in front of her. She began whispering to herself, but even with Assimilated hearing I couldn't make out her words from the edge of the clearing. Many of the others had chosen to retreat much further back into the woods, but the majority of the resistance leaders and quite a few Riftians had remained by the river to watch the Reader.

No one made a sound, beyond the soft rustle of the grass as someone adjusted their stance. No one spoke. Everything depended on her success. After several moments, a circle of white light appeared around Ama, and a similar light formed in a small ball in front of her palms. She tightened her features and chanted harder. As the ball of light reached the size of her hands, she flinched but kept going without breaking her concentration. It was like nothing I had ever seen, and I couldn't begin to guess how she accomplished it. My own ability, controlling the others, had come all too naturally. Scarily so. This, though. Ama was clearly putting in effort.

The light in front of her expanded and flattened, shimmering like the interior of a Doorway just before you walked through. The circle around her had grown high enough to encase her whole body, although she was still visible through it. As the Doorway took shape, Ama started shaking, and her arms trembled as if she was struggling to hold them out. The Doorway flickered and Ama grimaced and shoved her arms out even further, managing to keep her hold over the light.

When she fell to her knees, arms still extended, several people around the circle gasped and cried out. Fell's hand tightened around my wrist and I realized I'd lunged toward the Reader without thinking.

Ama's marks started flickering like a lightbulb on the verge of going out. She yelled, her voice echoing through the trees. Something was wrong. I shook Fell's arm and pointed. The comforting sunset orange of Ama's marks had begun to change. Starting at her fingertips and working its way up her arms, the orange faded into a stark and blinding white. The colored marks faded along her neck, and across her face. The result aged her, revealing wrinkles beneath the marks. A sheen of sweat dotted her brow, her face waxen. Then even her hair began changing to a shocking white shade, from the roots out.

"We need to help!" I lurched forward, only to find myself hauled back by Fell. He pulled me against his chest. The sudden entrapment only made me struggle.

"Let go! Something isn't right, we need to help her!" I turned to address him but his eyes were locked on Ama, wide and horrified. Still he held firm.

"Kena, we can't. She expressly forbade interference. If we stop her now, at best we'd prevent the Doorways from being opened, at worst we'd set off some sort of reaction and get everyone here killed. We have to let her try and see it through. This was her choice," he reminded me.

I stopped struggling, but tears fell as I watched Ama battle with the Doorway. Just when she was trembling so hard I thought it wasn't possible she'd hold it another second, I saw something new. Or rather, it was what I didn't see. Gasps rang out around the circle again, my own included.

Ama was fading away. Her hair, her marks, and the rest of her, from her edges in, were becoming transparent. With the same certainty Ama had always demonstrated when pronouncing the meaning of marks, I felt it deep in my bones. Ama wasn't just changing in shade; she was changing being. Like the songs outside her home, she was becoming a new concept or emotion entirely. Where the wind chimes played nostalgia, longing, apprehension, she was something else. She was the shade of absence.

I was pulled to the ground as Fell dropped to his knees behind me. His arms trembled and I could hear a sniffle as tears started, but he held on. He was right to. It took everything in me not to wrench myself free and run toward my beloved mentor. I'd thought that I had encountered suffering in the fights I'd engaged in so far, but having to watch Ama extinguish herself to help us, while we stood on the sidelines, tore me apart.

Ama didn't dissipate like dust in the wind. As the absence consumed her—I had no better words for it—a blinding light exploded outward. I cringed back, shielding my face with my arms. The light moved like a ripple in the water, out and over us all. I feared that it would burn, but it felt like a soft and comforting wind as it washed over us and then further into the trees.

I blinked after it passed, trying to regain my sight in its wake. As the spots on my vision faded, I stared into the middle of the clearing. In the center sat a perfect, shimmering Doorway. No tunnel needed.

But Ama was gone.

CHAPTER 29

Everyone slept outdoors in the clearing that night, bedrolls and blankets scattered across the greenery. Some, their Assimilations more suited for the outdoors, slept directly on the grass. A few of those from the Canopy were curled up like pampered dogs or cats, and I wondered if they were aware of the similarities.

The clusters of individuals were as varied as what they slept on. Some groups were solely from one Society, others intermixed by age with newer Assimilators together, or a few with a mix of those from all the Societies, uncertain where they fit.

While a few snored, many stayed awake, staring at the stars overhead or chatting. I lay on a mat next to Fell, watching the night sky, his hand holding mine. Soft laughter broke the silence between us. Maybe it should have felt morbid, sleeping near the spot where my mentor had left us, but it was also the place I felt most connected to her. I knew she was gone, but I couldn't bring myself to think of her as dead. The way she'd faded away, and then her light had washed over us was too different from death. It was as if her being had transformed, and then ascended into the skies of Lone. I couldn't bring myself to leave the Doorway. Freestanding in the center, with no tunnel leading to it, shimmering like a beacon of hope in the night.

"She wanted us to use it." Fell's words were soft, and he traced my hand with a thumb. I turned to stare into the reassuring constant of his blue and purple eyes.

"She did."

I wasn't ready to discuss it. But I knew I needed to be. I closed my eyes, blocking out even Fell's gaze as I took a deep breath, trying to center myself. I needed to grieve, but it would have to wait.

"The Spear will not leave us alone. I know we talked about figuring out Ama's secret to settlement and using it to run to a new planet, but that's not enough. Regardless of what the group chooses, some of us will have to mount a defense. We must fight. Not out of anger or a need for revenge, but to preserve what is good about the Societies."

I rolled to my side, opal and twilight mixing between us. He reached out one hand and cupped my cheek.

"I agree. The Spear is relentless."

"Would you have gone with me if I'd decided to leave it all behind?" I questioned.

He clasped my hands in his, allowing his marks to shine brighter. I'd become convinced that he did it consciously, to let me see his emotions. His control over them was too good for it to be accidental.

"Of course I would have."

I squeezed his hands back, not wanting to speak for a moment as I willed tears not to fall. It wouldn't be the first time I'd cried in front of him. But it didn't feel like the right moment. I had done enough weeping. I had done enough lashing out in blind anger. What I needed at that moment was a level head and a plan. I could weep when we were done.

I rested against Fell. I didn't sleep, but I let myself be comforted by his steady breathing through the night.

The mood was subdued as everyone readied to go through the Doorway in the morning. We'd both won, and lost. Not that it felt like there had been any victory. I brought my thoughts up to Fell.

"True, we haven't defeated the Spear. But we now know, or at least I think we know, every player at the table. No more surprises."

I hardly dared to believe it, but even so ...

"That's the Spear's doing, not ours."

"We set out to rescue the non-Assimilators, and that's solved. We wanted to free the delegates and other innocent Hub workers from the prison, and we did that. Sarah, Ariadna, Veronica and the others saved the children. Depending on how the Earthers handle what Digit did to their ships, we've probably disabled a few of them, at least. After what the rest of you have shared about Kaiser and the task force, I doubt they have the patience or skill to reboot those things. I'd wager at least a few groups will have gone for hacking holes into the walls to get out. We have accomplished several things we set out to do."

And yet it felt like it didn't balance out. I piled all the lives we'd saved on a scale in my mind against all those we'd lost. And it was laughable how uneven it seemed.

"It's not enough. We won't be done until the Spear is done, and—"

I paced the trees, running my hand over the leaves.

"And?" Fell prompted.

"At the time it felt like such a far-fetched goal, I'm not sure. If you'd asked me before we got to the Hub, it would have been all the things you just mentioned. If you'd asked me just after we'd run into that arena on the Hub, I would have said returning things to how they were. Salvaging the Coalition, the Societies as they'd been, with the exception of executing non-Assimilators."

Fell moved to me, wrapping his arms around me from behind and resting his chin on the top of my head. I felt my muscles drop as I let go of my tension and leaned into his comforting weight. True to character, he waited in silence for the rest of my response.

"But now, that seems wrong, too. The Spear is evil, and I hate what they're doing. Still, the system was clearly broken. Too many secrets, and too many misguided decisions. After all, no matter the cause, the Coalition approved killing non-Assimilators. They came up with the whole system of the Choosing, and dividing people in the first place. Things need to be different."

I turned in my Connected's arms, staring up at him.

"What do you think?" Fell always gave me room for my voice, and even if he was a man of few words, he deserved the same space.

"I think the Societies and the Coalition fell into the trap of believing good intentions and pride in their own planets meant the same thing as positive outcomes for the people they were supposed to be helping. Things have to change. Just in a way that doesn't leave violent individuals in charge who care only for what they themselves stand to gain."

A slight rustle prompted Fell to turn and step in front of me. His own movements didn't so much as disturb the grass beneath our feet.

Silas walked up to us, and I felt the pull of Fell's hands as I stepped toward the Verkenter.

"Kena, we've got almost everyone rounded up."

"Good. Then we can quickly move everyone through, and—"

"Kena." He waited for me to focus on him, my opal eyes locked onto his red before he continued. "*Almost* everyone. Your uncle is gone."

I pulled Fell with me, running through the trees and past the various sleeping areas where we'd all spread out in the woods. Silas kept pace with us. He motioned down at the empty bedroll Juliard had left.

"He took his scythe. But none of his other items. And I wanted to go to you first. I don't know what to make of this."

Juliard had used a folded-up grey Hub uniform as a pillow. It still lay at the top of his bedroll. And on that sat the ocala pouch, a piece of paper sticking out from it.

I reached down, pulling out the paper and unfolding it as I handed the pouch to Fell.

Niece,

We all make mistakes. I know I've certainly made many. Leadership comes with sacrifice. And so does righting our wrongs. I'm not asking you to understand. But I need to do this. Please know it doesn't change the love I have for you. I told you that long ago the Reader gave me two things. The first was the pouch. The second is under the Hub outfit. To my knowledge it's the only item she's ever handed out in the Twilight Grove that was made of combined materials. Ocala from the trees in the grove, and metal from the mines of Lone. I never understood the gift. I couldn't imagine why she'd impart the last of an extinct resource from an abandoned planet to me. I didn't know her direct connection to Lone at the time, of course. That, and the gift wasn't something I could use. Or so I thought. Now I realize I was meant to have it, but I wasn't meant to keep it. I was meant to give it. To you.

Juliard

P.S. I named my son Tiberius, after the brother I loved so much. The same brother who came back to the right side, before the end.

I took a deep breath, trying my best to put the P.S. from my mind. I pulled the jumpsuit up, and something metallic fell out, hitting the bedroll. Silas bent to pick the item up and held it out to me. It was immediately apparent what it was, and yet it still confused me. Made of twisting and overlaid pieces of the soft, leather-like ocala, and a steely grey metal, it was a circlet crown.

As I stared, Fell reached for it, with Silas handing it over. The forest walker, several inches taller than me, didn't even need me to kneel as he reached out and placed it atop my head. It slid over my forehead; a perfect fit.

"Are you guys coming or what?" Hale strode toward us, hand in hand with Nix. When he saw me, he let go of her and walked over, eyes wide. And then, he laughed.

"Please, *please* tell me you will be wearing that for the duration of this mess. Queen of the Alliance and Conspiracy Theory Princess indeed. This is too good." He thumped me on the shoulder, laughing so hard a tear trickled from his eye.

Fell and Silas were giving him side-eyed glances, but I smiled at my friend. I hauled him in close, hugging him tight.

"Thank you," I whispered into his ear.

Only Hale was able to take heart-wrenching moments and turn them into humor. I'd always laughed, but it was the first time I truly appreciated it for the skill it was.

"Any time," he whispered back before pulling away. "Hey, Serpentina! Get a load of this. You'll need to get yourself one of these." He called as he moved over to where the Rovers were grouped.

Everyone had gone around the clearing, gathering items and doing their best to camouflage the fact that we'd ever been there. The more confusion we could cause the Spear, the better. At least this was a skill multiple Societals excelled at. The Clan, for all their leaderless disarray, were the most adept.

"You learn quickly on that planet," Dex informed us, "that camouflaging your tracks in the snow is difficult but absolutely necessary if you don't want to meet a fearsome mammal set on taking a chunk out of you whenever you leave the mines."

He'd taken over instruction of the others left from his Society by default, but the role suited him. He may not have had Silas's gift for strategy, but he was forthright and capable.

One by one, the crowd dwindled. We moved with haste, but it still took a while to put us all through a Doorway one at a time. We'd sent Silas, the Crew captains, Sarah, and Vanya through first to explain the current situation to everyone who had been waiting on Tundra.

The clearing got emptier and emptier.

"Wait," I said as Fell stepped toward the line. "I want to leave something. For Ama. I don't even know that she died in a traditional way, since we have no body. It's more like she ascended into the air of Lone. But it feels wrong not to mark the space with anything."

I wracked my brain but had no ideas.

"If you don't mind waiting a bit longer, I think we can help," Hale said, walking over with Nix.

They wandered off into the trees, armed with their daggers and Nix's short sword, and true to their word returned some time later. Hale appeared to be carrying a pile of sticks and string in his arms.

"What's that?" I questioned, pointing at it.

He winked.

"You'll see."

Hale held the item steady as Nix grabbed a long cord from its end. It looked like they'd stripped and braided brush or grass to act as rope. After she tied it off, he released the pile of wood, and I heard the soft tinkling of music as it swayed in the breeze.

I felt my eyes grow watery with unshed tears.

"It's beautiful."

"It's perfect," Fell agreed as he approached my friend. Hale held out a hand, but Fell wrapped him into a hug instead. Hale allowed it for a few seconds before shoving him off with exaggerated movements.

"Hey, none of that. People will think you're starting to grow on me. Crypt keeper." But the sting had gone out of the insult. "You mentioned that she had those wind chime things when you first told me about her, so I just thought—"

"I didn't even know you could make something like this. How did you do it?"

Nix flipped one of the daggers she held in the air; it spun several times before she swiped it back toward her by the handle.

"Lots of action on a ship. Also lots of downtime below deck. Plenty of time to take up a hobby. And contrary to popular belief, Crew members are good for more than just drinking and brawling. Well, some of us."

Hale nodded, gesturing toward Nix.

"She's really good at wood whittling. Building. I picked up a few things from her."

"Picked *me* up as well." Nix bumped him with her hip and his cheeks reddened.

We stood for another minute or so, listening to the chimes.

"Kena," Fell's voice caught me off guard, "do you need more time?"

What I needed was for everything to be different, but I wasn't going to get that. I shook my head at him.

"No. I'll come back and visit her again, after we've won. I'm ready." I walked over to Fell, and he took my hands in his as we stood face to face. He leaned forward but didn't kiss me. Instead, he just leaned with his forehead pressed to mine, and somehow it was exactly what I needed.

"What if they find this and follow us through?" Nix asked.

"We'll have to deal with that when it comes, if it comes. We don't have another option right now. Not unless we want to wait here for them to hunt us down," Fell responded.

I dropped Fell's hand and stepped toward the Doorway, holding a hand out in front of it as I walked around the only way we had off of Lone.

"I don't think they'll be able to follow us. At least not this way. She did the same thing with the Doorway that she did with the book. It's shielded somehow. I don't know how she managed to add projection to it for them, and not the rest of us, but that's what she seems to have done. I'm almost certain the Spear won't be able to find it. They may come tromping through here, but they'll ignore its presence." It was just the sort of thing Ama would have thought to do.

I wondered for a moment, and only let myself linger on it for a few seconds, whether it had been that detail that pushed her over the edge. There was nothing to be done about it. Nothing was going to bring her back. All I could do for her now was to ensure her sacrifice wasn't wasted.

CHAPTER 30

The four of us linked arms as we approached the Doorway. Hale went through first. Then Nix.

"After you," Fell said, sweeping an arm out.

"No, I'll be right behind you."

I knew I couldn't linger long or Fell might panic, but I swept a final glance across the clearing. Once I set foot on Tundra, I would need to head straight into a quiet tent for concentration, and figure out Ama's journal.

"I will make you proud. But I will do it my way, embracing myself and my abilities," I promised the Reader.

I tensed my shoulders, bracing for the cold, and stepped through.

The frigid air hit me with force, not nearly as calm as it had been when we'd left. It sucked the air out of my lungs, and I wanted to curse in shock at the sudden change in temperature.

"Damned snow planet!" Nix stomped her boots into the snow, arms crossed as she hopped in place. Clearly, I wasn't the only one at odds with the environment.

No one was truly built for Tundra. After all, Assimilations were Society-specific, and the whole point of their origination seemed to be an ability to survive the host planet. Aside from some of the more mystical Riftian skills.

That aside, Dagan and Rover had the hardest time adapting to the snowy environment. Both had features of a somewhat amphibious or reptilian nature, and neither was equipped for a sub-arctic planet. Vanya and Hok veered off toward the supply area, determined to equip everyone as best they could. Coats were not distributed evenly, but by physical need.

"I hate this planet," Sarah grumbled as she walked past me. She stopped and took a few steps back over. "You have our support in this, Kena. You know that, right?"

I nodded. I did know. That, and a desire to protect the others, was the only thing that kept me going.

She shivered, then trotted off after the others.

Fell held an arm out to me and escorted me toward a line of tents. He led me to one of the smallest.

"This will be ours, for as long as we're here, anyway. I'll leave you to decipher the journal."

"You're not staying?"

"I'm afraid I might be a distraction. I'm available if you need me, but I'm going to work with the others. Between Dex's ability to cover his tracks in the snow, and my forest walking, I think we could increase the stealth of our group as a whole, just in case we do end up with some unwelcome visitors."

It was a good idea, and I wasn't going to take him away from it. After all, I'd been against the whole idea of Societies holding back from one another. If nothing else, this entire tragic war, as it had spiraled into, had forced at least the resistance to share with each other. They'd learned more about one another's talents and abilities in a matter of weeks than they had in generations of existing around one another.

After he exited I pulled a blanket around me and blew on my hands, rubbing them together to warm them. With nothing left to use as an excuse to waste time, I reached into my pack and pulled out the book.

It fell open in my lap, and when I looked down at the previously foreign symbols that had puzzled me, reading them was as easy as breathing. There, right in front of my eyes, were Ama's words.

I've perfected the ability. Now all I lack is the courage to see it through. Across my lifetimes I have hoarded knowledge. About Lone, and about the beginning of the Societies. The truth is not what most Societals think.

In the beginning, we had three planets. Dagan, Canopy, and the Rift. Everyone knows that; it's taught to all Blanks when they're educated at the Hub. What they don't know, and seem fine to live in ignorance with, is how Assimilation came to be. Their instructors give them some vague crock about it happening naturally over time, and no one seems to question that. Why would they, when the Assimilations themselves are so much more interesting to focus on? I doubt most are even aware that Lone's residents were nothing more than Blanks themselves. A term that didn't exist when I was growing up. There were no abilities, no enhanced senses. No one had gills or scales or tails. I love our true features, and that's how I see them, as much as the next Societal. But they're a lie. Or at least, their source is.

When we held the first Choosing, we hoped to uphold the same tenets the Coalition currently espouses. Monitoring resources, pooling our different natures for the cause of the greater good. But there were no adaptations. We merely hoped to survive and scratch out a living in our new homes. Assimilation came after, and only for the Riftians at first. Within the first year of our settling the planet, individuals started to glow. We could see and hear far beyond our original abilities. We'd become swifter, and surer-footed. There were variations in how each person wielded their newfound skills, but all had improved.

Dagan and Canopy, on the other hand, were struggling. Those on Dagan were barely surviving on the small archipelagos they had tried to claim as their home on an otherwise sea-filled planet. Traversing between them in the same small boats and kayaks that had served us so well on Lone resulted in the death of many to monsters of both the sea and sky. Storms pummeled them day and night, and many perished.

On Canopy there were beautiful plants and surroundings, as well as delicious foods. But also deadly ones. And more than that, the wildlife was fearsome. There were hundreds of different creatures, none domesticated, just waiting to turn the planet's new residents into prey. They needed help, and we on the Rift thought we could give it.

We set out to find the source of our good fortune. I was hardly an adult at that point, but determined to follow in my parents' footsteps. Others had begun construction on the Hub, but I hated the idea of moving two planets' worth of residents into a floating hunk of metal if we could find a way to salvage everyone's new homes. So we searched. And searched. It took two more years once we'd started. The Riftians loved the forests; we had no need to explore the caverns and caves. But that's where I eventually found what we were after. Even in the beginning, I was drawn to our markings, to cataloging them. Drawn to the feeling of power and connection to the Rift itself that they seemed to bring. And they drew me to the cavern. Past what is now called the Lake of Death, deep in the dark tunnels, I took a kayak. And past many twists and turns, rapids and narrow pathways, I found it.

I came through to a secondary cavern. Larger by several times than the one holding the lake. And it shimmered with glinting crystals along the walls. They ran in rivulets under the water itself. And they glowed. A cascade of colors and shades, some of which I've never seen before or since. Several others I've only ever seen mirrored in the markings of certain Riftians. But I knew, deep in my heart, that this was the source. Our planet had gifted us with our abilities. I told the others, and we hoped we could share them.

We just didn't realize what our gift would cost us.

I sat in the tent with the book open in front of me. I could see my breath in the air each time I exhaled, and it distracted me. I longed for the Rift's temperate forests. I might as well have wished my father back. For that matter, I might as well have wished that he'd never been the leader of the Spear. All impossible things. Just like what I'd dreamed and envisioned the Societies to be. I didn't have time to waste on the dreams of a young girl anymore.

The Societies held so many secrets, and so many things were different from what I'd expected. A few of the Societals, like Fell, were better than I'd ever imagined. But so many of them were worse. I dreaded what horrible journey the book might send us on.

"I take it we're still waiting on you to save the worlds?" Hale poked his head into the tent, a tentative smile on his face. "You know, you don't have to do this alone, Kena. I mean, obviously you have to read it yourself, but whatever it says, we're all with you."

He made his way in and sat down facing me, tucking his legs under him. As he reached out, I pulled his hand toward me and squeezed.

"Do you wish at all that it wasn't real? That we'd never come here, or they'd never come back for us? Things would have been so much easier."

He kept his hand in mine and stared at me for several seconds, then pulled back.

"No, Kena. It wouldn't have been. You and Juliard still would have been feuding, and you would have been off on your own without Verkent. The Societals would have been up here killing their non-Assimilators, and the Spear probably would have taken over by now—"

"Yes, maybe. But we wouldn't have known about any of it. And our lives weren't perfect, but we didn't know any better."

He shook his head.

"You're wrong. Tell me you didn't feel it, that pull of something else out there? It's what we dedicated our lives to believing in. Honestly, even I thought it was real, no matter how much I joked about it. You're sad about a lot of the consequences, about the people we lost, and about the illusions we left behind as well. You're tired. I get it. We all are. I wish there was an easier answer, and I would give up anything to swap and have it be me instead of you burdened with this. But that's just another thing that isn't true. It comes down to you. And you can do it. I know you can."

I dropped the book and launched myself forward, knocking him over as I hugged him.

"Thank you."

After several seconds I let go and scrambled back toward the book. Hale dusted bits of snow off his sleeves.

"Yeah, well. I can have the right words sometimes. Just don't expect it to become a regular occurrence. Get your glowing boyfriend to do that. Then I can go back to being the comic relief around here." His grin took the sting out of his words. "Speaking of which. He'd like to see you, too."

I heard the soft swish of the tent flap being lifted and felt the icy chill from outside sweep in with a vengeance. Hale exited, and Fell dropped cross-legged in front of me. He held out two bowls in front of him, and I knew if I had attempted the same thing they would have spilled for certain.

"You should eat," he said, handing one to me. It looked to be soup, the sauce red, with chunks of meat floating in it.

"How do we even have any food left?" I questioned.

He chuckled, and I nearly dropped the bowl. His laugh was deep, and I hadn't heard it since before we landed on Lone.

"It seems we're not the only ones who had our hands full. Several of the Societals here are rather industrious, and they took it upon themselves to find a food source while they waited for us to get back from the Hub."

"Why didn't those here just leave? Go back to their own planets and wait?"

"Fear of the Spear, most likely. We still have no idea about their full hold on the actual planets. Actually, more people have trickled in here since we were gone. Quite a few more. Tundra has become something of a refuge. But that's not the most interesting part."

I held the bowl up to my lips and sipped. The temperature alone was warm and comforting, but the taste was unbeatable. I downed half the bowl. Fell reached across and wiped a drop of soup off my cheek.

"Samell and Ariadna led a group to go look for food. And she came back with something."

His eyes sparkled, and I sensed he was enjoying holding me in suspense. I finished the soup and set the bowl aside.

"What exactly, other than delicious ingredients?"

"Well, Ariadna does have a new scar, courtesy of one of the local mammals."

I frowned, but he continued to smile.

"But she also has a new pet."

"Like a dog? A snake. Surely no one else is going to show up with a serpent here?"

He shook his head.

"Nope. I believe Hale referred to it as a 'freaking huge six-legged polar bear,' if I recall correctly."

"What?" I leapt up, tripping over my own feet in the process. Fell, of course, reached out and steadied me.

I sprinted past several of the tents and well away from the camp, but it was easy to find. A small crowd had gathered, and Ariadna stood facing a semicircle of Societals. Next to her, and towering over her, was a massive six-legged bear. That was as close a description as I could come up with. The snout was shaped differently, sharper and toothier, if such a thing were possible. The blackened rings around the animal's eyes continued and formed a pattern on the top half of its head.

Running down Ariadna's right cheek and onto her neck was a series of four angry red lines.

A hand thumped me on the shoulder, and I turned what I'm sure was a surprised face toward Digit. She was grinning from ear to ear.

"So cool, right? And look, scar twins!" Digit gestured between Ariadna and her own scarred face, with the Crew tattoo underneath it. "Did you figure out the book, then?"

A few people overheard her and started making their way over.

"No, I—"

"Just getting some fresh air before she goes back," Fell supplied for me.

"Yeah, that," I said, still dumbfounded by the bear.

"Fresh air, that's a riot," Sarah grumped as she joined the group. She wore a furry coat, and her snake poked his head out from the sleeve and hissed. Its breath puffed a small cloud into the air. Hok walked up and wrapped his bare arms around Sarah, who turned and smiled at him. "Then again, there are some benefits to this place. All the ways one can get warm, for instance."

His marks flared and I had to squint. Beneath his silver eyes I saw the red of his cheeks.

They wandered off to a tent, and I realized I needed to go back and actually get to work. Still, I didn't deny Fell when he followed me.

He grabbed my arm just before I entered the tent, spinning me back to face him.

He dipped his face to mine, pulling me in as our lips connected. I held onto him, seeking his warmth as his tongue ran over my bottom lip. I shivered, but for once it wasn't from the cold.

I stood in a daze as he pulled away.

"We should get inside," he said.

"Yes please." I realized how enthusiastic I'd sounded and was mortified to find my marks reflecting on the snow. He grinned.

"I wouldn't say no to that, but how about after you finish the book?"

"Oh, you're no fun," I teased, more light-hearted than I'd felt in ages.

As I moved past him and into the tent I yanked on his shirt, pulling him down toward me. I nipped at his bottom lip.

"Read quickly," he instructed as he followed me in.

CHAPTER 31

All around the lake and cavern, glowing crystals were embedded in the stone and dirt. We couldn't puzzle out what made them thrive, but we realized if we extracted them whole without breaking them, they kept their glow. If one broke, then it dissipated and the glow sort of floated away like dust in the air, and the crystals went dark. They're like plants that way, mirroring the Riftian trees. They're rooted into the planet. I felt each one, alive or dead. And I knew. I knew what we were attempting could work.

We approached the leaders of Dagan and Canopy. They kept the secret small at first. No one wanted to get up the hopes of the others. The Riftians, in the meantime, started covering our marks. There had already been talk from some of those residing on Dagan and Canopy that they ought to be allowed to move to the Rift. A second Choice. That made all the delegates nervous. It was too soon after Lone, and the situation was too similar. They didn't want an overcrowded planet full of desperate people. The crystals were our best shot.

Those on Dagan and Canopy had already been working on settling into their planets by force. Canopy had built up defenses around their towns, and Dagan had been fiddling with the ships we'd used to transport ourselves to the planet. They'd adapted some to be able to go under the water, and were toying with the idea of grand domes under the sea instead of the islands. We knew we needed to place the crystals somewhere hard to reach, to avoid anyone stumbling upon them and damaging them. It was the explorations of both groups that helped us.

Those on Dagan had an area underwater which they called the Deep. There was a drop-off where the depths of their sea increased drastically. Some of their more fearsome creatures, resided down below. We resolved to plant the crystals there. On Canopy they had an area on the planet referred to as the Wilds. They'd already decided not to settle there, deep in one of their many tropical forests. Part of their strategy was to avoid conflict with the wildlife, by preserving whole swaths of land without Societal interference. Once both sites were decided, we went to work.

At first, the attempts appeared to fail. The delegates from the other planets said they could secure the crystals in place, but they didn't take hold like they did on the surfaces of the Rift. They didn't grow. One of the Dagan pointed me in the right direction. They were fed up with the lack of progress and made a sarcastic remark that if the Riftians were so far superior at Assimilating to our planet that maybe we ought to be the ones handling the transplant of the crystals. They'd meant it as an insult, but the statement stuck with me.

By that point, I'd begun to realize that Riftians didn't just have physical changes. A few in the main grove had started to have visions, their marks wafting like smoke from a fire and their eyes going clouded.

All of us had noticed a change in how the other planets' residents reacted to us. Oh, they were well capable of being upset, as the Dagan had demonstrated. But our initial interactions with people were different. Our delegates were able to introduce and push through issues that would have typically been shouted down. We projected an air of authority, or trustworthiness.

I'd surmised that all our abilities came from the planet itself, so why not that? I went back to the cavern and removed some small crystals. At first I practiced on the Rift itself. I sequestered myself in the area now known as the Twilight Grove, away from the others. I buried the crystals beneath the trees, and as they grew, the grove changed. I decided to try my theory on the other planets. So, the next time the delegates made an attempt on Canopy, I went along. While the others were hard at work on the edges of the Wild, I snuck off on my own. I planted the crystal at the base of a tree, just one that spoke to me, and I willed it to take root. I tried to consciously project my desire onto it, as we had subconsciously been doing to the others. And it worked.

That was the beginning of everything.

"Time to sleep," Fell declared as I announced I'd reached the end of another entry. He grabbed at the book, starting to close it.

"No. Absolutely not. I've wasted enough time as it is today, not that I can regret seeing a space bear. For all we know, those Earthers' ships have already set course for somewhere else. I owe it to everyone to keep going."

I'd noticed the light in the tent had faded, but my opal marks were enough to read by.

I turned back to the book, but I didn't actually read. I waited for what he would say next, because I knew there would be something. Something comforting, or reassuring. But nothing came.

"Fell?"

His shoulders drooped, eyes downturned, focused on the floor of the tent. I moved over to him, which took little effort considering how cramped the space was. I took his hands in mine, and swept a strand of black hair away from his face. He gave a half-smile, but didn't meet my eyes.

"Fell, what's wrong? You're scaring me here."

He sighed.

"Kena. We don't have a plan. Not a good one. All of us with training experience, or any actual fighting experience, we haven't come up with anything. No matter how we try to consider the situation, the Spear has the advantage. Thousands of Earthers with those ships, and the ability to travel from one Society to the next, where largely peaceful people are waiting. The best Silas came up with was taking out the leaders. We know Bayard's in charge, but after our own experience I'm assuming there will be someone, or several individuals, from each Society running their own planet's contingents. Those individuals, and Kaiser or any other task force members, could be key people to target. If we can get rid of them, we might be able to overtake the rest of a leaderless Spear."

"And the rest of the Earthers?"

"That's where the plan falls back to you. We bargain. As much as none of us like it, I suspect everyone on those ships is either military of some sort, or valuable in some other way. Knowledge of technology like Digit, some specialists who could take certain materials off the planets. We can't come up with a way to beat them all. So we trade. We offer Earth whatever you find out about the settlement and send them off. This could be the best and only chance we have." Shades of blue and purple danced across the canvas inside the tent, arcing and dipping like waves in a stormy sea.

The plan put all the pressure on me to save us. Although I'd already put that on myself. I found myself loath to hand over the information. But he was right; if they couldn't think of another way to win, it was the best shot we had. I threw my arms around him, crawling onto his lap.

"You said, bargain the information to the Earthers. Because we know it's something they don't have. And we know the Coalition wasn't sure how to Assimilate on new planets, either. The Spear can't have all the information, but Bayard's calculating. He wouldn't have set his plan in motion without having at least a starting point." I let my thoughts run wild out loud.

"So, what are you thinking, then?" Fell questioned.

"He knows. I don't know how, but Bayard must at least know what he's looking for, even if he's not sure how to use it. Why else set this all into motion now?" I stared, unblinking, into Fell's eyes.

"Then we need to make sure and get to the rest of the information first," he said. I leaned against him with the book open in my lap, and his marks flared just enough to envelop the pages in vibrant light.

With comforting shades of twilight dancing across the pages, I dove back into my mentor's words, hoping they would be enough to save us all.

We still hit some snags. Not every Riftian was capable of placing the crystals. Only those who were able to garner some conscious control of their Assimilated ability of projection. And some of the damage had already been done. After all, the balance of power was off. The Riftians held the answers, and the others resented it. Along with placing the crystals, we stopped talking about our forests. We closed ourselves off.

Once the crystals began to take root and grow, the others Assimilated features of their own. Surprisingly different features from ours, but things that allowed them to survive and thrive in their new homes nonetheless. And it allowed us to settle other planets as the opportunities became available. The Hub was finished, and whole groups of workers were dedicated to just such an endeavor. Over time, knowledge of the crystals became privileged, known only to the

Coalition and select Riftians who helped plant them. The knowledge, like the items themselves, was fragile, and it was passed down verbally, with no written record.

For, while the crystals were planted, they weren't truly part of the other planets. On the other planets, they're an invasive species. Like any cultivated tree or flower, they're nurtured and encouraged to grow. I do think that now, with the ability I've gained since then, I'd be able to use projection to influence the crystals to meld with the planets themselves. That would ensure Assimilation forever, omitting the need to hide and protect the crystals, as we currently do. But it doesn't matter now.

Because I've failed. Failed miserably. Earth is gone. They're saying the settlers rebelled against the Hub, but I don't think I believe it. I knew several of those Societals, and I simply can't picture it. I believe others to be responsible. Others who are likely still among us. There have been whisperings of a radical group that wants to go back to Lone. The Spear, they call themselves. The fools. They have no idea what we did to each other there. And I assume no idea that the planet would render future generations Blanks. I've tried to influence the Coalition through the regular channels. To stop future ideas of settlement until we get this sorted out. I don't want to risk another Earth, and I don't want to risk knowledge of how we've Assimilated all this time falling into the wrong hands. This ability was for our survival, not so some radical group could utilize it to conquer and control. And after my upbringing on Lone, I have no doubt in my mind that's what they would do with such information.

But I've been outvoted. So, wrong or right, I've found a way around. I'm going to use my projection to make the Coalition forget. I'll do the same to the other Riftians who know about the crystals, and I'm hopeful that within a few generations no one will remember how we settled planets to begin with. I'll undo it if we ever figure out this group and their motives; if we can ever ensure settlement would be safe and unsullied again.

I knew how that had worked out. She'd accomplished her goal, but in the process she'd wiped her own knowledge of it. She'd had noble aims, but her mistake had meant that when non-Assimilators had started to die, she'd hidden the knowledge of how to save them from even herself.

There's only one potential loose end I can't get to. Perhaps two, although I hate to think about it. One of our own Riftians, Juliard, was the head settler of the group going to Earth. As such, he was privy to some of the plan. I don't think he realizes the significance, but he may put it together once Earthers fail to Assimilate. If there are even any of them still left alive. He knew I was coming down for some ceremony, and he knew it involved something I'd retrieved from the cavern that houses our Lake of Death. He was supposed to help scout locations for me to hide something of great import; he just didn't know what. And now he's gone, and his brother Tiberius is missing as well. I fear one or both could be involved in this return-to-Lone nonsense. And I wonder if they both know our secret. It won't matter, though, not unless they return. And if that happens, either we won't need to hide things anymore, or we'll all be in much more danger than we are now.

No matter what, I have to try. The very existence of the Societies depends upon it.

I slammed the book shut.

"What did it say?" Fell questioned after several moments of me glaring at the closed book in silence. I'd forgotten I was the only one who actually was able to read it. I relayed to him everything I'd learned.

"That's good. And bad. If it comes down to bartering with Earth, that sounds simple enough. We collect some crystals and hand them over. Although I'd vote we keep knowledge of where they come from and how we got them to a minimum. But what she said about integrating the crystals into the planets themselves, that's interesting.

And then there's the bit about Juliard. Do you think it's possible he's figured it out?"

The truth was I wasn't sure, and I told him as much. I wanted to regret telling Juliard about his son, but I couldn't. If I was being honest, Ama's plan relied on her ability to outsmart and out-projection the other Societals. But Bayard had fooled her, along with everyone else. She'd written that the brothers knew, or both might have known, something about the crystals. Had they had time to tell anyone before they left? Surely Juliard would have mentioned it to his family. It was highly possible Bayard already knew whatever Ama had told his father. After all, he'd all but admitted dedicating his early life to studying the brothers.

In my head and heart, I'd already made my decision.

"He's going to go after the crystals," I said, staring down at Fell's hands where they were wrapped around me. "This whole time we've underestimated the Spear, and it has cost us. Maybe in this instance I'm giving Bayard too much credit, but I don't think so. Especially now that Juliard's over there and giving him who knows what information. It never made sense. Bayard wanted to go back to Lone. He figured out where it was, and it's clearly habitable, so he could have just disappeared. He also wanted to take control of the Societies and their resources, and he managed to get Earth for that. But there's something else he said when he was ranting to me in Warrick's office, about the possibility of even taking more planets. That's got to be the piece he's still missing, and I bet you anything he's going to use those crystals to do it. Maybe I'm wrong, but I think we have to act as if I'm right. If he finds them first, our bargaining power with Earth goes out the window. That, and it gives him the ability to retreat to any random rock in the galaxy and just start over, if by some miracle we do beat him." I'd been rambling.

"I know," was all Fell said in response.

"You know?"

Fell reached out, taking one of my hands in his.

"I wanted to let you reach the conclusion on your own, because of what follows."

I sighed, looking first at the book, and then back at my Connected.

"We can't keep getting outsmarted by the Spear. We need to get ahead of Bayard and Kaiser, and I think I know how."

It was a guess, and a gamble, but it was also one of the few remaining options. As far as we knew, Bayard still had no idea about the location of any of our Tundra Doorways. If I was right, Bayard aimed to gain control of the crystals. We needed to do what Ama had suggested in her writings, and integrate the things into the planets themselves in a way he couldn't touch. That way, even if we lost, the Societies themselves were technically protected. I doubted anyone wanted to find out what a planet devoid of Assimilation looked like. And our best bet was to go where it had all began.

"I think we can try to do what Ama did with the book, but on a larger scale," I suggested.

Fell raised an eyebrow, his fingers absently tracing over my palm.

"You mean, hide the crystals somehow?"

"That, and more. We could make them a permanent piece of their environment, not something that can be rooted out. If Bayard can't remove them, or the Spear can't find them, we win. Either way, the Societies become untouchable."

He took my hands in his, opal and twilight shimmering together between us.

"Then I guess we should go tell the others we're going home."

NOTES AND THANKS

I would like to thank my family and spouse for all their support of this series. You all knew all the ins and outs of every Society before the first book ever reached the publishing stage. Thank you for listening to me think out loud all the various characteristics and connections in my mind.

Thank you to all of my early readers and my editors for your insightful feedback. This wouldn't have been the same book without you. Lizzy-thank you the insightful questions and predictions. Shelbs-thank you for the live reacts including the yelling and telling me you were going to throw the book at a certain point. Every author's dream.

If you are enjoying this series and want to stay up to date on upcoming releases, news, and general book appreciation you can connect with me here:

Website & Newsletter: nightlochpublishers.com

Instagram & TikTok: @reameswrites

Facebook: S. Reames Author

Other Books in This Series

Assimilation: The Societies Trilogy Book 1
Out Now
Serpentina: A Societies Novella
Out Now
Ascension: The Societies Trilogy Book 3
Releasing May 2024

Don't miss out!

Visit the website below and you can sign up to receive emails whenever Sydney Reames publishes a new book. There's no charge and no obligation.

https://books2read.com/r/B-A-CRDY-CAONC

BOOKS 2 READ

Connecting independent readers to independent writers.

About the Author

Sydney Reames has long been a lover of all things reading. Each time she's set loose in a bookstore she comes out with several purchases because "this particular book spoke to me." She is often found reading or writing while drinking what might well be considered too much caffeine. She loves swimming and spending time with her husband and two dogs. Both of whom feature heavily in her newsletter, the dogs, not the husband.

Read more at nightlochpublishers.com.